THE MYSTERY TOMB

THE NIGHTMARE COLLECTION

Eva Pohler

Eva Pohler Books
20011 Park Ranch
San Antonio, Texas 78259
www.evapohler.com

Publisher's Note: This is a work of fiction. Names, characters, places, and incidents are a product of the author's imagination. Locales and public names are sometimes used for atmospheric purposes. Any resemblance to actual people, living or dead, or to businesses, companies, events, institutions, or locales is completely coincidental.

Book Layout ©2017 BookDesignTemplates.com

Book Cover Design by Najla Qamber Designs

The Mystery Tomb/ Eva Pohler. -- 1st ed.
Paperback ISBN: 978-1-958390-55-9

You're going to get dirty. You may as well face it.
—SAMANTHA

Contents

The Mësingw 3

Rebecca 19

Kishku 24

Attie 36

A Secret Catacomb 40

Trouble 54

The Dream Catcher 62

A Secret Wedding 76

Another Wedding 79

The Charge 90

Human Finger Bones 92

A Still Wood 101

A Hidden Grotto 103

The Sacrifice 114

Ancient Spirits 116

Seven Clans 129

Beloved Bones 140

Jeannie's Story 154

Kukna's Womb 163

The Sacred Ritual 170

Grandma's Stories 185

The Rite of Misink 196

Grandfather's Story 213

Goodbyes 223

Return to Mother Earth 231

The Tribal Council 244

A Special Guest 254

Epilogue 261

    Chapter One: The Island 265

For my family.

The Mësingw

Samantha Beck stood, hunched over a screen, sifting through bones and dirt.

Her associate, Mark Farms, was bent over the screen across from her, photographing a scrap of leather with a digital camera. The two-by-four-foot wire-meshed screen lay atop two wooden sawhorses. Several of these were set up around their excavation site.

Samantha took off her dirty gloves and held up a sherd of pottery in the Pennsylvania summer sun. So far, two weeks on the site had turned up nothing. She doubted she'd be able to convince her professor to trust her again, so this might be her last chance to prove that her grandmother was a Lenape descendant. The landowner wouldn't let them stay indefinitely, and O'Neil, their department head, was sure to pull the plug any day now.

"Algonquian markings." She pointed to marks at the base of the sherd where an upward turned bow preceded a series of rectangular engravings, and her chest bloomed with hope. "I've seen these on Lenape pipes in Oklahoma. And here's another turtle. I still don't know what that signifies." She brought down the sherd and continued sifting through the screen, vaguely aware that the sun was going down.

"Look at this scrap of leather," Mark said.

"Is that the one the baby was wrapped in?"

Mark nodded. "But something's not right about this site. I agree with you. It's like they were moved." He took another photo.

Professor Ricardo Gomez's cell phone rang out across the excavation site.

Mark glanced over at the professor, who fumbled in the pocket of his blue jeans with his one free hand for his cell phone. "Maybe the professor can shed some light on this."

"The bodies *must* have been moved after burial, after decomposition," she said. "Like, in recent years."

But who would move the bodies, and why?

"Hello?" the professor said into his phone.

Mark shook his head. "You think he'll be on the phone an hour again?"

"The last call wasn't that long."

"We might have time for a quickie."

Comments like that made her wish she wasn't sleeping with him. "If these bodies were moved from their original resting place," she said, ignoring his comment, "I want to know why."

"Give us another four or five days," the professor said into the phone. "It's only been two weeks. No, but there's plenty of evidence to suggest…No. Yes, sir." He turned off the cell phone and stuffed it back into his pocket. "Bastard."

"What's wrong, Professor?" Samantha called to him from across the site.

The short, bony man walked around the excavation units in the ground toward his two graduate students, the brim of his straw hat waving in the wind, making him look like an old scarecrow. "Never mind that now. I think I've found what we're looking for."

Her mouth dropped open.

The professor held a small bandolier bag with its wide, beaded shoulder strap hanging like fully cooked lasagna noodles, its colors of orange and red and turquoise shining from beneath layers of dirt. She had never seen an artifact so perfectly preserved, so well intact.

The professor handed it over to her, and she took it in trembling hands.

"This bag is just like my grandmother's," Samantha whispered, her heart pumping.

"It gets better," the professor said.

Before he could explain further, a black pickup truck skidded onto their site from the dirt road. The driver's window lowered, revealing a man with long black hair and fierce black eyes.

"You guys need to clear on out of here!" He pointed to the tents and the screens nesting in the pasture at the edge of the site. "Get all this stuff out of here! Any arrangements you've made with my grandfather have been cancelled!"

"Who in God's name is this clown?" the professor muttered as Samantha gently laid the artifact on the screen.

Samantha followed the professor toward the truck. "Who are you?"

He gave her a once over and narrowed his eyes. "I should ask the same of you. My grandfather had no right."

"Just fucking great," the professor said.

Samantha gasped. "Do you even realize what we've discovered?"

"This is sacred ground, and those are my people! This isn't open for discussion."

Samantha's face flushed. If he was a descendant, then…

"Your people?" The professor moved nearer to the stranger. "Son, are you saying these bones belonged to your family?"

Samantha held her breath.

"You need to get the hell of my property!" the stranger shouted before driving off.

Descendant or not, Sam wanted to kill him.

"What in the hell was that all about?" Mark said.

"Let's not worry about him right now." The professor returned to the screen and lifted the bandolier bag up like a newborn baby.

Samantha watched as he reversed the inside lining.

"Oh God," the professor said beneath his breath.

"What?" Mark bent over to look at the artifact.

As they leaned over him, he whispered, "The seal."

"The Mësingw?" Mark raised his brows at Samantha.

"Really? Please don't joke with me." Samantha looked more closely at the beads on the lining. Beneath the folds of dirt, she could make out the half red and half black face: The Mësingw.

Her mouth fell open as Mark laughed out loud and patted her on the back. The professor met her eyes, and the two of them smiled before also breaking out into joyous laughter. Then she jumped up in the air, hugging herself. Mark ran a victory lap past the excavation units and all around the site, and she quickly followed, singing "Woohooo!" repeatedly as the sun continued to sink beyond the rolling hills.

"We've done it!" The professor shouted in the evening air.

"We've done it!" Samantha cried, too, returning to the professor, Mark not far behind.

She sank on the ground and covered her face with her hands. It had been such a long journey, and she had nearly given up. Tears sprang to her eyes. Her grandmother had been right: Their family was descended from a tribe that had branched away from the Lenape.

"The lost tribe," the professor said, tears streaming from his eyes. "My word, Samantha, you were right. My word, woman, you've discovered the lost tribe of Unikwëti!"

Samantha left the bathroom on the second floor of Gellermann Manor and danced in her robe toward what had been her room for the past two weeks. She couldn't believe four years of research had finally paid off. Her grandmother would be so pleased to know there was a way to join the modern tribe. And the professor would have to get tenure after this.

And what about her? Surely this would get her a job just about any-where, or at least somewhere good. She was so tired of living off her parents and eager to pay them back for all their generosity. At twenty-five years of age and still living with her parents, her days of feeling like a loser were over.

She hummed to the song playing on her iPod until, as she neared her door, the stranger from earlier appeared at the top of the stairs across from her. She'd had this part of the house to herself for two weeks, so it was a shock to see someone this evening. Her face flushed as she clutched her robe and pulled the tiny ear buds from her ears.

His long dark hair was wet like hers.

"Just great," he said.

She opened her mouth to speak, but nothing came out.

"You and the others are staying *here*?" He looked her up and down.

"Are you?"

He took a step closer to her. "I live here."

She backed up toward the door of her room. "Listen. Please don't make us…"

"I come all the way home from Iraq to find *this*."

"We've finally found the tribal seal on a bandolier bag that's just like my…"

He took a step closer, his face inches from hers. "You better start packing."

For a moment she thought he was going to kiss her. She stammered back and said, "Look, I'll just go get dressed." She entered her room, breathless, and closed the door.

Everyone else was already seated at the table when Samantha arrived at seven sharp. Brandon Gellermann wore a formal suit, as he had every evening since they'd been there.

He stood up when she entered. "Good evening, Samantha."

"Good evening. I hope I haven't kept everyone waiting." She took her seat beside him across from Mark and the professor.

The table was clothed with ivory silk trimmed with Chantilly lace. Samantha noticed a new setting tonight. Royal Crown Derby, Ashby pattern. China was her mother's love, after her family. Their home was full of collections from all over the world. Samantha turned her plate over. The maker's mark was green, indicating World War II production. This meant each of the pink flowers was painted by hand. Brandon had a valuable collection.

"Not at all." Brandon took his seat. "We're all just a little on edge tonight. I was just telling the professor that I wasn't expecting my grandson home for another month."

For the first time in two weeks, a fifth place had been set on the table next to her.

"Will he be joining us?" she asked, dreading the answer.

"Unfortunately, no," Brandon said. "Charles has been in Afghanistan for nearly six months, and tonight he wasn't up to company."

Relieved, Samantha twisted the napkin in her lap beneath the well-dressed dinner table as the butler entered with plates of salad. As she picked up her fork, Sam said to Brandon, "Your grandson didn't seem too pleased to see us."

Mark laughed. "That's an understatement."

Nodding, Brandon said, "Yes. He told me his feelings about the matter. I must say I never expected him to oppose your research."

"What does this mean?" Samantha asked, taking a sip of her water. "Do we really have to clear out?"

"I was just telling your professor that you may continue your excavation as long as you wish, but this is the difference: I want you to leave everything you find here with me."

"What?" the professor asked, with a touch of indignation.

"You may photograph as much as you'd like," Brandon said. "But I'm afraid that everything you find belongs to my grandson, for he is, er, a descendant of the bodies you have discovered."

"How do you know?" Mark asked.

"Charles's father was Indian, er, Native American. He died when Charles was eight years old. There used to be a large group of them living here."

"Here, on your property?" the professor asked.

Brandon nodded.

"Did you personally know and interact with them?" Samantha asked.

"Unfortunately, yes," Brandon said, his face turning red. And before anyone could ask more, he added, "Anyway, those bones are his ancestors, and the relics are his, too. And he doesn't wish for any of your findings to be removed from this property. In return, I'll reimburse the sum you paid to me for the use of my land. Every dime. Does that sound fair enough?"

"Hold on just a minute." Samantha brushed a strand of her long brown hair from her face. "First of all, your grandson is not the only living descendant of that tribe, and I can prove it. And second of all, you signed a contract agreeing to donate our most important findings to the university."

"Oh, dear," Brandon said. He turned to the professor. "Surely you understand my change of heart?"

The professor frowned. "Why did you agree to let us have the artifacts in the first place?"

"I didn't expect Charles to return from Iraq so soon," Brandon said. "I honestly had hoped…but now that he knows, my hands are tied."

"We have a contract," Samantha said again.

"I suppose I'll have to ask my attorney to sort out this matter."

"Does this mean you want us to leave?" Mark asked.

"Hmm. I'll speak to my attorney in the morning. Hopefully after breakfast, I'll have something to tell you."

After dinner, Brandon invited them all for cocktails in his study, as he had done each night, but only the professor accepted. Samantha was frustrated and not in the mood for company. As she and Mark left the dining room together and entered the foyer, where the winding staircase stretched up the expanse of the three floors of the manor, she said, "I think I'll go for a walk."

"Just imagine what Gellermann's grandson might be able to tell us about that tribe." Mark glanced up at the exquisite crystal chandelier, which sparkled like diamonds. "Brandon said Charles was eight when his father died. He may have learned some things about his people the tribes in Oklahoma and Canada can't tell us. Man, if only he would co-operate. It's a damn shame."

"I wonder if there are others, besides Charles."

Mark shrugged. "Seems likely." Then he added, "You might not realize this, but under most state statutes, the archaeological team has to get written permission from any known descendants of a burial site. Even though the Lebanon County Historical Society told us they didn't know of any, Gellermann's grandson might still have a case."

"Well, maybe he'll come around to our way of seeing things before we get into litigation. You never know."

"The eternal optimist, ladies and gentlemen." He grinned.

She gave him a smile.

"By the way, you look great tonight," he said. "Really sexy in that black dress with your hair down."

"Thanks." She scanned his wavy blond hair, handsome blue eyes, and tanned skin. "You look nice, too."

"Do you mind if I walk with you?"

Leave the guy alone, she admonished herself. She knew she shouldn't keep sleeping with him. The liberties he took with her because of it were too annoying. And she didn't want to hurt him. "I think I need some alone time. So much has happened today, I haven't even digested it all."

"Yeah, I know what you mean. I guess I could use some alone time myself now that you mention it." He kissed her cheek and patted her behind. "Good night."

Another reason to stop sleeping with him. She forced a smile. "Good night."

After he had taken a few steps up the stairs, he turned back to her and asked, "So what's 'petit mal,' anyway? Sounds familiar, but I'm not sure what it means."

She had been talking about her childhood seizures with him earlier.

"Petit mal seizures look like staring spells. An electrical storm would go off in my brain."

"No kidding?"

"Really. And it would last up to thirty seconds at a time."

"Would you fall down?"

She smiled and shook her head. "No. Nothing like that. I could stand and even walk. I just couldn't hear or see anything clearly."

"Damn. Not too fun."

"No. My teachers used to think I wasn't paying attention. Once I started taking medication—the right medication—everything changed. Now the doctor thinks I've outgrown epilepsy. I haven't been on meds for years."

"That's great."

"I brought it up earlier because you shouldn't be so hard on your nephew. I mean, what you were describing—the problems he's having at school and at home—actually sound familiar. It might not be his fault." They'd had a lot of time on the site to talk these past two weeks.

He smiled down at her and then continued up the stairs. "Thanks."

As Samantha walked through the foyer, she overheard part of the conversation between the professor and Brandon. She stood inside the doorway, on the verge of joining them now that she was rid of Mark.

"Excuse me for being so bold, Brandon," the professor said, both of them apparently comfortable with their coffee and cigars, each in overstuffed chairs on either side of an empty fireplace at the back of the room, and unaware of her presence.

Above the mantel behind them loomed a huge elk head, its glassy eyes watching over them. Samantha shuddered.

Brandon raised his eyebrows and waited expectantly for the professor's question, exhaling a stream of smoke that swirled up toward the ceiling. "What is it?"

"Well, I couldn't help but notice these past two weeks that you hold a strong emotion, something like contempt, in regard to the Native American people who once lived on your land. Am I wrong?"

Brandon avoided the professor's eyes. "No, Ricardo. Your observation is correct."

Samantha moved out of sight, not wanting to interrupt, and anxious to hear the old man's reply.

"I'm sorry. It's none of my business."

"I didn't always hate them. They were well liked by my family for over two centuries. I liked them, too. My wife and I both did until something terrible happened. Oh, dear. Forgive me if I don't go into details. It's too disturbing."

"Of course. I understand. I apologize for bringing it up. Let's talk instead about how you came to own that beautiful bronze of Beethoven in your foyer."

"Now that I would be pleased to divulge."

Samantha crept away from the study through the foyer toward the front double oak doors. What had happened between Brandon Gellermann and her ancestors that made him hate them all these years? She walked around to the back of the estate and down a steep hill to the small creek below. Steppingstones made the trek easier for her, and as soon as she neared the creek and was out of the light thrown off by the exterior fixtures around the manor, she pulled off her black pumps and carried them as she walked along the water to a large rock beside a tree. The thick trunk of the tree leaned over the running creek nearly parallel with the surface, and from the rock beside it, Samantha could sit and hold onto the trunk for balance as she moved her dangling legs through the cool water.

Two weeks ago, during a brief tour of the manor, Brandon had told her the name of the creek—Lethe, which was also the name of the river of forgetfulness in the Greek mythological Underworld. She had inwardly laughed at the irony given that she had come to be sure the Unikweti would never be forgotten.

Off in the distance, up the creek to her right, the hills seemed to roll up into darkness, to the end of the earth. The slight breeze over the water refreshed her in spite of the troubling turn of events.

She wriggled her toes in the water. The last thing she wanted to think about were her seizures, but Mark's questions made her recall her fourth grade teacher, plump and pear-shaped with gray curly hair swept up in a bun. She wore a red pantsuit that was too small, the buttons of her jacket threatening to pop, like her temper. She stooped over Samantha's desk. "Samantha, have you been listening?"

"Yes, Mrs. Bradley."

"Then tell me what I just said."

"If an object has more protons than electrons, it has a positive charge."

Several of the children had giggled.

"That's what I said a minute ago. I want you to repeat what I said last, just now. Who can say what I've just said to the rest of the class?"

All but Samantha raised their hands.

Mrs. Bradley put her stiff, cruel face to Samantha's ear. "Pay attention this time," she rasped. Mrs. Bradley stood upright, tugged at her tight red jacket, and called on the boy three chairs behind Samantha.

"Yes, Jack?"

"We measure the strength of an electrical current in amps."

"Got that, girl?" Mrs. Bradley spat, narrowing her cold eyes.

Samantha had nodded, fighting back tears. "Yes, Mrs. Bradley."

Samantha stared at Lethe Creek, wishing some things could be forgotten.

"Beck, that you?" a voice came from out of the darkness.

She straightened her back, pulled her legs together, and looked in the direction of the voice.

"Charles?" she whispered, unable to see the figure on the rocks behind the leaning tree.

"Not Charles. Tukihëla Nisha."

"But your grandfather said…"

"He's not too fond of my Native American side."

Somewhat frightened by the angry tone in his voice, Samantha glanced back at the well-lit manor on the hill and then back at the dark figure behind the leaning tree.

She climbed to her feet. "I didn't mean to offend you. I didn't know."

He took five steps toward her and stood in her view with the tree between their feet. He would only have to step over the tree to be next to her. The moon was behind him, and his face was in shadows. Samantha could not read its expression. She took another step back.

"I didn't hear you come down here," she said. "What do you want?"

"I want you to answer my question. Why can't you let them be? Why do you have to disturb and humiliate my ancestors like this?"

"I don't want to humiliate them," she insisted.

"You want to display their bones and their goods like animals in a zoo." He stepped over the tree and stood inches from her, bringing the fear back to her trembling body, but his voice became gentler. "How can someone so beautiful be so heartless?"

Did he say beautiful?

Hang on. Did he say heartless? No one had ever called her heartless.

She backed away, gathered her shoes from the rock, and hurried a few steps up the hill from him before turning to say, "You're the heartless one. I want to give those people a voice. You want to stifle their contribution to modern society before they even have a chance to make it."

She reached around her face and bunched her windblown hair in a single fist. "Well, I won't let you do it." Then she turned and walked away, back up the hill to the distant manor.

Back in her room, Samantha changed into her comfortable nightshirt, grabbed her cell phone, and climbed into bed. How dare he, she thought. How dare he try to stop her from learning about her people?

The silver-framed photograph on the antique nightstand fell back, so she set it upright.

She realized now, upon closer inspection, that this was a picture of Tukihëla's mother, Rebecca. Brandon had shown her another portrait down in the music room. This photo was taken when she was a girl of ten or so. Two barrettes pinned back blonde curls, and grey eyes narrowed in a scowl. Rebecca lifted her little chin defiantly as she stood in her plaid dress in the front of Gellermann Manor holding a red dachshund. Samantha put the photo back on the nightstand beneath the antique Tiffany lamp and sat against her pillows on the bed.

Samantha sighed in the full-sized antique oak poster bed and sank into the cream satin linen, as she stared at the enormous window opening on to the front of the estate. She turned off the Tiffany lamp so she could gaze out the window and the starry landscape and forget the man who called himself Tukihëla Nisha.

She decided to look up his name in her Algonquian dictionary, so she flipped back on the lamp and grabbed the book from her bag.

Tukihëla meant "awaken." She leafed through to the N's. Nisha meant "two."

She slammed shut the book and returned it to her bag on the floor by her bed. She flipped off the lamp, closed her eyes, and pleaded with the river of forgetfulness. Why couldn't she get the image of Tukihëla Nisha out of her head?

When the image refused to leave, she took up the cell phone and called her grandma to tell her the news of the day's discovery. She was going to wait until morning, but then remembered it was still only seven o'clock in Texas.

Plus, her grandma's voice would cheer her up.

"So those skeletons you found are without question ancestors of mine?"

"I believe so, Grandma. I'm ninety-nine percent sure they are. We haven't gotten the DNA test yet. I've sent samples of my blood and fibers from several of the bones to our lab."

"You should use my blood, or your father's."

"What does it matter?"

"You're right. Of course, it doesn't matter. Anyway, I'll have to come up and see the place for myself!"

"Not right now, though I'd absolutely love that. There's a bit of a kink in our plans. Another descendant has appeared, and he doesn't like what we're doing."

"Oh, dear. That's too bad. I hope you won't let this obtuse person stop you."

"You know me."

"That's right. So I won't come now, but I will come eventually."

"I'd like that."

"A fellow descendant? I really must meet him."

Samantha imagined her boisterous grandmother meeting the solemn Tukihëla Nisha.

"By the way, it was our discovery of the Mësingw that provided the final proof," Samantha added.

"You mean Misink, don't you?"

"Isn't that what I said?"

"No. I've told you before, you need to say 'sink,' like a kitchen sink."

"Grandma, I know what I'm talking about. I interviewed lots of folks in Oklahoma. They even spelled it for me."

"M-I-S-I-N-K. Short for Misinkhalikàn."

"That's not what they said. Oh, it doesn't matter, anyway. It's the same guy, I'm sure of it, with the face that's half red and…"

"Half black. Look, I know what I'm talking about, too. My Grandma Kexi told me a story about Misink. I told it to you when you were little, but your mother didn't like it. She was afraid my stories would undermine your Christian values."

"But you're Christian."

"I know, I know. Well, we both know your mother can be a bit ridiculous. Anyway, shall I tell you the story again?"

"Absolutely."

"Alright then. A long, long time ago there lived three boys no one loved, not even their parents. People threw rocks at them and called them names, and no one knows why. One day when they were out in the woods, a hairy-looking person with a face painted half red and half black jumped in front of them and said he was Misinkhalikàn. He said he would protect them from the others. So, they followed him to the sky, and he showed them his home, promising them strength and power.

"Years later, after they had been accepted by their tribe and had become leaders, they would often hear Misink's peculiar call, 'Ho-ho-ho!' and they would follow the sound to the middle of the woods where that great hairy person would be herding the deer."

Samantha interrupted. "Ho-ho-ho? Like Santa Clause?"

"Exactly."

Samantha shifted on the bed and pulled back the duvet to slide beneath the covers and listen more comfortably. She lay down on the pillow. "Go on, Grandma."

"Anyway, about this time, for some unknown reason, the Unikwëti had stopped their bi-annual worship ceremonies. Ten years went by without a single tribute to the spirits. Then a great earthquake came upon their land and lasted for twelve moons. They built a new long house of bark and worshipped all winter, praying for help.

"In the spring, they heard the peculiar cry of Misink through the forest, 'Ho-ho-ho!' The three men who had once befriended him followed his sound and met with him in the forest, where he gave them instructions for a new ceremony to ensure their safety from earthquakes and other doom.

"Misink told them they must create a mask using paint, half black and half red like his face, and he would put his power into the mask so whoever would wear it, Misink would be there among the people. The man must carry a turtle-shell rattle, a bandolier bag, and a staff. Misink told them he would keep the deer close by if they would pay homage to him through this ceremony at least once a year."

"How cool. So did they? Did our people pay homage?"

"Yes. Twice a year. Once in the fall and once in the spring. Grandma Kexi told me Misink comes to warn humans when we are not living in harmony with the other creatures and with Mother Earth."

"What a great story, Grandma."

"You remember years ago—I can't remember—when all that talk came out about Bigfoot?"

"That was before my time, but I know what you're talking about."

"I remember wondering to myself if it wasn't Misink whose footprints were left behind and whose big hairy body was caught on tape. Maybe he'd come to protest cruelty to animals—you know, testing on them needlessly and such."

Samantha laughed. "Who knows, right?"

"It just might have been Misink!"

CHAPTER TWO

Rebecca

Rebecca slid the eight-foot aluminum boat from the bank of the creek, hopped in with a bucket of live perch she had caught that morning, and paddled up the creek toward her drop lines.

She couldn't believe Daddy was going to send her to Hartridge after all. She didn't want to go away to boarding school. She wanted to stay here where she could run her lines every day and play with Sandra and Nancy up in her tree house when they came to visit their grandparents in the spring.

The hot summer sun had yielded to a cool evening breeze, and Rebecca now wished she had worn long sleeves. The small pool of water that had leaked into the bottom of the boat soaked into her shoes and socks and chilled her.

Daddy had said she needed to learn how to become a smart and proper young lady. Hadn't she become one already?

I know more than most ten-year-olds.

She eyed the first drop line—a bit of twine tied to a willow near the bank of the creek. At the end of the twine was a shad stripped on a straight hook and probably a nice catfish by the way the twine was moving in circles. She paddled toward the willow.

What's more useful, playing piano and doing embroidery or catching dinner?

Her father used to set and run the lines with her, but a year ago he had broken his hip in a skiing accident, and though he had undergone a hip replacement, he wasn't comfortable paddling in their little boat.

He'd fish with her from the bank with rod and reels when they wanted perch, but she now set and ran the drop lines herself.

She heard a rustling in the nearby brush and looked up as she approached the willow. She didn't see anything.

That sounded bigger than a squirrel. Could it be a deer? A raccoon?

She grabbed the willow and flung the rope that was tied to her boat around a branch to keep the boat from drifting while she checked her line. She heard the rustling again and looked up.

When the rustling stopped and she still didn't see anything moving along the brush, she pulled the catfish into the boat.

"Far-out! That's a four-pounder for sure!" she cried.

She waited for the flapping fish to settle down. Then she pinched the shaft of the straight hook with needle-nose pliers and grabbed the catfish beneath its poisonous fins with her other hand, leaning her weight on the fish to keep it still. Then she broke the tip of each of the three fins, removed the hook from its mouth, laid the fish in the bottom of the boat, and baited the hook with one of the perch from her bucket.

"You're the biggest I've caught in a while," Rebecca said to the catfish, tossing the line with its wiggling perch back into the water.

The fish lay at her feet, worn out and gasping.

As she paddled up the creek toward her next line, she heard rustling along the bank again. She paddled so she wouldn't drift back, but she kept her eyes on the bank.

She found nothing on her second and third lines, so she quickly baited and moved up the creek to her fourth, which she could see had something pulling on the end of it.

As she flung her rope around the branch of a tree and tied on, she heard the rustling again, and this time, when she looked up toward the bank, a strange painted face stared down at her. Half of the face was red and the other black. Bearskin draped around the figure's shoulders.

She screamed and toppled back, nearly falling from the boat.

Quickly, she untied the rope from her boat and tossed it overboard. She snatched her paddle and used it to push from the tree, allowing herself to drift downstream. Then she paddled away, catching glances of what she now realized was just a man, but a scary man, nonetheless, running along the bank, following her.

When she reached the place where she had docked, at the rock by the leaning tree, she heard Zugi barking on the bank at the painted man.

"Good girl!" Rebecca yelled. "Get him, girl!"

Although Zugi's red, hot-dog-shaped body was not all that threatening, the barking accomplished what Rebecca had hoped: Daddy was bearing down the hill from the back porch, calling to her.

"Rebecca? Everything okay down here? Zugi? What's the matter, girl?"

The painted man disappeared.

"You look adorable," Rebecca's mother told her as they stood together before the mirror in Rebecca's dressing room.

Rebecca didn't like the stiff material of her plaid school uniform. She rather liked the knee-high socks and new shoes, but the dress smelled funny and felt itchy.

"Now let's pin back your hair, so we can see your pretty face."

Rebecca flinched from her mother. "No. I don't want barrettes."

"But you won't be able to see." The mop of golden curls fell into Rebecca's eyes.

"I can see."

Her mother put her hands on her hips and sighed.

Rebecca didn't mean to make her mother angry. She wanted to hug her and tell her how much she would miss her and please, please don't make her go away to school!

"I'm asking you to wear these barrettes for your own good. Now please do as I say. You exasperate me."

Tears streamed down Rebecca's cheeks. "Yes, Mama."

"Quit crying like a baby over these silly barrettes."

Rebecca pushed her mother's hands away from her hair. "I'm not a baby!"

"I didn't say you were a baby. I said to quit acting like one."

"I'm not a baby! I'm not even going to miss you when I'm gone! The only one who loves me in this whole wide world is Zugi!" Rebecca ran from the room calling for her dog.

"Zugi? Where are you, girl?"

"Rebecca! Come back here!"

Rebecca ran from the house.

"Zugi?"

She followed the steppingstones down to the creek where she heard Zugi barking.

"What's the matter, girl?" Rebecca stayed back, afraid she would find the painted man she had seen a few days ago. She had told Daddy about him, and he had said not to go to the creek without him. "Zugi!" she called from the side of the hill. "Come here!"

Then Rebecca heard music coming from the creek. A single instrument, maybe a flute, sounded from the trees.

Zugi stopped barking.

"Zugi?"

She crept a little further down the hill toward the creek and the melody lifting up from the trees and into the wind and sky.

"Hello? Who's there?"

The music stopped, and a teenage boy jumped from the oak tree in front of her with a flute of wood in his hand and said, "Me. Attie."

Rebecca thought he must be at least sixteen, much too old a boy to be talking to her, but she asked, "Are you the painted man?"

"Misink? You saw Misink?" and with that, he ran up the hill and into the woods.

Rebecca had seen the Indians many times, but never had she seen them so close to her house. And never before this week had she seen the painted man whom even the Indians apparently feared.

Moments later, Rebecca's mother hastened down the hill. "You come to me when I call you, young lady!"

Instead of running away, Rebecca charged up the hill and flung herself against her mother, wrapping her arms around her waist and sobbing uncontrollably.

"Don't let Daddy make me go. I want to stay here!"

"Now, now." Her mother plopped onto the grass in her soft, flared pants and pulled Rebecca onto her lap. "That's enough crying." She smoothed the curls away from her daughter's face and kissed her cheeks several times. "You know Mama and Daddy love you, don't you?"

Rebecca nodded, clutching Zugi as the dachshund added herself to their bundle on the grass.

"Daddy and I want you to go to Hartridge so you'll be able to get in to the best universities. We want you to have all the best chances for success. We want you to have choices when you're older, so you can be happy doing what you want to do."

"But I'm happy here."

Her mother kissed her again and gave her another hug. "We'll visit weekends, and you'll come home for Christmas and summers. Just give it a chance, will you?"

Rebecca shrugged. "What choice do I have?"

Her mother pulled them up to their feet, patted her daughter and Zugi, and said, "Now let's go take that photograph, shall we? I want to remember the day my little girl started becoming a young woman."

Rebecca held her mother's hand as they walked up the hill.

"Will you wear the barrettes for me?" her mother asked.

Rebecca groaned. "Okay, Mama."

CHAPTER THREE

Kishku

Friday morning, Samantha awoke to her beeping alarm. She had a miserable night with little sleep and troubling dreams. The Mësingw, or Misink, she couldn't decide which she should call him, had found her and had descended upon her, smothering her, crushing her, choking her. She hadn't been able to breathe.

Now, she flopped back down on the satin pillow thinking how silly the dream had been, a hairy Big Foot with a painted face.

A few minutes later, she forced herself from beneath the covers and walked in her bare feet and nightshirt across the hardwood floor to the closet to fetch the robe hanging from a hook on the door.

On impulse, Samantha passed the bathroom door down the interior balcony from her room to peer inside Rebecca Nisha's abandoned suite at the end of the hall. The day she had arrived, Brandon's butler, Jes, had explained, as he had helped her with her luggage, why that room always remained closed. The suite had once belonged to Brandon's daughter and had not been used since her death. To Samantha's surprise, the door was ajar this morning, and the windows were open, and a thick fog hung throughout the room, illuminated by the morning sun. As Samantha entered, her eyes followed a sunbeam to the mantel over the rock fireplace.

There, in a painting, Rebecca, probably age sixteen, sat behind a desk in her boarding school uniform with a stoic look on her face. The blonde wavy hair was painted back in a ponytail except for one long strand that cut across her grey eyes. Samantha stepped closer and looked into the eyes that gazed down at her.

"You were beautiful," Samantha whispered.

The fog wrapped itself around Samantha. For several seconds, she stood transfixed on the painting.

She blinked, as if waking from a dream. "Did I just have a seizure?" she whispered to herself, wiping spit from her chin and feeling disoriented.

The sound of footsteps prompted her from the room and down the balcony toward the bathroom.

Tukihëla greeted her from the back stairs. "Good morning, Beck."

"Tukihëla," she said, hoping he had not seen her in his mother's room.

He took a few steps toward her, wearing khaki Dockers and a green polo shirt, quite a different look from the jeans and boots and t-shirt of the previous evening, but still a good one.

"You remembered my name."

"Yes. Tukihëla Nisha." The first name had its emphasis on the second syllable: Tu KEE hala. The second name sounded like three syllables: Na EE sha. "I recognize the Lenni-Lenape dialect. I looked it up in my book. Do you know what it means?" She casually leaned her elbow on the cherry wood balustrade, attempting to hide her embarrassment.

"Of course."

"It's rather ironic, don't you think?" she asked.

"Why is that?" He raised his thin brows as he waited for her to explain.

"Never mind," she said, lowering her eyes. "It would only offend you."

"Then by all means, let me have it." He gave her a radiant smile, so unlike his demeanor the previous night.

She hesitated. "It's just it seems to me the last thing you want to do is 'wake up.'"

His grin became a wry smile. "I don't want to wake up the dead, in any case."

She stood from the balustrade and opened the bathroom door, turning her red face away from him. "I'm sorry. I don't know you well enough to suggest such a thing. I suppose we think differently, that's all." She started to close the bathroom door, but Tukihëla stopped her.

"Beck?"

She peeked back at him from behind the door. She wanted to hide. "Yes?"

"I want you to understand where I'm coming from. Can we go to breakfast, just the two of us, away from the others?"

"Divide and conquer? Is that it?"

"Exactly."

She knew she was up for the challenge. There was nothing he could say to change her mind about fighting for her right to continue her research, even if his good looks did have her stomach in knots.

"Meet me in the foyer in about a half hour?" he asked.

"See you there."

He was waiting for her in the circular drive beneath the giant sycamore.

"Hello again, Beck," he said, opening the truck door for her.

"Hello," she climbed in while he went around to the other side. Was he really going to call her by her last name? He probably thought he was being distant. Or maybe it was the way he spoke to everyone. She stifled a giggle. If he knew it was her nickname back home—her old tennis team not to mention her own father called her that—he might be less inclined to use it.

"Ready?"

"Where's the seatbelt?" Samantha asked, looking behind the seat and along the passenger side of Tukihëla's pickup. "Is it broken?" It was difficult to disguise her trembling hands. Why was she shaking so?

"Yeah. Sorry about that." Although his seatbelt looked like it was in working order, Tukihëla did not belt himself in as he turned the key in the ignition.

"Wait a minute," Samantha objected. "Don't tell me you don't ever wear seatbelts."

"No, I don't."

"You know, there is a law about this."

"Why is it anyone else's business?"

She folded her arms. "I thought you were smarter than that."

"Right." He started to pull from the drive.

"Wait a minute," she objected again. "I'm not going anywhere without a seatbelt."

"The middle one works," he said with a grin as he applied the brakes. "Do you want to sit in the middle?"

Inwardly, she groaned. She would feel stupid sitting over there beside him like a teenager out on a date.

"Well?"

She slid over despite her burning complexion and fastened the belt, hating how aware she was of his body.

He shook his head as he pressed his foot to the accelerator. Before he could pull out of the drive, Samantha noticed his necklace come untucked from beneath his shirt. It was the Mësingw on a round piece of petrified wood. Her hand reached out of its own accord and held it, shocked as much by the sight of the seal as the heat of his throat against her knuckles.

"It's the Mësingw!" she said.

His hand flew to hers and clutched it as his foot hit the brake again.

They rocked forward and back.

"I'm sorry," she muttered. His hand squeezed around hers in a defensive gesture, nearly crushing her fingers. "Let go." She could barely breathe.

He released her hand and tucked the ornament flanked with bones back beneath his shirt.

"It's the tribal seal, the image we've been looking for all this time." She didn't add it had tried to suffocate her last night.

"It's Misink. Short for Misinkhalikàn."

"That's what my grandma calls him! The Lenape of Oklahoma call him the Mësingw."

"Your grandma?"

"Yeah. That's why I'm here."

He arched a brow, but she held her tongue, not wanting to make him angry again.

Tukihëla parked in front of a cute café on a street lined with shops and full of tourists. After sliding across a booth from one another and giving the waitress their order, Samantha said, "So tell me what you know about that burial ground."

"Grandfather says never to tell stories in the summertime. You'll have to wait till it gets cold."

"Ahh, Grandfather. You mean the Lenape people." She smiled.

"You know about Grandfather?"

"Of course. I've been studying the Lenape for four years now. They were known as Grandfather to the other tribes because they were among the first Native Americans to meet and sign treaties with the European settlers."

"That's right," he said, clearly impressed.

"They signed the treaty with William Penn in 1682, and I believe the first treaty they signed with the U.S. was in 1778, or something like that, shortly after the American Revolution anyway, at Fort Pitt."

"You know your history."

"The U.S. was going to establish an Indian state, and at its head would be the Delaware nation, with representation in Congress."

"And as we know, that never happened," he said dryly.

"Do you say Lenape or Delaware?"

"Lenape, because that's what we call ourselves. Delaware was a name imposed on us by the Europeans." He leaned back in the booth. "So go on. I'm interested in hearing your version of the Lenape people."

"Okay." She blushed, feeling like a schoolgirl about to be tested. "European settlers continued to push the Lenape and other tribes west, so they settled in Indiana Territory, but then in 1818, signed another treaty giving away their land there. From Indiana they went to Missouri, then Kansas, and finally to Oklahoma by 1867."

The waitress brought them their coffee.

"Thanks," Tukihëla said. Then, he turned back to Samantha. "They may have signed treaties, but you know they had no choice. They were tricked. The white settlers refused to leave their lands, and even though Native Americans raided and killed to protect their homes, the white settlers kept coming."

Samantha dumped several packets of sugar into her coffee and stirred. He sure had a chip on his shoulder, which she wouldn't have expected from the grandson of a man as wealthy as Brandon Gellermann. Rather than argue about the ethics of European immigrants colonizing America, she changed the topic back to the burial mound on his grandfather's land. "We believe those bodies we discovered to be a chief, his wife, an infant son, and eight warriors buried around them. It seems they died in battle. We found weapon fragments buried with them as well."

Tukihëla smirked. "Why do you assume it was a battle, Beck? That's history for you. You can make it anything you want. They weren't warriors. They were farmers—men and women. It was typhoid."

"How do you know?"

"My father told me."

"And how did he know?"

"His father told him."

"All right, let's assume you're right." She didn't want to argue. "Tell me more."

"Well, you've only covered those who left. Not all Lenape left Pennsylvania." He took another drink of his coffee.

"So, they stayed here?"

He nodded. "The Gellermanns came with a group of Germans from New York in the early seventeen-hundreds. They purchased the land from a Pennsylvania governor, but they recognized innocent people were being displaced."

"The Lenape."

Tukihëla nodded. "Unlike other landowners, the Gellermanns worked out an arrangement with the Lenape, and the two families lived in harmony. For a while, anyway."

Their food arrived: steaming pancakes, scrambled eggs, sausage, and biscuits.

"Were those bodies moved from an original burial ground, sometime after decomposition?"

"I don't know what you're talking about." He stabbed at his pancakes and shoveled some into his mouth.

They both ate without talking for several minutes. She hadn't realized how hungry she was, and he was suddenly angry with her again. His moodiness unsettled her, so she had to build up the courage to tell him what she'd wanted to say from the beginning. She was afraid he wouldn't believe her.

Finally, when her plate was nearly empty, she said, "Those bodies we uncovered may be my ancestors, too."

He looked up at her in disbelief.

"My grandmother, Gale Adams Beck, is the daughter of Alice Smith and Walter Adams married in Indiana in 1919."

"So?"

"And Alice was half Lenape."

"Go on."

"Alice's mother married a white man named Raymond Smith here in Lebanon County in 1879. Alice's mother's name, as it appears on both her birth and marriage certificates, was Kexi Kishku. She was born in 1861 right around here. My grandma says they called themselves Unikwëti, which means 'The Ones.'"

Tukihëla's eyes widened.

"What is it?" She straightened in her seat.

"And you're sure?"

"Yes. I've traced the bloodline from my grandmother. I'm still waiting on a DNA test, but…"

"That means we're both of the Turtle."

"What?"

"You should be ashamed." He pushed his plate away, took his wallet from his back pocket, and threw money down on the table. Then he stood to go.

She grabbed money from her purse and laid it next to his on the table and then followed him from the diner. "Listen," she said at his heels. "My grandma can't join the modern tribe without proving her heritage."

He stopped and faced her in the parking lot. "What?"

"In order to join the modern Lenape tribe in Oklahoma, you have to have had ancestors living there before 1906. Grandma knows she's Lenape, but she can't prove it. That's why I'm here."

He turned and walked toward his truck. "I can't help you."

During the ride back to Gellermann Manor, Samantha clamped her legs shut to avoid rubbing against her angry driver. Occasional bumps in the road made it impossible, though, and she clenched her jaw with each touch. Why couldn't he understand her desire to know her ancestors? Why must he be so secretive and bitter?

When they arrived at the dig, they found it abandoned.

Samantha climbed from the truck. "Where's my team?"

"Do you want me to leave you here or not?"

A patrol car drove up.

"Samantha!" the professor called out to her. "The bandolier bag is missing from the tent. Do you know anything about this?"

As the others climbed out of the patrol car—a young officer, Mark, and Brandon—Samantha looked questioningly at Tukihëla.

"I took nothing that wasn't already mine," Tukihëla said.

"You don't understand, son," the professor said. "That artifact belongs to the government by federal law. Once your grandfather agreed—"

"I'm not your son. And my grandfather has no authority over any of that." He gave Brandon Gellermann a hateful glance. Then he moved closer to the professor and stood face to face with him. "They belonged to *my* family, not his."

The professor appealed to the police officer. "Sir, this man has virtually admitted to stealing the bandolier bag. Can't you arrest him?"

"Now wait a minute." Brandon limped toward the officer.

"I admit nothing," Tukihëla growled.

The officer spoke, his chocolate complexion slightly pink. "You don't have to say anything without an attorney, but I'll ask you anyway. Do you have this bandolier bag in your possession, sir?"

Tukihëla stared at the young officer before he spoke. "Yes."

"And is it true that the owner of this estate made an agreement with these archaeologists?"

Tukihëla narrowed his eyes first at his grandfather, and then at the police officer. "Yes."

"Then I'm afraid, sir, you will, uh, have to come with me." The rookie officer was tall and thin. He had a hard time hiding his trembling hands as he took the cuffs and placed them on the angry half-Native American. "You have the right to remain silent. You have the right to have an attorney present. Anything you say may be held against you in a court of law. Do you understand your rights?"

Tukihëla nodded.

"Do you have to handcuff him?" Samantha asked.

"Yes, M'am. Just till he calms down."

"But sir," Samantha appealed to the officer. "We won't press charges if Tukihëla returns the bandolier bag. There's really no reason to arrest him."

The officer paused. "Is that so? You plan to return the stolen item?"

Tukihëla kept his eyes fixed on Samantha.

"I plan to return nothing," he finally said.

Samantha, Mark, and the professor sat on couches in the library, where they sipped warm cups of coffee Jes had left for them moments before.

"What a jerk," Mark said. "He thinks he's being all noble, but I wonder what he's really after."

"He thinks he's doing the right thing," Samantha said. "He's trying to maintain respect for the dead."

"But we've already excavated," Mark continued. "What is he protecting them from?"

"Unless there's more to be found," the professor said. "Maybe he's afraid we will stumble upon something else."

They sat in silence pondering this before Samantha said, "That bandolier bag will do none of us any good in police custody. I've got to try to talk some sense into him. Maybe we should offer a compromise."

"What do you mean?" the professor asked.

"Maybe we should offer to end our research and to restore the tomb in exchange for the bag. It's all we need, really."

"But what if there is more?" Mark asked. "What if there are greater things here? This doesn't sound like the Samantha Beck I know. How in the world can we turn our backs now? We may have an important discovery right beneath our noses."

The professor spoke up. "Mark's right. We've come all this way. We may be able to learn some things about these people no one has yet discovered. Why should we stop when we may be on the brink of something that could make us famous worldwide?"

"Is that all you two care about? Fame?"

The professor sighed.

"Come on," Mark said. "That's not fair. Don't you want to be known and respected by the top archaeologists in the world? It's about respect."

"What about the respect we owe one of the few living descendants of that tribe? What about his respect? And hasn't the fact he's known about this fourth tribe all along taken just a bit of the glory out of this project for you guys? I mean, we really haven't discovered anything."

"Not at all," Mark insisted. "This tribe remains unregistered, and we don't know he understands the true significance of his ancestors and what their existence here means to the modern Lenape tribes."

"Give me a break!" Samantha cried out.

"This isn't helping our situation," the professor said calmly. "Look, the police will be arriving soon to search for the bag. If we're going to try to talk some sense into the younger Gellermann, we better head down to the county jail now."

"His name is Tukihëla Nisha," Samantha said. "And I think I'd better go alone, Professor. You two will just make him more defensive."

Mark objected. "You seem to bring out the worst in him without even trying. I don't see how you'll have any more luck than the rest of us."

"No, she's right," the professor said. "Let her go alone. Maybe as his fellow descendant, she can appeal to him in ways the two of us cannot. We'll all go back to the site after lunch. There's bound to be more there, otherwise Tukihëla wouldn't be trying so hard to stop our research."

Mark gave her a hurt look just as Brandon entered the room.

"Excuse me," Brandon said. "I thought you might like to know: The police have arrived with a warrant, and they're searching the premises now."

CHAPTER FOUR

Attie

Rebecca stood outside her parent's bedroom suite.

"I don't want her to see me like this, Brandon! Get me my wig," her mother said.

"We can't hide it from her anymore. She's sixteen years old. She's bound to have already guessed what is going on," her father said.

"I want her to remember me as I was, when I was beautiful."

"You're still beautiful, my darling."

Rebecca looked through the small crack between the door and its frame and saw her father kneeling beside the bed, holding her mother's hand. She couldn't see her mother's face, but she could hear her sobbing.

"I wish you would have woken me up before you left to go get her. Where is she? She's not out in the hall, is she?"

Her father kissed her mother's hand and said, "You can't avoid her all summer. Once you finish this round of chemotherapy, you'll be back to your old self again. You'll see. But it'll take several more weeks."

Chemotherapy? Then that meant…

Rebecca ran down the hall, down the back stairs, through the kitchen, and down to the creek. She sat on the rock near the leaning tree and sobbed. Zugi caught up to her, and Rebecca held on to her old and blind dachshund as her body shook with tears.

She couldn't believe her mother had cancer. Why hadn't anyone told her? And why wouldn't her mother want to spend every possible second with her?

***

Dusk had fallen along the creek where all was quiet except for the song of the crickets. Rebecca and her father sat in lawn chairs on the bank, each holding a rod and reel.

"I felt a bite," Rebecca said, "but it's gone away."

"It would mean a great deal to your mother."

Rebecca reeled in, saw the worm was still on the end of her hook, and gently cast back into the creek. "I don't mind," she finally said. "If it'll make her happy."

"It would indeed." Then he jerked his rod. "Got another one."

"Looks like you have all the luck."

Her father reeled in the perch. "It's smaller than the others, but it'll do."

"We don't have to put the lines out if you don't want to," Rebecca said.

"We'll put them out now, if that's alright with you. We've got enough bait for seven, no, eight lines. I'll walk along the bank and help where I can."

Her eyes lit up. "You sure?"

"Sure, I'm sure. Come on. We don't have much time."

She grabbed her tackle box and the bucket of perch, shoved the boat into the water, and hopped in. She was hungry for fresh fried catfish.

As she paddled upstream to the first tree, an Indian came down toward them from the house.

"I've finished planting those pots of chrysanthemums for you, Mr. Gellermann. Should I start mowing the front yard tonight? It's nice and cool, see?"

The Indian glanced at Rebecca in the boat and smiled but didn't say anything to her.

"Yes, Attie. See what you can get done tonight. Oh, and Mrs. Gellermann would like some pansies on our bedroom balcony. Maybe you could get some from town tomorrow?"

Rebecca held on to the leaning tree to avoid drifting down the creek in the boat. She watched the Indian as her father spoke. She recognized him as the boy with the wooden flute years ago. Now he was a grown man, at least twenty-two or twenty-three, but she didn't feel so much younger anymore. She smiled back at him.

"Sure thing, Mr. Gellermann," Attie said.

As the Indian turned to walk away, Rebecca called out, "Do you still play that wooden flute?"

Attie faced her, "Sometimes. Not so much anymore."

Rebecca's father raised his brows. "You two know each other?"

"No, Daddy. Not really."

"Attie, this is my daughter, Rebecca. Rebecca, Attie. He's been doing some gardening around the place for your mother and me. He's good with plants, and, as you know, your mother loves to have flowers around."

Rebecca nodded. "I've noticed them. They're beautiful."

"Thank you, Miss," Attie said, blushing. "Good luck with the fishing."

Rebecca watched as Attie turned back up the hill, his hands covered in potting soil, his flared jeans raveling at the hems. She liked the way his body looked and would have watched him until he disappeared if her father hadn't interrupted her thoughts.

"We better get started, Beck. It'll be dark soon."

***

"Keep your eyes on the elk, over my head," Mr. Davenport said again. "And try not to fidget."

"I'm sorry. I'm trying my best," Rebecca replied.

Sitting at her father's desk in the study, she could see through the windows flanking the fireplace and would rather look there than over the mantel at the scary dead elk looking down at her.

She hoped her mother liked the painting. It sure hadn't been fun sitting still for three whole days.

Mr. Davenport studied her again as he lifted his brush in the air. "Can't you give me even the suggestion of a smile?"

"My mouth is tired. Can't we take a break?"

"I told your father I'd finish today. Just sit still. It won't be much longer."

Attie walked by the window outside and crouched over a flowerbed. Rebecca straightened her back and strained to see him over the lounger in her way.

"That's a nice smile," Mr. Davenport said. "Can you hold that for me? But look up, at the elk."

Mortified by the thought of Mr. Davenport seeing the cause of her smile, Rebecca obeyed. But the smile vanished from her face the moment her eyes left Attie. Then a strand of her blonde hair fell from her ponytail. Before she could brush it away from her eyes, the painter cried, "Leave it! Hold it, just like that!"

CHAPTER FIVE

A Secret Catacomb

A tall and beautiful young woman kissed Tukihëla inside the cell of the Lebanon County Jail just as Samantha entered from the lobby.

"See you later, Tuki," the woman said.

Of course, he would have a girlfriend. Why was she surprised?

The deputy said, "We'll have to detain Mr. Nisha as long as the ladies are gonna visit."

Samantha wished she hadn't been so haughty to the others on her team. She might have felt less nervous if they'd come with her.

The woman smiled as the deputy unlocked the door and let her out. Samantha entered the cell. She jumped at the sound of the bars slamming shut. Then she was alone with Tukihëla.

He searched her eyes, unabashed, waiting, with the patience of a predator.

At last, she spoke. "I've come with a proposition." She stopped at the sound of thunder.

"It's coming this way," he said of the storm.

"I want the bandolier bag—not for the sake of my career, but because it's the only way I can prove my grandmother is Lenape. It has the seal, the Mësingw, which proves the tribe is the Unikwëti."

"Why should I trust you?"

She met his eyes. "We—the archaeological team, that is—are required by law to restore the tomb and the human remains once our research has ended. If you agree to give up the bandolier bag, I promise to return everything else to the burial ground in addition to the human remains and to discontinue my search for any other possible signs of the Unikwëti.”

“Do the others agree as well?”

She hesitated. “Not yet. But I know I can convince them with a little time.”

“If the others agree. But I won’t turn over the bag until I get it in writing with all three signatures.”

So there is more, she thought. “I’m afraid of it going into police custody. I’ve heard they sometimes lose things. It would be a disaster. Please reconsider.”

“Don’t worry. That bag will never be found unless I want it to be.”

She looked at his mouth as the thunder raged, louder this time, and wondered how a kiss from him would feel. She cleared her throat and backed away. “You’re sure?” she asked.

“Yes.” He turned away and ran a finger along the bars of the cell. “We might have been friends, don’t you think?” He looked at her again.

“In another life, maybe.” If he weren’t so stubborn, they could be friends now. She held her breath as she imagined it.

He squared himself to her. “Get the others to put in writing what we discussed, and I’ll hand over the bandolier bag.”

“Really? Oh, thank you!” she said, shocked by his cooperation. “Thank you so much!” In her excitement, she put her arms around his neck and hugged him.

He stiffened, and she quickly backed away as the blood rushed to her cheeks. “Deputy!” she called out. “I’m ready!”

Samantha awoke from Misink’s death grip to find a darkening sky outside her window. She knew Tukihëla had likely returned after Brandon posted bond. She was partly glad the team of police hadn’t found the bandolier bag during their search of Gellermann Manor, for she worried about its being mishandled, or worse, lost, while in police custody. She moved her book from where it lay across her chest and sat it on the nightstand beneath the Tiffany lamp. It was dusk, and through her window there was a faint glow from the setting sun over the rolling hills in the distance.

Feeling restless, she thought some night air might do her good. She felt lightheaded from the headache medication she had gotten from the butler an hour ago—like the effect of a couple of glasses of wine—but she decided to put on her sneakers and walk it off in the cool summer breeze that had come with the passing of the storm.

She grabbed a flashlight from her bag and, after peering over the cherry wood balustrade to the foyer for signs of others about, headed down the back servants' stairs. Outside, the air was crisp, so she buttoned up her blue cotton shirt and folded her arms across her chest. She took a deep breath.

"Mmm," she sighed aloud. "What a beautiful evening."

She made her way down the hill toward Lethe Creek. She walked through willows, cypresses, and hemlocks until she reached the part of the creek where it narrowed. Then she jumped across and started up the hill on the opposite side. Although parts of the landscape were thick with brush, and some of the hill had high grass, most of the rocky terrain on this other side of the creek was open and spacious.

A swishing sound startled her. She laughed upon seeing a frightened squirrel taking refuge in a nearby tree.

The hills began to get steeper and rockier, so she walked more cautiously, looking discriminately at the ground that appeared in her small circle of light. The coming nightfall was dark enough to slow her down on the rocks. Halfway up the hill, she thought she heard voices, so she stopped to listen.

"I don't know why you can't take my word for it," she heard a woman's voice say.

"It's not that I don't trust you. I just want to know exactly where it is. And I need to talk to you about something else, but down there, where it's safe."

The wind garbled the voices, but she thought one sounded like Tukihëla's.

"I'm the only one besides you who has been down there since last April," the woman said.

"I hope you're right," the man replied, and Samantha knew it was Tukihëla. She softly stole up the hill.

"Someone's coming," Tukihëla whispered.

As she approached the top, she glimpsed, in her beam of light, a woman vanish into the hill. She'd seen that woman somewhere before.

"Hello?" Samantha shined her flashlight all around the area, but she couldn't find a trace of the two people.

"Hello? Is anyone there?" she asked again.

She waited several minutes before descending toward the creek. She must have been seeing things. She did feel a little light-headed.

How could two people have vanished into thin air?

As she neared the creek, she suddenly realized where she had seen the woman on the hill. It had been the same woman who had kissed Tukihëla at the county jail.

Samantha entered the dining room early the next morning wearing a summer dress and sandals, her hair twisted up in a big brown clip. She was determined to convince mark and the professor to accept Tukihëla's terms. Everything depended on it.

Tukihëla came up from behind her. "How are you feeling today? Headache gone?"

She gave him a puzzled look.

"Jes mentioned it," he said off-handedly.

"I'm better, thanks." Then she met his eyes, her heart pounding. "A nighttime stroll did wonders for me." She couldn't believe what had just come out of her mouth. Why did she have to say anything at all about it?

"Come across anything peculiar last night?"

"Squirrels, jack rabbits, and one ass, which fled when I called out to it." Her face flamed, and she swallowed hard.

He chuckled and shook his head. "My sister said she saw you, but I couldn't see a damned thing. It was too dark."

"Your sister? What would you be doing out in the hills at night with your—" It suddenly hit her. The bandolier bag. They were out there hiding the bandolier bag! Then a second thought occurred to her: The woman at the jail was his sister.

It hadn't been his girlfriend.

So? Why did she care?

"She and I like to hike in the evenings together. We've been doing it since she was really young."

Brandon entered the room. "I'm sorry I'm late," he said. "I've been on the phone with my attorney all morning. Where are the others?"

The professor and Mark followed shortly, and they all sat down. Jes brought out juice, coffee, pastries, and fruit.

"Charles, did I hear you say you saw Claire last night?"

"Yeah."

"How is she doing these days?"

"Does she live nearby?" the professor asked.

Brandon said, "Claire is a nun in the convent up the road, right here near our property."

"We passed it driving in," the professor said.

"My great-grandfather was a convert and gave the land to the church," Brandon explained. "You might enjoy the history sometime. It's a very old building, dating back to the seventeen hundreds. It produced quite a scandal in my great-granddad's day."

"What kind of scandal?" Mark asked.

Brandon chuckled. "Most folks around here had come to America to escape the religious intolerance of the Church in Germany, and here my great-granddad was inviting the enemy in."

Everyone at the table laughed at Brandon's joke except for his grandson.

"The Pennsylvania Dutch, my ancestors were called," Brandon continued. "None of them came from the Netherlands, though. The other early settlers misunderstood the German word Deutsch for Dutch."

"I don't think they want a history lesson," Tukihëla said.

"Are you kidding?" the professor said. "We're archaeologists."

"As I was saying, Claire has lived at the convent ever since she was in kindergarten, after her mother died. She and Charles shared the same father but had different mothers. So, tell, me, Charles, is she doing well?"

"Yeah, I think so. We enjoyed a nice hike in the hills last night. It seems Samantha was out, too, but it was too dark for us to find one another."

"Goodness, my dear. Was that wise going out alone so late at night? What if you had fallen and sprained an ankle? Or worse?"

"I'll agree with that," Mark added.

"Oh, don't worry about me," she replied, trying to hide her excitement. She couldn't wait to go back and search for the bag. If she found it, she wouldn't need to convince the professor or Mark to accept Tukihëla's terms.

Wearing gloves to protect her hands from the rocks, Samantha climbed the hills full of excitement. The sun was directly above her, shining its rays over the rolling landscape, but its glare only hindered her search.

Samantha found the side of the hill where she had seen Tukihëla's sister disappear into thin air. She overturned a few of the stones in the vicinity but, after nearly an hour, did not find the bandolier bag.

She came upon some yellow jonquils and daffodils near a large boulder, so she stooped to breathe in their sweet aromas. Their perfumed scent brought an added pleasure to the peaceful surroundings. As she leaned against the boulder on the side of the hill to enjoy the wind against her cheeks, she decided the Pennsylvania countryside was the prettiest she had seen in all her travels around the world. She had been on more than half a dozen digs during her academic career over the last five years thanks to her parents' generosity, including places such as China, Russia, and Africa. They had all been amazing, but this was her favorite.

Samantha turned to look over the hills behind her when she saw fresh mud covering the top of the boulder.

How would mud get all along there?

She touched it, sniffed it. It was definitely mud (thank goodness).

Someone has moved this rock. Could this be it? The place they hid the bag?

She grabbed a thick branch from the ground and wedged it beneath the boulder. As she pushed down with all her weight against the branch, the boulder rolled to the side, revealing a small, dark opening.

She leaned inside to take a closer look, and as her eyes adjusted to the darkness, she realized it was some kind of cave. Cautiously she climbed through the opening. A four-foot drop surprised her, and she fell on her knees.

"Aaah!" she cried. Even though the floor of the cavern was solid rock, the fall frightened more than injured her.

To the right of the entryway by the light from the opening, she saw what appeared to be a statue carved in the rock. She felt her way to it and touched it with her hands. Her heart drummed rapidly. She couldn't believe her good fortune. She felt the curve of a face and shoulders in the stone. Is this what Tukihëla was protecting?

Below the statue on a shelf in the rock, a dozen or so votive candles in glass holders were clustered together, with a lighter placed beside them. The image reminded Samantha of the vigil and novena candles lit before a life-size statue of the Blessed Mother at St. Mark the Evangelist Church in San Antonio. Samantha took off her gloves, shoved them in her pockets, and flicked the lighter.

She lit several of the candles. As she peered around the cavern, she nearly lost her breath.

"Oh my God!" She breathed. "Oh my God!"

With a lighted votive candle in hand, Samantha made her way around what she now realized was a catacomb. It was approximately twenty feet by forty feet and about fifteen feet high in most places.

Thirty or so stone tombs, ornately decorated with carvings and artifacts, occupied most of the cavern floor. Samantha held the candle beside some of them to inspect them more closely. Some of the engravings were rectangles with geometrical shapes, similar to those on the sherd she found and to those she had seen on pipes in Oklahoma. Some were of nature—animals, flowers, and vegetation. Each one was unique. She saw the Misink seal on many of the tombs. And again the turtle. She wondered what it signified.

We're both of the turtle.

Samantha gasped when she recognized a pair of hand-carved snowshoes made of redwood. On a smaller tomb—a child's tomb—she saw a miniature canoe made of birch wood, probably crafted by the child's father. Ever so carefully, she touched the canoe. She pictured the child, whom she imagined as a girl, and sighed. These were her people, the people she had been looking for all of her life!

Decomposed quillwork and badly decayed leather artifacts lined the tops of other tombs. Some of the artifacts looked intact and well preserved; others looked as though they might crumble at the slightest touch.

She felt along the back wall, holding the candle close. On it she saw figures and writing. As she inspected more closely, she recognized Algonquian words and an illustration of human forms with bags on their backs.

Below this were more words and illustrations of similar design. Images of the same woman at the entrance to the catacombs with snakes wrapped around her feet and torso and a wreath of flowers adorning her head appeared in several places along the wall.

At the bottom, she found an illustration of a Wampum Belt with two human figures shaking hands. On the left side of the picture were more Algonquian words.

"The peace treaty with William Penn!" Samantha gasped. She recognized the belt, for she had seen a picture of it in her research many times. It dated back to 1682.

"It's some kind of record," Samantha whispered. "I wonder how old." Her heart raced like a jackrabbit and her hands twitched with excitement.

What in the world have I come upon? And what in the world do I do now?

Later that evening, the professor, Mark, and Samantha huddled together at a table in a restaurant in Myerstown.

"Okay guys. Just listen," Samantha said after she and the rest of her team had ordered. "Tukihëla says he's got the bandolier bag where no one will find it. Even if the police do find it, it will be in their custody until the hearing, and then, if there's a trial, even longer. Who knows how long it will take to settle all of this?"

"You got that right," Mark said before taking a sip of his beer.

"We're not getting anywhere soon, and, in the meantime, the cost of the attorney and court fees and traveling expenses are all going to add up," she continued. "I think we need to seriously consider a compromise."

"What kind of compromise?" the professor asked as he loaded up his fork.

"Tukihëla will turn over the bag if we promise to return all our findings to the burial ground and end our research on his grandfather's property." Then she added, hesitantly, "And we have no real cause to believe there is anything more significant to find." Her stomach tightened. She didn't like lying to them.

"There's got to be, or he wouldn't be acting like this."

"Not necessarily, Mark," said the professor, before taking a drink of his water. "Let's think about this carefully. I think we ought to wait and make our decision when the date of the hearing isn't so far off."

"But…" Mark began.

The professor didn't let him finish. "We don't have to decide tonight. Keep in mind that if we don't find that bag and legitimize these past two years of research, you lose your scholarship, I lose my career, and Samantha's grandmother won't be able to prove her ancestry to the modern Lenape tribe in Oklahoma. We may have to forfeit the other possibilities to save our hides."

Mark frowned. "I guess we ought to think more about this before we decide."

Samantha and her team returned to Gellermann Manor and bid one another good night at the base of the winding stairs. The professor headed for the study looking for Brandon, Mark went up to his room to read, and Samantha went through the kitchen and out the back door and took the steppingstones down to the creek.

She sat on the flat rock beside the leaning tree, removed her sandals, and let her legs hang down in the water. It was cold, but it felt good after a few minutes. Twirling her legs round and round, she gazed at the twinkling stars. Was it family loyalty or something else that had prevented her from telling the others?

"Watch out for snakes," Tukihëla called to her from a distance.

She looked back at him. "Good evening."

"Good evening. Do you mind if I sit with you for a while?"

She hated how nervous he made her feel. "Not at all. The water feels great." She scooted over on the rock, toward the leaning tree, and he sat beside her. He removed his flip-flops and rolled up his jeans to his calves so his feet could join hers in the ice-cold water.

"Ooh," he said. "That's cold."

"It feels wonderful."

"Yeah, it does."

They smiled at one another.

Then he said, "It seems you have a knack for finding my secret places."

She moved her feet through the water without answering.

"I know you were down there. I just need to know what you and the others plan to do."

"The others don't know." She gazed at the stream.

"They don't know? But weren't you just with them?"

She nodded.

"You didn't tell them?"

She shook her head.

"Why not?"

She shrugged. "It didn't feel right."

He studied her. "What do you mean? You are going to tell them, aren't you?"

"I haven't decided what I'm going to do yet." She felt stupid admitting this to him. Wouldn't her hesitance make her attraction to him obvious?

"I don't understand."

She met his gaze. "Neither do I."

He looked at her mouth.

Blood rushed to her cheeks as she realized she was also looking at his.

She took a deep breath. "I can't explain. But, I can tell you today has definitely been the most exciting day of my life. Those catacombs are amazing. Do you know anything about them? Like how old they are?"

"Yes, I know everything about them."

"I'm all ears," she said, giving him a bright smile.

He crossed his arms and sighed.

"What's wrong? Why can't you tell me? What are you afraid of?"

"I just don't want anyone to destroy them."

"Destroy them? I'm an archaeologist."

He didn't reply.

"You won't own this land forever," she added. "What will become of them decades from now? If they were registered, it would be against the law for anyone to remove or deface any part of them. They would be protected. Forever."

"I don't have much faith in the government. As it is now, so few know about it. Someone would have to stumble upon the entrance by accident."

"Like me?"

"You found it because I stupidly led you to it. It's not the kind of place a visitor stumbles upon. You were looking."

"What about a developer when the property is sold by your descendants? How do you know your children and grandchildren and great-grandchildren will feel the same about this land and those catacombs as you do?"

He climbed to his feet. Then he wormed each foot back into its flip-flop. "Look, I'm sorry. But, what are you going to do?" he asked. "Are you going to fight me in court?"

She looked down. "I don't know." Then she looked up at him squarely. "Can't you at least consider the possibility of sharing the catacombs with an archaeologist?"

He turned away, toward the water, thrusting his hands in the front pockets of his jeans. "As far as I'm concerned, the only difference between an archaeologist and a grave robber is that..." he paused.

Her face flushed. "What?"

"Never mind."

"Say it." She jumped to her feet, holding her shoes, waiting.

She could see he didn't want to say it, but he did. "The archaeologist calls it research."

"Thank you." She started up the steppingstones, clenching her jaw. He was infuriating.

"Beck."

She stopped and turned to look at him, narrowing her eyes. She waited for him to speak, and, when he didn't, she turned toward the hill and made her way to the manor.

Samantha entered the kitchen from the backdoor and was about to take the back stairs to her room when Brandon poked his head in from the foyer.

"Oh, hello, Samantha. Why don't you join the professor and me? We're just now having our coffee. I'll have Jes bring you a cup." He looked around the kitchen. "Jes?" Jes entered from a side door. "Ah, there you are. I called for you, but I don't think the speaker's working."

"Sorry, sir."

"No worries. Samantha will now be joining us. Coffee all around, please."

"Yes, sir. My pleasure."

Brandon looked like he wouldn't take no for an answer, so Samantha thanked him and followed him to the study.

"Hello, mija," the professor said. He sat in one of two leather chairs beneath the big elk head.

"Hello, Professor."

Samantha picked up a framed photo sitting on the hearth before the empty fireplace and immediately recognized Rebecca, seventeen or eighteen in the photo, standing on the beach beside an older woman, likely her mother. They both had big smiles and big hats and flowing white bathing suit covers. The waves raged behind them.

"Those are my girls," Brandon explained. "That picture was taken just before my wife's last relapse. We had such a good time together, the three of us, on that trip to Ocean City. I took the picture."

"Relapse?" Samantha asked.

"My wife, Jeannie, had cancer."

"I'm sorry," Samantha said. "My grandma on my mother's side also died of cancer."

Brandon cleared his throat. "Jeannie didn't die from the cancer. No, er, she hadn't gone into remission again, but the cancer's not what killed her."

"What did?" the professor asked. "If you don't mind my asking."

"The, er, the, uh, Indians. But please let's not talk about this sad subject. Ah, look, here's Becky's, er, excuse me, Samantha's coffee. Thank you, Jes. I'll take just a bit more, too."

Samantha took the warm cup and smiled politely as Jes refilled the men's cups with steaming coffee, but her smile faded with the butler's exit as she fought the desire to ask Brandon Gellermann more.

Had her ancestors really killed his wife?

CHAPTER SIX

Trouble

Rebecca ducked behind a tree and watched Attie strolling toward the creek from the manor. After he had passed by her and had entered the woods a few yards ahead, she crept from the tree to follow.

Her father had once told her she could explore as much as she wished to the west and south of their property, but the northeast belonged to the Indians, and because they worked hard and paid the Gellermann's a percentage of their farm earnings, they deserved the respect of maintaining the boundary between them. The eastern wood she now entered was that boundary.

Although she loved her father and wished to obey him, she couldn't find any harm in sneaking a peek at the Indians to see what Attie did when he wasn't gardening for her parents. Before now, she'd been too afraid of the Indians, but at seventeen she now felt she had been silly to be afraid.

And she really didn't believe Attie would let anything bad happen to her.

She climbed up the hill through the brush, glad for her high socks and sneakers and denim jeans. She lost sight of Attie, but she could hear him crackling on sticks and rustling through shrubs toward the Indian grounds. She stole forward carefully so he wouldn't hear her.

At last, she came to a clearing and was surprised by the two dome-shaped houses, side by side, each as large as a barn and covered with bark. They stretched across the back of the clearing and were surrounded by people. Three old women prepared food near a campfire. One shucked ears of corn, one plucked the last feathers from a chicken, and the third kneaded dough. Five small children ran around playing, while three older ones returned with some of the men from the fields carrying tools. Rebecca scanned the scene for Attie but couldn't find him.

"Why did you follow me?" a voice came behind her.

She jumped and turned, backing up to a tree.

"Attie! You scared me," she said.

His hands were covered in soil up to his elbows, and he dripped with sweat. His jeans, just as filthy as his hands, had holes at the knees. His boots cracked with dry mud. His shirt, open at the buttons, flapped in the slight breeze, exposing a strong chest and abdomen.

"Why are you here?" he asked again.

"Curious, I guess."

"But you've never come before?"

She shook her head.

"Then why today?"

"I don't know." She shrugged. "I guess because I'm no longer afraid."

"Why were you afraid?"

She shrugged again.

"How old are you?"

"Eighteen," she lied. What was one more year?

"The first time I saw you, you were a scrawny kid."

"But I'm not anymore," she said.

He looked her over. "I see that."

She blushed. "So, are you going to show me around or not?"

"Follow me."

He led her to the old women and spoke to them in another language. Then he turned to Rebecca. "Not many here speak English."

"Why do you?" she asked.

"Because I want to. Most of the others don't care to learn. When I was younger, I worked for a man in town. I learned English there, in his restaurant."

The women nodded at Rebecca as Attie told them her name and then he beckoned her to the first of the dome-shaped houses.

"Don't the children go to school and learn English?" Rebecca asked as they crossed through some kind of game the little ones were playing.

"No. A few have left us, and they go to the schools. Some have married Americans or gone through the immigration office. But we who stay here and live on our homeland, we are not Americans, so we cannot attend the American schools."

"I don't understand. Why aren't you Americans? You live in America, don't you?"

"It's more complicated than that."

He opened the door of the first house they came to. "These wigwams are homes to many families, but we only sleep inside. Everything else, we do out here."

The wigwam was divided by wooden beams into six outer rooms—three on each side—which opened into one larger center room. The outer rooms appeared to be bedrooms, with bunk-like beds along the exterior wall. A higher shelf over the top bunks contained wooden bowls, baskets, pottery, animal skins, and flashlights, a transistor radio, and a stack of notebook paper. The animal skins hung from the shelves as well as from some of the inner beams of the center room, where dried meat, blankets, and colorful belts also hung.

The center room ran the length of the wigwam, but the back section had two stalls where two horses stood looking at her. A circle of woven mats lay in the middle of the building, and lying on one of these was a sleeping dog, who had raised his head when they had first entered, but had gone back to sleep. Leaning against some of the center beams were spears and other weapons, and across from these, to Rebecca's great surprise, was a baby, hanging vertically in a kind of crib, sleeping as soundly as the dog.

"The men are coming in from the fields to eat. We wash up in the creek, where some of the women are cleaning many of our things."

"What things?"

"Bowls, clothes, blankets. I don't know. I'm always at your father's house working. I just come back for the food."

She followed him out of the wigwam and past a chicken coop to a part of the creek she had never seen.

"The water runs faster up here," she said.

A half a dozen women sitting on the bank, scrubbing and talking and laughing and nodding, looked up when Rebecca approached. They weren't much older than she.

Attie said something to them, but they continued to stare at Rebecca without smiling.

Some articles of clothing hung from the trees—shirts, jeans, skirts. Some looked dry and others still dripped with water from the creek. Others sat in a bundle beside the women who continued to stare. Without warning, a man emerged from the water, naked, and walked past her, grabbing a clean pair of jeans blowing on a tree limb. As she turned to look away, she saw Attie strip down, kick his dirty clothes into the bundle beside the women, and walk into the stream with the other men.

Rebecca turned around and ran home, through the woods along the creek, and didn't stop running until she was inside the kitchen.

Jes looked up from his cooking and asked, "Everything okay?"

She nodded and rushed upstairs to her room.

The next morning, Rebecca tried to avoid Attie, but he found her when she was helping Jes bring in the groceries in front of the house beneath the giant sycamore. Jes had gone inside.

"Why did you go so suddenly?" Attie unloaded empty terracotta pots from the bed of her father's old pickup.

Her face turned red. "I guess I was embarrassed."

"Why?"

"Because you were naked."

"I don't understand."

"I'm not used to that. Americans in general don't do that."

He cocked his head to the side. "The body is something beautiful, unless you are old. Why cover it up?"

She smiled. "If you feel that way, then why wear clothes at all?"

"To protect my skin from the sun and the rocks and the dirt." He closed the tailgate and knelt beside the pots, filling them with potting soil. "Our bodies aren't as durable as those of most other animals. That's the only reason for clothing."

She remembered him naked. "Hmmm. I'll have to think about that." Then she turned to carry the groceries inside.

"What are you smiling about?" Jes asked playfully.

"Hmmm?" Rebecca felt the blood drain from her face. "Nothing."

Later that day, Rebecca stood before her dressing room mirror gazing at her body.

"It's just a body," she whispered. "There's nothing naughty about it."

She didn't want to be a prude. Attie had told her the human body is beautiful. She supposed she was beautiful.

"It's natural," she whispered, turning to look at her backside. "There's no reason to cover it up."

She walked around her room, getting used to her own nakedness. She twirled and pirouetted and glided across the hardwood floor, snatching glances in the full-length mirror.

If only Attie could see her now, she thought, laughing.

She went to her window and saw him in the yard, mowing. She pressed her breasts against the windowpane, willing him to look up and see she understood, she wasn't ashamed, and she had transcended the cultural barriers.

A knock on the door surprised her, and she fled from the window and jumped into bed, pulling her covers over her.

"Who is it?"

"It's Mama. Can I come in?"

Rebecca panicked. "Just a minute. I was just changing into my new bathing suit."

She stepped into the yellow bikini and opened her bedroom door.

"What do you think?"

"It's a bit skimpy. But I guess that's the style. That's all we saw at the shops yesterday." Her mother crossed the room and sat on her bed. "Didn't we have fun?"

Rebecca nodded. "I wish we could do that more often."

"Well, I didn't want to say anything until Daddy got things finalized, but now that everything's settled, I have good news. We're going to Ocean City for two weeks, and we're leaving in three days!"

Rebecca's face fell. "Two whole weeks?"

Her mother stood up and adjusted her wig. "I thought you'd be pleased. We haven't been in ages."

"Of course, I am, Mama. Are you sure you can handle it? Are you strong enough?"

"Absolutely!"

Her mother kissed her cheek and left the room saying, "Better start packing!"

Two days later, Rebecca stood on the balcony of her bedroom in her yellow bikini watching Attie digging in the backyard, replacing a busted sprinkler head.

This is it. Today's the day.

She grabbed the white terrycloth robe from the bed, stuck each arm through a sleeve, and left her room.

By the time she reached the backyard, Attie had already quit for the day and was walking toward the woods by the creek. She ran down the hill.

"Attie!" she cried. "Wait up!"

He stopped and looked up at her.

When she caught up to him, she asked, "Do you like my new bathing suit?"

"It's nice," he said, scanning her up and down.

"You want to go swimming?"

"That's where I'm headed now. I need to wash up before eating."

Her heart pounded against her chest. "No, I mean swimming with me, away from the others."

He gave her a puzzled look. "You want to go swimming with me? The two of us? Alone?"

She nodded, unable to hold back the huge grin spreading across her face.

"Does your father know?"

She shook her head.

"Go ask your father. I don't want to get in trouble and lose my job."

She hadn't expected this answer. She had expected him to sweep her up in his arms and carry her into the water.

"But I'm eighteen," she lied again. "I'm a grown woman, able to make my own decisions. I don't need my father's permission."

"Is that how the Americans do things?" He started walking again, up through the woods.

Rebecca followed.

"Yes," she said. "Once you turn eighteen, you no longer have to listen to your parents."

"That seems foolish. The Lenape never stop listening to their parents—and grandparents as well. As long as they are living, we seek their advice. You go ask your father, and I will go ask mine."

She jumped in front of him, blocking his path. "No! I will not ask my father, because I know what he will say. But I would disagree with his answer. He would be wrong, because he would be thinking of money and society and things that don't matter."

"Money and society don't matter? You have a lot to learn." He walked past her.

"Attie, stop and listen to me. I like you. Don't you like me?"

He stopped and faced her. "You are the most beautiful girl I've ever seen. And the sweetest, too. I like you a lot."

Her heart blossomed, and she wanted to shout hooray. Smiling, she said, "Then let's go swimming!"

He frowned. "But we are from different worlds. We should seek the advice of our fathers."

Disappointment welled in Rebecca's eyes. "My parents and I are leaving tomorrow for two whole weeks. We're going to the beach to spend time together. As soon as I return, I'll have to go back to Hartridge for my last year of school."

"You're leaving?"

She nodded as a tear tumbled down her cheek.

He wiped away her tear with a knuckle. "Why are you crying?" His voice was tender.

"Because I'll miss you."

He took her face in his hands and touched his lips to hers.

When he looked at her, he smiled. "I've gotten dirt all over your face."

"So take me swimming."

"Let's go." He took her hand and led her to where the woods were thick—a place neither the Lenape nor the Gellermanns could see.

CHAPTER SEVEN

The Dream Catcher

Well after dark had settled on the horizon, Samantha changed into jeans, took up her field gloves, flashlight, and lantern, and headed up the hill across Lethe Creek toward the catacombs. In two days, the judge would decide the immediate fate of her research on the Gellermann land, since she'd been unable to get the professor and Mark to settle for the bandolier bag, and although she expected a favorable result, she wanted to take a harder look at this fantastic discovery just in case things went wrong for her and her team.

She felt razor sharp tonight, but it was the adrenaline and not a good night's rest. Misink had returned again and again, upsetting her sleep.

Her heart drummed with excitement as she neared the boulder. She set down her flashlight and unlit lantern and heaved the great rock aside. Then she shined her light in the opening, making sure no creatures were visiting tonight, before taking up the lantern and climbing inside.

Once she found her footing in the dark cavern, she lit her lantern and was struck by the awesome sight. Previously, she had seen it only in snippets—as much as a little votive could light at one time. But tonight, with the help of her lantern, she could view all at once the structure and enormity of the room and its contents—the utensils, jewelry, and clothing adorning the tombs, the art on the walls—and she could observe two small tunnels branching off from the center, one on each side.

Before she could study the numerous artifacts, her eyes were drawn upward to the back wall, to the record. Now she could see the whole wall, and the beauty of the artwork amazed her. Setting the lantern on one of the higher tombs, she moved closer toward the wall to inspect it. She wished she had brought her Algonquian book so she could look up the words and images, but she had been in such a rush, that she had left it on the nightstand beneath the Tiffany.

Unlike the ceiling and other sides of the great cavern, which were lined with various rock formations that looked like columns, ribbons, and stumps, the back wall was smooth and appeared less damp.

She reverently touched one of the pictures matching the statue near the opening—a woman wrapped in snakes wearing a floral wreath. Her swollen belly indicated she was pregnant, and her hands, painted red and raised palm upwards, gave her the appearance of praying. The picture was carved into the stone and painted.

"That's my great-grandmother," Tukihëla's voice suddenly carried into the chamber from the opening.

Samantha jumped and whirled around. "You scared the heck out of me."

"Sorry." He climbed into the cavern and made his way through the tombs to her side.

Delighted that he didn't seem angry with her, she determined to find out from him what she could. "The statue is your great-grandmother, too?"

"No. Just that particular symbol by those dates. The one above it is Táskëmus, my great-great grandmother."

"The others we found out in the pasture, who are they and why aren't they buried here?"

"They died of typhoid, and the tribe feared the disease might infect this catacomb. They are Chief Kishku and his wife, Saca, their baby, Wëli, and a handful of devoted farmers."

"I see. Kishku. My great-great-great grandparents."

"And mine."

She looked up at him. "So we're cousins."

He moved nearer to her. "Distant ones."

"Are you certain the bodies of Chief Kishku and the others weren't moved at some point?"

"I couldn't tell you before. It wouldn't have made sense. But about four years ago, several of us tried to bring them here. It was a fiasco. We were ill-equipped. The bodies were falling to pieces. We didn't realize what we had undertaken, so we ended up leaving them there."

"I see." She looked away, back to the wall of figures. "Why is this same symbol used for each of your grandmothers? It's the lady at the entrance, isn't it?"

"I don't know. I'm still catching up on a lot I missed growing up with my white grandfather. Around age twelve, a few years after my father died, I was forced to live in the manor with Brandon. I missed out on a lot. When I went to college, I took a class that made me want to get back in touch."

"Oh."

He pointed to the wall. "I guess that symbol means female or mother. The statue at the opening is of Mother Earth, Kukna. I suppose the tribe saw all women in this way."

"But look here, this is a female symbol, and it's different from the others." She pointed to a bare-breasted farmer carrying a basket of corn on her head.

"That's not a female symbol."

"What are these?" She pointed to the breasts.

"Oh yeah. You're right." He smiled.

"What are the words below the pictures? Can you read them?"

"Táskëmus, which means 'mockingbird.' That's why there's the bird. Born in 1865 and died in 1884."

"She was young—only nineteen." She cleared her throat and looked back at the bird symbol. "I wonder what killed her."

"Probably childbirth. My great-grandfather was born the same year as her death."

"Poor woman. So then, this one here is your great-grandmother?" She pointed to another symbol of the lady and the snakes.

"Yes. Sami, also called Wáxëna, or 'Windsong.' That's what the swirl-like symbol means. She was born in 1900 and died in 1918."

"My God, she was young, too. Eighteen." Samantha gently caressed the symbol with her hand.

"I guess people didn't live as long back then."

"I guess not. Okay, so that's your grandfather?"

"Yes. Koko Nisha. His name means 'rabbit.' See the symbol? Can you see it's a rabbit?"

She nodded.

"Born 1918 and died 1975."

She did the math. "Let's see. Fifty-seven. That's not too bad. Young by today's standards, but a heck of a lot better than eighteen or nineteen. Wait a minute. He was born the same year his mother died. I bet she also died in childbirth. Damn, I'm glad for modern medicine."

"This is my grandmother, Ana, also called Kéxiti because she was so small, born 1922 and died 1940."

"This is strange. Each of the women in your family died young. Don't you find that odd?" She glanced back at him.

"Maybe a genetic defect?"

"But none of these women were related. This is your father's paternal bloodline. It couldn't be a shared defect in the women, unless they practiced inbreeding."

He shook his head. "No. Only the Turtle are, were, permitted to inter-marry, and there had to be a degree of distance."

"Maybe something was wrong with the babies. Maybe they all had large heads or were all breech."

"My mother also died in childbirth. Rebecca Gellermann Nisha—that's her symbol there." He pointed to an image resembling a wave. "Born 1962 and died in 1980, the year I was born."

"This is really strange. This seems too odd to be a coincidence. Something caused each of these women to die young. Do you have any other living relatives, descendants of this tribe, who might know the reason behind these deaths?"

"I have an uncle and several cousins in New Jersey and a handful of cousins here and in Maryland. I suppose I could ask around."

"In the meantime, I'll see what I can learn about birthing techniques and genetic birth defects causing the death of the mother. You might also check your medical records—if you have any—to see if you were diagnosed with any problems at birth."

Tukihëla didn't reply.

"What can you tell me about these symbols here?"

He paused. "Listen. I don't feel comfortable divulging all the details to you. How do I know what you will do with the information?"

"You don't trust me."

"Why should I?"

"You're right. You shouldn't. I still don't understand what good there is in keeping all this hidden."

"I made a promise to my father—your cousin. Why isn't that good enough?"

She looked away. "I don't know." Then her eyes caught a row of dream catchers sitting on a high shelf across the cave. "Look at these. They're beautiful and so well preserved." She maneuvered across the cavern and looked more closely. "These are new. These hoops are made of willow, recent willow."

"Yes. I made them."

"All of them?" There were at least a dozen tucked neatly on the shelf of rock.

He nodded. "I gather my materials nearby and sit among these ancient spirits crafting them. They don't take long to make once I find everything I need. I make them for the convent. The nuns sell them in their craft show and use the money to help orphans."

She raised a brow at him.

"What? I don't hate the Church or anything just because I don't belong to it. I think it accomplishes a good many things."

"I always get the Crusades and the Inquisition thrown at me."

"So, you're Catholic?"

"Out of custom, out of respect for my family. I see the religious stories metaphorically, though. I wish women had greater leadership roles. And I can't defend the Church against its darkest times in history."

"All institutions have their skeletons."

"You sound like an archaeologist," she smiled. "But I wasn't questioning your generosity to the Church. I was wondering about your use of 'ancient spirits.' Just how ancient do you mean?"

He shrugged.

She lifted one of the dream catchers from the rock. "These are so beautiful. Where did you learn to make them?"

"My father taught me when I was young. The Chippewa taught his grandfather, as part of some kind of trade." He took the dream catcher from her and explained. "You take young willow bark and bend it about six inches in diameter all around. You can use bloodroot, sinew, or cordage from different plants for the webbing." He showed her how to loop the roots around the willow hoop to make the web design. His hand brushed against hers and made her tremble. "You put a bead made of rock, like turquoise, lapis lazuli, or quartz and you put it here, to represent the spider. And you leave a small hole in the center for the good thoughts to come through."

"What happens to the bad thoughts?"

"They get caught in the web, and then, with the first morning sun rays, they perish."

"Maybe I need one to catch my bad dream." She shuddered. "Then maybe I'd get a bit of sleep at night."

"You haven't been sleeping well?"

"I never have nightmares. None I remember anyway. Just lately. I think it's because I've been nervous, stressed, you know?" She wrapped her ponytail around her finger.

"Yeah, I know." He smiled grimly. "What happens in your dream?"

She shook her head. "It's weird. Always a little different, and yet the same. It always ends with the face of the Mësingw, or Misink, as you call him, trying to kill me."

Tukihëla chuckled. "Sorry. I'm not laughing at you. Your dream reminds me of what my cousins used to say to me when I was young. They'd say I better be good or Misink would get me."

"Why did they say that?"

"To correct me when I misbehaved. Occasionally one of our tribe would dress up as Misink, with his face painted half red and half black. He'd drape himself with a bearskin and do a funny dance. We children were afraid of him, so the older kids and the parents would use that fear to keep us in line.

"He'd come before a big hunt, or at the birth of a baby. That's all I remember."

"My grandma says he comes to keep the harmony between humans and the rest of nature."

"That's right." He gave a gentle smile. "He warns us to kill only what is necessary, and to use every part of what we kill, to waste nothing. Otherwise, he will haunt us."

Samantha touched Tukihëla on the arm and then let her hand drop away. "Thanks for sharing your stories. They make me feel more connected to my past."

"Here," he said, handing over the dream catcher. "Take it. You never know. It might work."

She gave him a grateful smile, though she knew such a thing to be nothing but folklore and superstition.

Two days later, the three archaeologists, shocked by the judge's decision to put a restraining order on them until after their hearing, secured their findings as best they could beneath the tent and drove the van back to San Antonio to await the hearing, which was four months away.

Now Samantha sat with her parents at a late breakfast after a peaceful night void of any haunting by Misink, even though the dream catcher had remained, unpacked, in her luggage on the floor beside her bed.

At the smaller table in the breakfast nook, nestled in a bay window looking out onto a colorful Texas garden, Samantha told her parents about her trip. Through the window, bright petals glistened in the morning sun, and two hummingbirds visited the feeder hanging from a nearby oak. An orange cat belonging to a neighbor suddenly jumped from the tree and scattered the dancing birds over the pool.

"Wow, Beck. You amaze me. It makes me want to fly out to Pennsylvania and see for myself." When he was excited, her father's round face and round eyes often reminded Samantha of Jiminy Cricket, from Disney's Pinocchio.

As she took a bite of the steaming blueberry muffin, Samantha thought how much more eager her father would be if she told him about the catacombs.

"Your grandma will be thrilled to hear the details," Luther added. "She's coming tomorrow."

Dorothy interrupted. "Will you be able to attend Marta's wedding next Saturday?"

"Oh, that's right. Yes. I will."

"I can't wait to see Grandma's face when you tell her your news," Luther said again.

"Well, it might not amount to anything if my team doesn't win the hearing in September and we end up going to trial. Without the bandolier bag, we have no proof."

"That reminds me," her mother said. "A man called early this morning to tell you he's bringing the contract and the bag sometime next week."

Samantha jumped out of her chair. "What? Who, Mama? Who called?"

"I can't say his name. Tookalahisha?"

"He's coming to San Antonio?"

"Well, that's what he said, Liebling," Dorothy replied. "He said the professor would know what he was talking about."

"Mama! Why didn't you tell me before?"

"Ach, I was going to, and then you started on about your findings, and I forgot. But I've told you now, haven't I? What's the big deal?"

"Mama! If the professor has truly agreed to sign, then, then, ahhh!" She threw up her hands and went looking for her cell phone.

"O'Neil won't fund anything past our current dig," the professor explained to Samantha over the phone. "He said we have the proof we need, so we should sign the contract to get the bag back from Nisha. I'm sick as hell over it, but there seems to be nothing I can do. Unless you can convince your daddy this is a worthy investment."

"No. He doesn't have that kind of money floating around." She knew she could change O'Neil's mind by revealing details about the catacombs. She teetered on the edge of divulging her knowledge of them to the professor. This would be a sure way out of their dilemma. They could get money from anywhere in the world, both public and private. She and Mark could get jobs anywhere, too. Any institution would be pleased to have them. They'd be set for life.

What was holding her back?

"Anyway," the professor said. "We're scheduled to meet Nisha on campus in my office Friday at two o'clock."

Samantha spent the next few days conducting research at the campus library, hoping to discover some insight into the untimely deaths of the women in Tukihëla's family. She began by reading books devoted to maternal deaths and birth defects, but nothing in them seemed to provide any answers. One article had at first seemed promising with its discussion of a possible genetic tendency in babies to attach too low on the placenta, causing the placenta to rupture before delivery, but when Samantha understood this almost always resulted in the death of both the baby and the mother, she realized she was on the wrong track.

She was about to give up her search when a classmate sitting on a padded bench said hello, and, as they were talking, Samantha's eye happened upon a stack of books on the nearby coffee table.

"Hey, Jasmine, what's this?" she asked her friend, taking the top book from the pile. Its title was *Dating and Nuptial Practices of Ancient Native Americans*.

"Oh, I'm working on a paper for the summer term. I haven't really chosen a topic, but I found a bunch of book titles when I Googled 'mythology' thinking I might write something along those lines."

"Do you mind if I take this one?"

Her friend shrugged. "That's fine. You've just helped me to eliminate one topic from my list."

Back in her bedroom listening to the music playing over her iPod, Samantha rummaged through her backpack looking for the notepad she had been using to take notes at the dig. As she felt around the bottom for a pen, her hand hit upon something sharp and foreign, something square and made of glass. She pulled it out. It was the picture of Rebecca Nisha, the one from the nightstand in her room at the manor. How did it get into her book bag?

The three archaeologists met with Tukihëla in the professor's office Friday afternoon. Mark stood in the cramped room, hanging over Samantha like a great palm tree. Stacks of books and papers, a box of paper-clips, several old memos that should have been tossed, and two stained coffee mugs littered the top of the professor's desk so there was little room for the contract.

A leather satchel lay across Tukihëla's lap, and inside this was the bandolier bag.

He didn't hand it over right away. Samantha feared he had changed his mind. She even asked, "Are you having second thoughts?" and he shook his head, though still gripping the satchel, making no move to empty it of its precious contents. Eventually, after seeing the contract signed by the three archaeologists, Tukihëla gave the bag over to the professor and signed his name: Tukihëla Nisha, A.K.A. Charles Gellermann.

The meeting ended on a celebratory note with a conference call to O'Neil. The team was so pleased with the bureaucrat's promise of future funding that they decided to go out for happy hour drinks and appetizers, inviting Tukihëla to join them.

Tukihëla hesitated and then, like a sudden change in wind, accepted.

At the club, Samantha felt like a rope in a tug of war between Mark and Tukihëla. She was shocked, when after a dance with Mark, Tukihëla asked for a turn. She had another shock when he masterfully twirled her around the dance floor, and, as she clutched and tried to follow him (in strappy sandals not meant for such dancing), she felt uncomfortably aware of Mark's eyes following her every move. Both men smelled and looked good. Both men possessed qualities she admired. She liked Mark—had always liked Mark—but her body responded to Tukihëla.

Later, when she and Mark had returned to the bar for a second round of drinks, Mark leaned in for a kiss, but she pretended not to notice and turned her head.

Just as she finished her drink, Tukihëla came up for another turn and the dancefloor and pulled her in close for a waltz. Their bodies brushed against one another, sending shocks of heat across her skin. She bit her lip and gazed up at him, only to look away and sing with the music pouring from the speakers.

By her third drink, she felt less self-conscious in Tukihëla's arms, and after her fourth, she didn't mind when he held her captive on the dance-floor.

She felt a tap on her shoulder just after ten and found the professor and Mark standing behind her.

"Come on. Let us take you home," the professor said. "I want to make sure you get there safely before all the drunks get out on the road."

"I'll get her there safely. You have my word," Tukihëla replied.

"Come on, Sam. Come with us. Please," Mark said.

"But I'm not ready to go home yet. I'll see you later."

Mark leaned in closer to her. "Come on. I don't trust this guy."

"Let's go, mijo," the professor said to Mark. "Let's let the lady dance."

Samantha avoided Mark's eyes as he and the professor left the club.

After a while, she asked Tukihëla how he came to be such an excellent dancer.

"My people had a lot of dances we had to learn, for different occasions. They were built into our worship. So, when I went to college, I made a deal with the dance professor. I would teach her these tribal dances if she would teach me all she knew."

"You dated your college dance professor?"

"She was never my professor."

"You didn't answer my question."

But he didn't have to.

After the bar closed at two, Tukihëla drove her to her parents' home. They both grew quiet without the safety of the loud music and thick smoke between them. When he parked in front of her house, neither spoke or made a move to get out of the truck.

The large historic mansions of Olmos Park and the tall sprawling oaks brooded over them, blocking most of the stars and moonlit sky from their view. The narrow streets closed in on them, making Samantha even more aware of how close she sat to Tukihéla in the middle seat, the two of them alone with the sound of their breathing and the whistling leaves.

Finally, full of adrenaline and alcohol, she said, as she nervously flicked at one fingernail with another, "I can't say I don't think of those catacombs every time I look at you."

"I know." He gripped the steering wheel and gazed out at the empty street.

"But I know I would have liked you even if they had never existed." She bravely glanced over at him.

"I know." He wouldn't meet her eyes.

"I really like you. Your stubborn pride and the way you whirl me around the dancefloor, and your beautiful dream catchers, and, God, your devotion to your father and your ancestors—our ancestors—and, and your deep love for your grandfather, even though there's that wall."

He raised a brow at her.

"Yes, it's obvious you love your grandfather."

"But?"

The alcohol had loosened her lips. She couldn't stop herself. "But, well, I can't explain. I'm an archaeologist, and, well, you and I see things differently. You see me as a grave robber. You said so yourself. No, just listen. I'd never give up. I'd always try to convince you to let me publicize the catacombs. And if you ever gave in, you'd hate me for it, and if you didn't, I'd grow to hate you." She wrinkled her brows. "How did you know there was a but?"

"Women never reveal their true feelings unless they are followed by a but."

"How is it you know so much about women?" she teased.

He didn't reply.

Right. The dance professor.

Samantha didn't know what to say.

"Ride back with me, to Pennsylvania tomorrow."

She gave him a surprised look. "What?"

"You were going to fly out with the professor and Mark Monday anyway, right? To start the reparations?"

"Yeah. Now that our team has the money."

"I'll save you the airfare."

"Why did you drive all this way anyway? Why didn't you fly?"

"Long story. Look, I'm not asking you to marry me, just to make an otherwise boring drive a little more interesting."

She blushed. "I've got my mother's best friend's daughter's wedding tomorrow in Fredericksburg. Or, I'd say yes."

"I'll wait for you. We'll leave Sunday, then."

"What? Really?" Her heart danced.

He nodded.

"This is crazy." She took a deep breath. "Okay, but only if you come with me to the wedding."

"And meet the whole family?"

"Your family, too, remember? Well, my father and grandmother are related to you anyway."

He laughed. "All right, Beck."

Then he leaned in and gave her a soft kiss. Samantha beamed, waiting awkwardly a minute longer, and then scooted across the bench seat, jumped out, and waved goodbye.

"I'll call you in the morning from my hotel," he said.

"It *is* morning." She laughed and waved as he drove away.

<u>CHAPTER EIGHT</u>

A Secret Wedding

"You're going fishing dressed like that?" Rebecca's father asked.

She turned on the grassy hill leading to the creek and looked up at him standing on the back porch still wearing his Sunday suit. Beautiful daffodils bloomed all around her. Dressed in her prettiest white summer dress, carrying a bouquet of jonquils in one hand and her favorite rod and reel in the other, she smiled at her father, though she was on her way to secretly marry Attie.

"I'm making a trade with the Indians," she said. "I'll be home soon."

"You're trading your favorite fishing pole? What are you getting in return?"

"Jewelry, Daddy. I'm not so fond of fishing anymore. It's no big deal."

"I can take you shopping for jewelry, if that's what you want." He thrust his hands in his pockets and lifted his chin. Rebecca wondered if he knew what she was doing.

"I want Indian jewelry. It's one-of-a-kind. You can't get it in any store."

"Hold on. Wait a minute." Her father entered the back door of the manor.

Rebecca froze, a lump forming in her stomach. She would be leaving for Hartridge in the morning, and she wouldn't go without marrying Attie. The Indian marriage would keep Attie from taking another in her absence. Next year, when she returned from school, and after she turned eighteen, she would convince her parents to give them a traditional wedding. But she knew they would not give their permission today.

Her father emerged from the house. "Let me take your picture. You look lovely standing in those flowers, like a painting."

Rebecca smiled with relief for the camera and then waved goodbye and turned away, down the hill toward the Indian grounds.

As Rebecca entered the eastern woods by the creek, she wondered how the tribe would react to her using a fishing pole in place of an ear of corn in the wedding ceremony. Attie knew what she was doing, and though he had laughed at first when she had told him her idea, he had given his approval. A Lenape bride usually gave an ear of corn to the groom to symbolize that she would bake the maize into bread, and the groom presented a bone, to show he would hunt and bring home the meat. But Rebecca had told Attie she hadn't the slightest idea how to bake bread, and that if the symbols were going to mean anything, she would have to use a fishing pole.

Hopefully he explained this to the rest of the tribe, she thought as she walked through the woods.

They were waiting for her when she entered the clearing—all of the women of the tribe. The oldest woman, large-breasted, wrinkled, and hunched over, approached her with a smile and put a deerskin cape trimmed with quillwork around Rebecca's shoulders.

Rebecca didn't want to cover up her pretty white dress, but she was grateful for this sign of acceptance.

Another woman placed a wreath of flowers on her head.

Where were the men? Where was Attie?

Rebecca followed the group of women through the clearing and down the other side of the woods, over the creek.

"Where are we going?" she asked, though she knew no one could understand her. She wouldn't have worn sandals if she had known she'd have to hike her way to the wedding ceremony.

As the group made its way through the brush along a well-worn path, Rebecca heard music. It sounded as though it was coming from the ground.

At last, they came to a dark cave. The younger girls entered first, carrying flashlights. The older women beckoned to Rebecca to follow the girls.

The music sounded from the cave. The beat of the drum sent shivers up Rebecca's spine.

She followed the girls down a long corridor, sloping further into the ground.

When at last, the girls in front of her stopped and looked at her, she moved through them to the front at the edge of a cliff and saw the rest of the tribe gathered below.

"Oh my God!" she cried.

CHAPTER NINE

Another Wedding

Saturday afternoon, wearing a fitted pink rayon gown, Samantha stood in a pew at St. Mary's Catholic Church in Fredericksburg, Texas. Her mother stood on one side of her, and Tukihëla on the other, as they awaited the procession of her mother's friend's daughter's bridal party.

Tuki.

He had asked her on their way to Fredericksburg to call him Tuki.

"My sister will be amused when she learns I attended mass," he whispered as the first bridesmaid made her entrance. He looked spectacular in his brand-new suit, bought just for this occasion.

"Count on it being a long one, too," she whispered back. "German Catholic weddings always are."

When the father of the bride kissed his daughter's cheek and handed her over to her husband-to-be, Samantha felt her stomach tighten. She stole a glance at Tuki. She imagined the two of them, together, before the altar, becoming husband and wife. Yeah, she was feeling really stupid, but she couldn't help herself.

She turned her attention to Marta, who said her vows in a blabbering of sobs. Samantha could feel Tuki's eyes on her, so she looked down, afraid to meet his gaze.

At the reception in the Lady Bird Johnson Park Pavilion, Tuki sat with Samantha's father while her mother dragged Samantha around to reintroduce her to many of her Fredericksburg friends she hadn't seen in years. The newlyweds had just cut the cake, and three bridesmaids in their matching green sleeveless gowns were handing out platefuls to each of the guests.

The park pavilion was the size of a large warehouse with sides that opened like garage doors. On this hot June afternoon, the sides were open, allowing a faint breeze to circulate among the three hundred or so guests. White Christmas lights hung from the high ceiling and along lattice behind the cake and gift tables near the entrance. Long buffet tables, once spread with food, made a cross configuration in the center of the room, and, along the two open sides of the building, even longer buffet tables covered with white tablecloths and real ivy runners were now peppered with cups of beer and wine. Some of the metal folding chairs had been pulled from the tables and moved to the outskirts of the dance floor as the local band on the stage at the back of the building prepared its instruments and equipment for a live performance.

When her mother had finally finished with her, Samantha found Tuki sitting at the table alone.

"I'm sorry about that," she said, taking the chair beside him. "My mother can be so embarrassing."

"It's not hard to understand why she'd like to show you off to her friends."

"But she doesn't ever say a word about my archaeological accomplishments. Nothing about the lost tribe. She'll comment on my choice of fingernail polish before she'll say anything about what's been going on in Pennsylvania." Samantha sighed. "Maybe she's waiting on the DNA test before she makes a big deal over it all. I had to send in another blood sample because the first was apparently contaminated."

"They aren't her ancestors, they're yours. And your father's. Now he's an interested man. If he hadn't needed a bathroom break, we'd still be talking."

"Really?" She leaned forward in her chair.

"Yeah. It's been great. Did you know his grandmother, Alice, Kexi's daughter, taught him how to play Pahsaheman? I couldn't believe it when he described it. It's exactly like we used to play it, my cousins and me, when we were young." He rested his chin in his hand, his face only a foot or two away from hers.

"Pahsaheman?"

"Unikwëti football. Only, the boys play against the girls. The boys aren't allowed to carry or throw the ball—only to kick it—and they can't grab or tackle the girls. But the girls can basically do what they want."

"Sounds like my kind of game."

He smiled. "I must have been nine or ten the last time I played, just after my father died and before Claire went away."

"Went away? What do you mean?"

"When her mother died, she was only five or six. My grandfather took her from our people and put her in his convent to be raised by the nuns."

Samantha saw his face suddenly twist with the memories. She wanted to talk to him about it, but this didn't seem like the right time or place. To distract him, she asked, "Why don't we dance? The *Grand March* is about to begin."

"The what?"

She shrieked playfully at his dismay over having to learn a new dance. She stood and pulled on his arm. "You'll see. Come on. They're lining up now."

After the *Grand March*, Samantha enjoyed teaching the hesitant, but ultimately cooperative, Tuki the *Chicken Dance* and the *Cotton-Eyed Joe*. Then they broke off from the group and danced to a mix of different kinds of songs, Tuki more than capable of taking the lead.

Laughing, she asked, "The college dance professor?"

He gave her a nod as he twirled her under his arm and then pulled her in close.

"This is crazy," she whispered.

She could tell he knew she didn't mean his moves. "I know."

A sobering moment came much later, when the bride gleefully flung her bouquet to a group of girls and single women ranging from age four to sixty-five, with Samantha unwillingly among them after having been coerced by her well-meaning mother. The flowers hit her in the face, and though she could have easily snatched them up and won the contest, she let them bounce against her chest and fall to the cement floor, where they were scooped up by an eager teenager.

Tuki laughed and shook his head, and when it came time for him to join the boys and other single men for the garter toss, he stood silently on the outskirts of the group, a token among them, apparently even less eager than Samantha to win.

A few minutes later, after sitting quietly across from one another at their table, both finding their cups of beer a bit more useful and necessary, Tuki asked if he could drive her home, back to San Antonio.

"We need to get an early start tomorrow," he muttered.

"You sure you still want to do that? I mean, drive together?"

"Why? You don't?"

"It's not that. Believe me." She looked courageously into his eyes, for only a moment, and then looked away. "I'm just not sure of the good of it."

"Come on, let's go. We have an hour to discuss it."

During the ride back to San Antonio, while she sat close to him in the middle seat of his truck, Samantha brought up their traveling plans again.

"It's probably not too late for me to catch a flight out on Monday."

"Do it. If that's what you want to do, then do it." He kept his eyes on the dark road.

She studied his profile. After a minute, she said softly, "Please don't be angry. I'm only trying to do the right thing. To do what's best. For both of us."

"I know." He looked at her.

She didn't know what to say.

"Listen." He returned his eyes to the road. "Why can't we enjoy these two weeks? When you're not busy with the reparations, I can tell you more about our ancestors and you can tell me more about your side of our family, and then, when it's time for you to go, you go."

"Because I'm afraid."

He looked at her. "Of me?"

She shook her head. "I've never had a broken heart."

His hand curled itself around her knee.

"Have you?" she asked.

He shrugged.

"You have."

He finally nodded.

"When?"

"In college. When I was at Harvard."

"You went to Harvard?"

He nodded again.

"The dance professor?"

"Yeah." He took his hand from her knee and returned it to the steering wheel.

"Will you tell me what happened?"

"You really want to know?"

"Sure, I do."

He was quiet for a while. She thought he wasn't going to tell her, but then he broke the silence. "We dated about a year while I finished up my master's. Then I finished my degree, got a job, and left for Iraq."

"That's it? That's your story?"

He shrugged. "I knew she'd never leave Cambridge."

"I see."

"She was older anyway. It wouldn't have worked."

She asked why he went to Iraq.

"The engineering firm I work for sent me to help rebuild the infrastructure in a few major cities."

A little while later, he said, "I dread that long drive all by myself, Beck, but I guess you're right."

She nodded with moist eyes.

They were quiet the rest of the way. When he parked in front of her house, she said good night and climbed from the vehicle, shuddering before the dark, empty house. Her parents were staying in Fredericksburg after the wedding, so she'd be alone. She looked at him and waved, wishing so badly she could ask him to stay the night. As he pulled from the curb, the tears came.

She had to call him the next morning with her tail between her legs, but with a strange feeling of elation. "There are no available flights out of San Antonio. Can you take me as far as Dallas?"

Samantha sat beside Tuki in the middle seat of his black Chevy pickup late Sunday morning about an hour outside of San Antonio. "This is interesting," she said without looking up from her book.

"What is?"

"It says here the girls of some ancient Native American tribes, once they reached the age of fourteen, would paint their faces with a special design that would let others know they were unmarried."

"Sounds a lot cheaper than using wedding rings after the fact."

"Oh, hush." She laughed. "And less comfortable, too. Note it's only the females who had to wear the sign. The males got off easy."

"Well of course."

She laughed again. A few minutes later, she said, "Oh, listen to this. I know I've read this before—I think in a book by Joseph Campbell—but I had forgotten until now. Snakes were viewed as something positive, as a symbol of rebirth, because of the shedding of skin. Now I understand why our Unikwëti ancestors depicted the Mother Earth with snakes around her torso and feet."

"Mother Earth, Kukna, is a beautiful, life-giving spirit. She represents creation, birth, and eternal life.

"I remember when my aunt was about to give birth, she was dressed all in white, like the Earth goddess—with a crown and everything. The tribe held a ceremony around her for good luck. Then she went into this temporary, makeshift birthing house built just for the occasion. We had a midwife, I think. I was too young to understand everything. I just remember it was a lot of fun—the party, I mean. I'm sure it wasn't fun for her."

Samantha laughed. "Not if she didn't have drugs."

"She may have." He laughed, too. "We did pass the ceremonial pipe around, you know."

Samantha covered her mouth and giggled.

"Yeah, even after the baby was born, that party lasted well into the night."

"Well, at least you can't say our ancestors didn't love life."

He nodded. "That's true, you know. Not only *human* life. Our ancestors valued the lives of the animals and the plants as well. Whatever was killed became a god, and when it was eaten, it was like Holy Communion is for the Catholics. All of the meat must be eaten or dried, the hide tanned, the tusks, teeth, and bones made into ornaments or weapons, because you couldn't throw away part of a god."

"That's why you wear the small bones around the Misink ornament, because they came from something special you killed and ate?"

He shrugged. "No. I was very young when my father gave this to me. He just told me to always wear it, that it had once belonged to my mother." He touched the necklace beneath his shirt before returning his hand to the steering wheel.

A few hours later, Samantha was pulled from her quiet thoughts by a sudden bump in the road. The truck continued to drive unevenly.

"Feels like a bad tire." Tuki slowed the truck and took the next exit off the highway. He found a filling station and pulled in.

Samantha waited while he climbed out and walked around the vehicle, inspecting it.

"Flat tire," he mouthed through the windshield at her.

Rolling her eyes, she climbed from the pickup.

"It's okay. I've got a spare," he assured her. "That will get us to Dallas."

She stood behind him and watched as he took the spare from the bed of truck, found the jack and other tools in his toolbox, set the jack in place, and began pumping near the back passenger side.

"What can I do?" she asked.

"You can help me get this tire off," he said as he removed the hubcap.

Together they pulled off the tire and rolled it to the tailgate.

After he had finished and they had put the flat tire in the back of the truck, they started for the Dallas airport, with plenty of time for Samantha to make her flight.

"Oh no," he said, before he had pulled out of the filling station.

"What now?"

"The spare's no good."

"What?"

"The spare's going flat. I'm surprised I didn't notice it as I was putting it on. It's not going to get us there."

"Geez."

They sat for a moment in the truck. Then he went into the filling station to ask about a garage. She watched as he disappeared into the store and then reemerged.

"There's a place around the corner." He climbed back into the truck.

Carefully, he drove down the access road and took the first right, where Jon's Paint and Body Shop appeared behind a handful of scraggly mesquite trees.

"I won't be able to get to it right away," one of the men in the garage said after Tuki explained what had happened. He wiped his grimy hands on a dirty rag and then stuffed the rag into his back pocket. He was short and squat in his blue coveralls, which bore his name, "Red," on a beige patch, probably for the red locks curling from beneath his baseball cap. "It'll be at least an hour before I can look at it. I promised this other guy his car by noon."

"Any tire dealers nearby?"

"None open today."

Tuki turned to Samantha. "You'll have to take a cab the rest of the way."

"A cab for two hours? Won't that cost a fortune?"

"Or you can wait and drive with me the rest of the way. It's up to you."

"Um, there's no cab service in this town," Red informed them. "You'll have to order one from Waco, and that'll take about forty minutes."

Samantha looked at her watch. "That would be pushing it, but it might work."

Tukihëla frowned.

"What?"

Red looked on, so Tuki ushered her further away, back out toward the truck.

"Listen. It's up to you, of course, but I think you're being silly. We're two adults. Cousins, no less. I think we can control ourselves the rest of the way."

"I know we can control our bodies," she snapped. "It's my heart I'm worried about."

He squeezed her shoulders. "Maybe something wants us to ride together."

"What? Spirits?" Samantha's heart sank with regret over her sarcasm as soon as she saw the hurt in his eyes.

He released her and turned back toward the garage. "Yeah, go ahead and order that cab for us, will you, Red?"

"Sure thing."

"Wait." She caught up to him. "I'm sorry. I didn't mean that. I'm just nervous. That was a terrible thing for me to say."

"I'm glad you said it. It reminds me how different you and I really are."

"Wait, please." She took his shoulders in the same way he had taken hers.

Samantha started to speak, and then didn't. She released his shoulders and turned away, back toward the truck to get her things.

"What?" he said, following her. "What were you going to say?"

"I was going to say that…" She didn't face him. She reached the truck and leant against the driver's door, looking, but not looking, through the windowpane. "Whether we ride together or not, whatever we do, it doesn't matter anymore. The damage has been done. My heart's already broken." Her throat tightened.

He stood silently behind her.

After several minutes, she whipped around to face him. "Aren't you going to say anything?"

He spoke tenderly. "What do you want me to say, Beck? That I understand how you feel? Well, I do."

"That's right. You do. The dance professor."

He shook his head. "Naw. This is different."

Searching his eyes, she put her hands to her mouth. "What are we going to do?" she whispered.

He stood close to her, his body touching hers. He took her face in his hands, so both of their sets of hands held her face.

"Cancel the cab," he said softly.

She froze as the adrenaline rushed through her body.

"And I'm going to spend the next two weeks convincing you the catacombs are better left alone."

She dropped her hands. "And when you fail?"

He shrugged. "What have I got to lose by trying? If I fail, I fail." He gently covered her mouth with his.

She closed her eyes and leaned into him, savoring the kiss and the moment she knew couldn't last.

CHAPTER TEN

The Charge

Dizzy from the humidity inside the deep caverns, Rebecca looked down at the tribe gathered below. A center fire was surrounded by four water drums, upon which four young men beat a slow cadence. Other men played turtle shell rattles and wooden flutes. Attie stood next to his father at the far end of the cave wearing deerskin trimmed with the same quillwork as that on Rebecca's cape.

Attie was smiling, so everything must be okay, Rebecca thought.

The oldest woman handed Rebecca's fishing pole over to another woman and then led Rebecca down a path to the floor of the cavern. The music increased in volume as she neared the ring of tribesman surrounding the fire. The woman led Rebecca to the center and danced around the fire. She pulled at Rebecca's arm and nodded, indicating Rebecca should imitate her moves.

Two shakes down, two shakes up, twirl around, clap. Two shakes down, two shakes up, twirl around, clap.

As Rebecca maneuvered around the fire, the rest of the tribe danced in their places in the human ring and chanted:

"He-ya, he-ya. Unikwëti hach ki? He-ya, he-ya. Unikwëti hach ki?"

Rebecca felt dizzy and faint from both the humidity and the dancing, but just when she thought she couldn't go on, Attie caught her and held her close.

"Hello, there," he said smiling. "Are you okay?"

"Never better," she said, and it was true, now that she was in his arms.

Four months later, on the day she returned home from Hartridge for the winter break, Rebecca, still wearing her school uniform, tight now around her belly, stood inside the Lebanon County Jail. Attie's father gave her a stern look as he exited, and she entered, the cell with the help of the deputy. Once inside, she jumped at the sound of the bars slamming shut behind her.

Attie looked at her warily from across the cell.

"This is all a big mistake. Daddy has agreed to drop the charges."

"How could you lie to me, Beck? Is this how the Americans do things?"

"If Madame L'Ponte hadn't interfered…"

"You have no one else to blame but yourself."

She hung her head. She knew he was right. "I'm sorry."

"Now your parents hate me."

"They don't understand."

"They think I forced you."

"No. I told them the truth."

"I've never been treated so badly as your father treated me."

She moved near him, only a foot of air between them. "I'm so sorry. Please forgive me. I love you, Attie. I didn't mean for you to get hurt."

"You put my whole tribe in jeopardy. If my people are discovered, they will be forced to either become citizens or move to a reservation."

Rebecca covered her belly with her hands as the tears streamed down her cheeks. "I've ruined everything. You don't love me anymore." She took a step back, looking at him through a veil of tears.

CHAPTER ELEVEN

Human Finger Bones

Sitting across from one another in a booth at a Mexican restaurant a half a mile from Jon's Paint and Body Shop, Samantha and Tuki talked over enchiladas, refried beans, and Spanish rice. He asked about her schooling.

Samantha said, "I went through a scholarship program at Trinity University. My mom wanted me close by, so I didn't even apply to other schools. And I have no idea yet where I'll go for a doctoral program, if I choose that route. Trinity doesn't offer one."

"You must be pretty smart."

"I didn't always think so. When I was younger, I suffered with epilepsy. I went undiagnosed for years, and my teachers thought I wasn't paying attention."

"Man."

"Enough about me. Tell me something about you. What was your major?"

"I double majored in engineering and political science. Then got a master's in engineering."

"And then took a job for a firm that sent you to Iraq fresh out of college."

"That's right. Do you want to tell the story?"

"Sorry. What was it like? In Iraq?"

He shifted in his seat. "Well, I worked with a group of civil engineers on rebuilding." He shook his head. "It's never going to happen. As long as there are insurgents there—and there will always be insurgents there—the electricity, sewage, water—all those things we Americans take for granted—will never be the same."

Samantha finished up the last of her rice. "Did you see a lot of bloodshed? Bombing?"

"Just one, but it was enough."

"What happened?"

"I was waiting at the clinic for a friend of mine. I was playing around with a deck of cards when I noticed this little Iraqi girl—couldn't have been more than six years old—watching me. Her mother had a crying baby in her arms, and the little girl was bored and wanting attention, so I showed her a card trick. I showed her a card, shuffled the deck, and then made the card appear on the top of the deck—it's an old trick, really easy. You probably know it. Anyway, the little girl is amazed. I soon realize she wants the cards. Well, I give them to her, not sure if she'll give them back, but she was a little girl. What could I do?

"So, she tries to do the same trick, and when she shuffles the cards, they fly everywhere, all over the damn clinic. Before I can get up to help her, she runs down the hall away from me, like she's afraid she's going to get in trouble. I called out to her, but she wouldn't come. Next thing I knew, a bomb exploded right in front of me, from the direction of the little girl. Her mother, who was still sitting across from me, looked at me with terror. I ran through the smoke looking for the girl. It was awful. It was the worst day of my life. That was the hardest thing I've ever had to do, carrying that little body back to her mother."

"Oh my God. How terrible!"

"I'll never forget the look the mother gave me, letting me know it was my fault her daughter died."

"But you know it wasn't. Right?"

He shrugged, and Samantha thought she saw his hands trembling on the table.

They had finished eating, so the waitress came and took their plates, leaving the check in the center of the table.

Then Tuki said, "To me, death isn't the end of us. Our death has meaning to others, especially if we are young when we go. I spent but a short time with my father, but he continues to influence me. He lives on in me."

Samantha leaned forward. "Yes. You're right. I never thought about it that way, but, in a way, I suppose that's what I'm trying to do as an archaeologist. I'm trying to enable past civilizations to have an impact on the modern world."

He smiled at her. "Naw," he shook his head. "You're just a grave robber," he said jokingly.

She narrowed her eyes at him, but before she could say a word, he leaned over the table and kissed her.

Five hours later, as they approached Texarkana, Samantha finally asked the question she had been dying to ask.

"Why don't you and your grandfather have a better relationship? Did something happen?"

Tuki didn't answer. She wondered if she had crossed a line, but a few minutes later, he said, "We were close once. In my early teens, he was cool. I could talk to him about anything. He let me drive the car whenever I wanted. He completely trusted me."

"Should he have?" Samantha teased.

"I was a pretty good kid, believe it or not. But I didn't understand how much my grandfather had suppressed the Unikwëti side of me."

"That sounds a bit strong. Suppressed?"

"He raised me Catholic, called me Charles, and prevented me from attending powwows. Hell, I didn't even know about them. I lost track of my cousins and aunts and uncles. He brainwashed me. I didn't know it until I went to Harvard and was able to get back in touch with who I really am. He sent me there thinking he'd won. What a shock when I came back to visit that first Christmas, and he found the Native American half of me stronger than ever.

"You don't seem to think I know a lot about the registered Indian Nations. But I see where the government continues to fail and disappoint and hurt people of Native American descent. Whites continually try to 'civilize' what they see as a savage race without recognizing the true wisdom and talents these people have always had, long before the first European settlers came. My people and I vowed to never allow our most sacred places to be known by the government. We have managed to protect them. I wish you could understand. You're one of us, after all."

"But your grandfather…"

"He could have sent Claire to any private boarding school in the world, but he sent her to a convent. He wanted to exorcise her."

"Did he succeed?"

"Not completely. She's definitely a converted Catholic, but she hasn't forgotten her Unikwëti heritage. I haven't let her."

"Why do you suppose he wanted to do that? What has he got against the Unikwëti?"

He changed lanes to pass a slow clunker. "He's just racist, that's all. Some people are just like that. It comes from ignorance. He probably thought he was saving her."

She shook her head. "I can't believe that of Brandon. He seems so open-minded."

"It's a front. I'm telling you."

"Does Claire have an Indian name?"

"Wisawtayas. It's a kind of bird——a golden finch."

"Wi-SAW-ta-yas?"

He smiled. "Very good."

As Tuki drove the truck into Little Rock, Samantha felt sleepy.

Now Misink was shaking her and screaming at her in a language she couldn't understand.

She screamed.

"What in hell? Wake up!"

She looked at him, glanced around the truck. She sat up and covered her mouth. "I had the dream again," she muttered. "It was terrible. I was having a baby, I think, and Misink was hovering over me, strangling me. Only this time, he, uh, he looked like you."

Tuki looked mortified. "Well, you're awake now. It was just a dream. Christ, you scared the crap out of me. Come on. Let's stay the night here. Do you need all of these bags?" He climbed out of the truck and helped her down.

"Um, just that cosmetic case and that suitcase there." They carried their luggage toward the hotel office. "Man, that was so real. So terrifying."

"You should have brought your dream catcher."

"I did."

He looked surprised.

"But not for the reasons you think."

"Of course." He smiled.

"What? Why are you smiling like that?"

He shook his head but didn't answer as she opened the door for him.

"One room or two?" the man behind the counter asked.

Tukihëla looked at Samantha.

"Uh, two," she answered.

"Shit, shit, shit!" Samantha muttered as she went around the room flipping on lights. What had possessed her to say two rooms? She had been caught off guard and hadn't been sure what to say. If she had said one, she would have been opening herself up to heartache. As it was, they were downright crazy getting to know one another when they had opposite views about the catacombs. Neither of them would ever change. Sex would only further complicate matters, wouldn't it?

An hour later, around eleven thirty, after a long warm shower and a half an hour of television, Samantha lay in her bed unable to fall asleep. She cradled the dream catcher against her and tried for the millionth time to forget about Tuki lying in bed across the hall.

Not a minute later, she heard a knock at her door. Through the peephole she saw Tukihëla in his robe with his arms crossed.

She opened the door just a bit and asked, "What's wrong?"

"Did I wake you?" His long hair was wet, just like hers.

"No. I can't sleep."

"Me either. So, I was thinking I'd show you how to hang the dream catcher to see if it helps keep that nightmare away."

"Oh. Okay. Come in." She opened the door all the way, even though she hadn't covered her nightshirt with a robe.

He pulled a length of string from his robe pocket.

"Where did you find string at this hour?"

"I carry some in my toolbox in my truck. Where's the dream catcher?"

"There." She pointed to the bed.

He met her eyes with a smile. "You were going to sleep with it?"

"I didn't have any way of hanging it." She blushed.

He took it from the bed and looped the string through two different loops of sinew close to the willow hoop. Then he fastened each end to the light fixtures on either side of the double bed, so the dream catcher hung parallel in the center right over her pillow.

"Now climb in and make sure your head is beneath it, okay?"

"Okay, I will. I promise. Thanks."

"Go ahead and get in. I want to make sure it's not uncomfortable for you. Maybe you want it a little higher up."

"Okay." She got into the bed, pulling the covers around her. The man-made web hung about two inches from her face. "That does feel kind of weird. Can you make it higher?"

He refastened the string to a higher point on each fixture. She looked up at him hovering above her as he retied the thread. She'd only have to reach her arms up to embrace him.

"How's that?" he asked.

She cleared her throat. "Good."

He sat on the edge of her bed and looked down at her. "I hope you sleep well tonight." He leaned down and kissed her on the forehead.

Without thinking, she reached up around the back of his head, like the fronds of a closing leaf, pulling his mouth down to hers. Soon he was on top of her, with the covers between them.

Just as she was about to take his lips again between her own, she saw Misink tumble from beneath his robe and lunge at her. She screamed.

Tuki sat up quickly, bumping into the dream catcher and then setting it right again. "What is it? What's wrong?"

"I'm sorry," she giggled. "It was your necklace. It came at me just like Misink in my dream." She took the harmless ornament between her fingers, still lying down on the pillow as he bent over her. Then she noticed something peculiar about the bones flanking either side of the ornament. She sat up. "Oh my God!"

They bumped heads.

"What now?" He rubbed his forehead as she rubbed hers.

"Sorry about that but look at these. These bones on your necklace. These are human bones. Phalanges. I'm sure of it."

"What the hell are phalanges?"

"Finger or toe bones—in this case, finger."

"Human? You're sure?" he studied them. "How can you be sure? Don't many mammals have similar bones?"

"Come on. I'm an archaeologist."

"You're a twenty-something grad student. That hardly qualifies you as an archaeologist."

Her face flamed.

"I'm sorry. I didn't mean that. I just can't believe my father would give me a necklace with human bones on it."

"Do you think our ancestors might have been cannibals?"

"What? No, man. No way. Uh-uh."

"You know, what you said about our ancestors' beliefs about killing for food, how the thing killed was a spirit, like a god? Well, for some past civilizations, they did the same thing to a brave enemy defeated in battle."

"I never heard stuff like that about our ancestors."

"Are you sure?"

"Yeah. I'm sure."

"You were eight years old when your father died. Then your grandfather took over raising you. Do you think it's possible your father might not have had the chance to teach you all about their customs?" She sat further up in the bed.

"These would have to be very old bones, dating back to way before my father or grandfather or his father was born. Maybe it was a family heirloom from a less recent ancestor who did such barbaric things. I don't know." He leaned back, fingering the bones.

"We can find out how old they are."

He looked at her dead in the eye, still holding the bones between his fingers. "How sure are you? How sure are you that these are human?"

"The closest relative is the ape, but I can't imagine how a Native American living in Pennsylvania would have access to the phalanges of an ape."

"But it's possible?"

"Remotely."

"How can we know for sure?"

"We'll have to send them to the lab. We can find out how old they are as well as what mammal they came from. Are you willing to do that?"

He stood up and headed for the door. "I'll think about it. In the meantime, try to get some sleep. Hope that thing works."

"Yeah, me too."

She sighed, supposing accusations about cannibalism in the family would sour the mood.

"Lock this deadbolt behind me."

"I will. Good night."

"Good night." He closed the door. She climbed from the bed, hitting her head again on the dream catcher. She went to the door and locked the bolt, then crawled back beneath the covers and tried again to go to sleep.

CHAPTER TWELVE

A Still Wood

Rebecca stood beside Attie, each of them looking toward the creek they could hear but no longer see in the darkness.

"We should go away from here," he said softly. "Your parents don't like me, and my father doesn't like you."

"But I could never leave my mother. And I like it here. I can't imagine living anywhere else." She rested her hands on her swollen belly. The baby would come any day.

"It's the same with me. This is my homeland. I've never known another. But I want peace. I don't feel peace anymore." He threw a stone into the dark creek. There was no sound of stone hitting water. The crickets were also silent. The entire wood stood still except for the flow of the water.

Rebecca took a step closer to Attie. "Once the baby comes, our parents will change. They'll soften and finally see how much we love each other."

Attie did not reply. Like the wood, he stood silent.

"You do love me, don't you, Attie?"

He turned and looked at her, placing his hands on her belly, his warm touch moving through her to their child. The baby kicked, causing Attie to flinch in surprise.

"Wow," he smiled. "He's strong, like his father."

"How do you know it's a he?"

"If it's a daughter, she's willful like her mother."

Rebecca smiled.

A few moments later, she frowned.

He hadn't answered her question.

CHAPTER THIRTEEN

A Hidden Grotto

"The professor and Mark and I drove through the Great Smokey Mountains National Park on our way up several weeks ago." Samantha said. "I'd love to see it again. That okay with you?"

"Won't your team be waiting for you?" Tuki asked from behind the wheel.

She shook her head. "They won't be able to get started today. They probably won't arrive until this evening, and they'll spend most of tomorrow getting the site ready."

"I don't know."

"Oh, come on!"

"Well, I'm in no hurry."

"Sweet!"

As they drove toward the Visitor Center, they could see the Meigs Falls cascading down the Smokey Mountains.

"Oh, isn't that beautiful? Let's hike through one of the trails," Samantha said. "One of the shorter trails. I think we could finish in an hour. Wouldn't you like to stretch your legs after being in the truck so long?"

"Sure. I could go for that."

He waited while she changed from her sandals into socks and tennis shoes in the cab of the truck and then they went into the Visitor Center to pay their entrance fee.

The park offered eight different trails to falls that couldn't be seen from any other view and several more moderate and strenuous hikes down to rocky crags or bald mountains overlooking splendid mountaintops.

Samantha looked over the map from the Visitor's Center as they walked back to the pickup. "Hey, why don't we do an unpaved moderate hike? What do you think?" she asked.

"Sure."

"What about Rainbow Falls?"

"That's over five miles. We won't finish in an hour." Then he added, "What about Andrews Bald? There's not a fall there, but it's a shorter hike, and it says you can see Fontana Lake. I bet it's spectacular."

"Sounds like a plan!"

They took the truck down Clingmans Dome Road to the trailhead and began their hike.

After they walked a half hour down the well groomed and gently rolling trail, tucked under towering oaks and spruces and covered with loose gravel, Andrews Bald came into full view.

Beyond the lush foliage appeared several majestic sloping layers of misty grey rock against the afternoon horizon. The cool breeze chilled the two hikers as they looked out as far as their eyes could see over a seemingly never-ending expanse of mountain. To their right appeared a stream that pooled into a small basin below them. Samantha climbed from the trail to dip in her hand.

"Oooh! That's cold!"

"Look over there," Tuki said, as she climbed back up to the path.

To their extreme left, on the other side of a cliff, a forty-foot slope appeared dense with colorful azaleas, half in shade and half in sunshine. The chilling breeze carried their scent, mixed with the fresh pine below, up to them, beckoning them.

"Let's climb down there," Samantha said. "Oh, they're absolutely gorgeous! Come on!"

"I wish I had my camera," he said as he followed her off the trail down a risky path from the crag. "Are you sure about this?"

"Yes! Come on!"

Samantha slid down a steep slope onto more stable rock, and from this view appeared a huge field of azaleas. She jumped from the rock and ran through them feeling like Julie Andrews in *The Sound of Music.*

At the end of the field of flowers, she wedged herself in a narrow crevice where two giant mountains came together, and the view took her breath away. She stood there in awe until Tukihëla caught up to her.

"Oh my," he whispered at her back.

Fontana Lake sparkled hundreds of feet below, and several mountaintops they couldn't see from the trail towered above them.

She turned and looked up at him. "Makes me want to sing."

He laughed.

"Let's go further down," she said.

"But—" It was too late. His objections fell on her back.

She giggled inwardly, knowing she was taking risks and scaring the hell out of him.

They climbed down the rocky terrain through the crevice down from the tall wall of rock and saw it now leaned out over them, hiding the small ten-foot waterfall cascading from the neighboring mountain crag. Behind the fall, which they could only now hear thundering against the rocks, was a grotto carved into the rock flanked by more azalea shrubs of bright pink.

"It's absolutely wonderful," Samantha whispered into Tukihëla's ear, so he could hear her over the roar of the fall. "Let's go inside."

He grabbed her arm. "We're far from the trail, Beck. I'm not sure this is safe. In fact, I'm sure it's not."

The rocky descent to the grotto behind the fall looked dubious even to the less experienced climber.

"I can't go through life regretting I didn't do this," she said.

"If you even have a life to regret."

"Please. It's only a few more feet down, and see that ledge over there? If I fall, it won't be far."

"That's if you make it to that ledge. Otherwise, it's hundreds of feet straight down into Fontana Lake."

He held her close. She could smell his skin, his sweet breath. She liked his need to protect her, but her instinct was to run.

She frowned. "Okay. If you really don't want to go, we don't have to."

"Wait a minute. I guess it's safe enough, if we're very, very careful. Let me go first."

He put his right foot down on the steep slope and bent his knees, leaning back, allowing his foot to slowly slide down as he held onto the jagged side of a nearby cliff. He looked up at Samantha. "Be sure you hold on here and regain your footing at the base of this shrub." He stepped from the slope onto a lower crag jetting from the grotto, just outside the little fall.

An icy mist chilled Samantha, exhilarating her. The adrenaline surged through her. She wanted to shout.

Tuki reached above for her hand and helped her down beside him onto the crag jutting from the grotto. The crag came out about four feet from the tall wall of rock and formed a natural bridge along the inside of the fall into the shallow cave. The two of them looked up at the fall with awe as they walked behind it into the cool nook. Samantha sat on a bench of rock where some of the water pooled into a shallow lip in the bottom of the cave.

"I want to put my feet in!" she hollered to him over the sound of the roaring fall as she removed her shoes.

"It'll be cold as ice!"

"I know! Refreshing, huh!"

She dipped in a toe, only to pull it back out with a squeal.

"I told you, Beck!" He sat on the rock floor across from her, watching.

She stuck out her tongue, playfully, and thrust both feet in. "Ahhh!" she shrieked. She lifted them back out and walked from the pool over to where Tukihëla sat shaking his head at her. Then she sat beside him and gazed at the fall, every bit of the view on the other side blocked, except for the azalea bushes on either side and a tiny sliver of one of the taller peaks across the bald quay below.

Then she lay down on her back on the moist rock with her head on her hands, fingers laced behind, elbows jetting out, aware she was lifting her breasts.

"I bet no one can see in here," she said.

He met her eyes before she quickly looked away.

"Don't you think we're completely out of anyone's view? Even from the trails across the way? I bet even people with binoculars can't see us inside here. What do you think?"

He smiled and shrugged. "I suppose you're right." He looked away.

"I want to always remember this day," she said, moving onto her elbows with her legs stretched out. "Don't you?" His indifference emboldened her.

"Yes," he looked her over. "I don't think I'll ever forget it."

She hesitated as his eyes penetrated hers. She bit her lip and frowned.

"What's the matter?" He moved his face closer to hers.

"I, uh," she licked her lips, looking at his mouth.

It was all the invitation he needed.

They spent that night in Roanoke, in one room, in one bed, with the dream catcher above them, after hours of lovemaking. As Samantha fell asleep, her last thoughts before the unconscious took over were not peaceful.

She was deeply, completely, and unforgettably in love with a man she could not have.

Tuesday evening after dinner, Jes greeted Samantha and Tukihëla at the double oak doors, taking a suitcase from Samantha's hand.

"Welcome back, Mr. Nisha, Miss Beck. Just set everything here, and I'll be sure to put them in your rooms. Dr. Gomez and Mr. Gellermann have retired to the study with their coffee and cigars, if you wish to say hello. And the young man has taken an evening stroll down by the creek."

Tuki gave Samantha a look of alarm. Once the butler left them standing together in the foyer beside one lone suitcase, he whispered, "You don't suppose Mark's out there looking around, hoping to find something, do you?"

Samantha frowned. "I don't know, but I doubt it. Plus, it's like finding a needle in a haystack."

"Maybe we should go after him."

"Shouldn't we say hello to your grandfather and the professor?"

Before he could reply, the professor and Brandon entered the foyer from the study.

"There they are!" Brandon said cheerfully.

"Hello, mija." The professor patted Samantha's back and then shook Tuki's hand. "Good evening, Tukihëla. Good to see you again."

"We were a bit worried when you didn't arrive for dinner," Brandon said.

"I'm so sorry," Samantha said. "We should have called."

"Nonsense, my girl. I'm just glad you're finally here, safe and sound. Are either of you hungry?"

Both young people shook their heads.

"Actually, I was just thinking about taking a walk out by the creek. Care to join me, Beck?"

"What did you call her?" Brandon asked.

"Beck. It's her last name."

"That's not very polite, my boy, dropping the 'Miss.'"

"It's okay," Samantha came to his defense. "Really."

Brandon's face paled. "That's the same name your father used to call your mother."

Samantha felt her own face turn red. "I'm pretty tired," Samantha said. "I think I'll go and get ready for bed. I have to be up early in the morning, right Professor?"

"That's right."

"Brandon, thank you so much for your generous hospitality," she said. "Good night, everybody." She gave Tukihëla one last glance before she turned and ascended the winding stairs.

"Hold up there, mija!"

She waited for the professor to catch up to her on the stairs.

"You might be interested to know we have a press conference first thing in the morning at the site."

"What?" she asked with a huge smile on her face. "Are you serious?"

"All the major networks will be there. O'Neil arranged it."

Samantha frowned. Tuki wasn't going to like this one bit.

As soon as Samantha was alone in her room, she found the backpack Jes had carried up for her and took out the framed photograph of Rebecca. She looked at it again before replacing it on the nightstand. It must have fallen into her bag. There was no other reasonable explanation. She set it down and started to unpack her things when she heard it fall over on the nightstand.

Damn that frame. The stand must be no good. A foggy aura wrapped itself around her, and she dropped to the bed. She lay there for several seconds, feeling tired, and then finally pulled herself up from the bed to change. She took up the frame again and frowned. The glass over the photo had cracked.

After she had gotten ready for bed, Samantha sat propped on pillows, listening to the music playing over her iPod as she read the library book she had taken from Jasmine. She had to struggle to keep her mind away from tender thoughts of the grotto in the Smokey Mountains.

The passage depicted a matrimonial ritual in New Guinea, dating back to 1000 A.D. The book described the ceremony in great detail, including the passing of the pipe and the singing of religious hymns, but what disturbed Samantha was the custom that followed. Dressed in a gown made of corn silk, head crowned with jewels, the bride and her new husband were led willingly to a small house of heavy logs, built specifically for the nuptial consummation. As the newlyweds copulated, they knew the tribe members would drop the side beams of the house, causing the uppermost logs to fall on the couple, crushing them to death.

Samantha gasped.

The book read: "There is a union of male and female again, as they were in the beginning, before the separation of the genders took place, before the divine became human. Death and begetting are one and the same. And so the couple becomes like a god, their bodies fished from the logs and roasted and eaten by the tribesmen. Their bones were then made into ornaments to be adorned by both persons and important animals. It was done the same way to a woman chosen to give birth. She became a god during delivery and was crushed after the baby was taken to safety. Then she was consumed as Holy Communion."

Tuki had to see this.

She jumped from the bed, taking the book with her down the hall to the west wing. She rapped on Tuki's door, softly, so as not to wake the professor and Mark, whose rooms were also located in the west wing.

"Tuki? Are you up?"

She saw a light come on and spill beneath the door, so she turned the knob. Finding it unlocked, she pushed open the door and saw him sitting up, sleep-filled eyes squinting against the side table lamp he had just switched on.

"I'm sorry to wake you." His bare chest, illuminated by the lamp, beckoned to her. She looked away, at his room, which was twice the size of hers. A rock fireplace and sitting area were to the right of a king-size poster bed, and several uncovered windows flanked French doors at the back, leading to a small balcony overlooking the creek and hills below.

"Come in. It's okay."

"I've come across something disturbing in this book. It reminds me a little of the story you told me about your aunt, when she gave birth. Listen." She sat on a chair beside his bed and read him the passage, trying not to steal glances at his chest and the firm body lined by the thin cotton sheet.

He frowned. "I don't see what you're getting at."

"You really don't? Almost every woman in your family died after giving birth. They each bear the symbol of the Earth goddess on the wall in the catacombs, and, like your aunt, may have been dressed in a gown of silk and crowned with bronze and jewels."

"Are you saying each of those women was killed by my family?"

"No, I'm asking you if you think it's possible."

"God, no. Absolutely not. That's crazy. I can't believe you woke me up for this."

She stood up. "Think about this for a minute. The other three tribes of the Lenape are not known to have ever practiced such a ritual, but if our ancestors resided here on this very spot for thousands of years, it might be possible some ancient customs, unknown to the other modern tribes, were maintained."

"Hell no! Are you crazy? You act as though these people aren't your own family. This is disgusting."

"Quit being so ethnocentric. It's only disgusting to you because you aren't entrenched in the ancient culture."

He climbed from the bed. "You look here. Don't accuse me of being ethnocentric. Jesus Christ."

"Listen, according to the book, the newlyweds died willingly, looking forward to becoming gods. It was an honor. A noble sacrifice. Like Jesus. If you think about it—you're familiar with the Catholic dogma of transubstantiation—ancient Christians were also accused of cannibalism. After all, Jesus said by eating his body and drinking his blood, Christians can enter his father's kingdom. Maybe the women, after they gave birth, were—"

"Stop, Beck. Just stop. Christ, enough is enough. You know, you were right. This was crazy. You're not going to change. How could I be so stupid?"

She opened her mouth, but nothing came out.

He narrowed his eyes. "When you came through that door tonight, I thought, I thought maybe there was a chance. Maybe this thing between us was something real. But you won't let up. You'll never let up." He turned his back to her and raked a hand through his long black hair.

She glanced at his bare back, longing to lay her cheek against it. His thighs, his hips—outlined by the thin pajama bottoms—and the strong dark arms had been hers, all hers, only hours ago. She stood and wiped her eyes with the back of her hand, unable to prevent the hand, her whole body, from trembling.

As she was about to leave the room, she stopped, turned back, and said in a low, calm voice, "You had a chance to know them. You had an opportunity to learn something about our family. Why can't you understand my need to do the same?"

His hands flew above him in anger as he turned to meet her gaze. "Learning about them is one thing! Making up ghost stories about them is another! I think you just want a good story! Something that will make you famous!"

She opened her mouth wide with astonishment. "I can't believe you!"

When he said nothing in return, she raced from the room.

She hadn't gotten far down the hall when she turned and ran back and said in a controlled, but sad, voice, "By the way, the professor told me tonight that a press conference has been arranged for tomorrow morning out at the site. I just thought you might want to know."

She raced away, this time for good.

CHAPTER FOURTEEN

The Sacrifice

Rebecca lay on a table in the center of the wigwam. Over her swollen belly, she could not see her feet, only the horses in their stalls staring at her with fear.

The pain between her legs made her scream.

The horses winced and whinnied.

Somewhere below her, the dog whined.

"Attie! Where are you?" Rebecca cried.

The old woman beside her spoke in a language she did not understand, but her voice was soothing.

The pain between Rebecca's legs magnified, so she pushed. The woman's eyes opened wide with fright. She shook her head, shouting. One of the horses bolted back and hurt itself on a cedar beam.

Then Rebecca felt a rip, like a knife between her legs. She bore down and screamed as her flesh tore from end to end and a bath of blood fell between her legs.

The old woman cried out, "Attacullakulla!"

Rebecca felt herself growing weaker, weaker, unable to stay awake. She closed her eyes.

"Beck! Wake up! Tukihëla! Please! Tukihëla!"

She opened them and closed them again. She could not keep them opened. But they were opened long enough for her to see Attie looking down at her, his face half black and half red, the bearskin rough against her arm.

"Her blood!" he cried to the old woman as Rebecca drifted, drifted, drifted.

Then Rebecca heard the dim sound of a baby crying far off in the distance, and she smiled.

CHAPTER FIFTEEN

Ancient Spirits

There were no chairs for the fifty or so journalists and photographers gathered outside of the tent on the dig early Wednesday morning, so the archaeological team made do by standing on their metal folding chairs so the members of the crowd could see and hear them.

The professor first provided a general statement, summarizing Samantha's research of her family history, the many letters she sent out to people in this area, and the site they studied prior to this one. He spoke of Brandon Gellermann's reply, which led to the excavation of this site and what they had uncovered. He held up the bandolier bag, explaining its significance. Then, clearing his throat, he offered an opportunity for those gathered to ask their questions.

An older, balding man wearing thick glasses directed the first question at Samantha. "What's it feel like to be reunited with your long lost relatives, young lady?"

Samantha smiled. "Wonderful. I can't begin to describe it."

"Can you try?"

"Well, I don't believe in miracles, but if I did, this would be one. My grandmother didn't really think I could do it."

The professor then took a question about carbon dating and the age of the tribe discovered.

Leaning against his black Chevy pickup truck, Tuki watched, unable to conceal his disapproval. Samantha knew this was exactly what he had wanted to avoid.

Samantha was asked another question, this time by a tall woman. "Are there any other living descendants besides you and your grandmother?"

Samantha glanced back at Tuki. "Well, there's my father, of course. And there are bound to be others living in this part of the country, but I have yet to learn all of their identities."

Mark spoke up. "Well, that's one of them right back there."

The entire crowd turned in the direction of Tukihëla standing, flabbergasted, in front of his truck.

"What is your name and what do you know about this tribe, young man?" someone asked.

"Did you or your parents personally know any of the people buried here?" A couple of cameras flashed.

"What about their customs and beliefs? Were those handed down to you?"

Tuki climbed into his truck and drove away.

Following a long day of photographing in the hot summer sun, the archaeological crew enjoyed the evening meal around Brandon's formal table. Tukihëla did not join them.

Although Samantha was tired from a sleepless night—the dream of Misink had returned—she chatted now with the rest of the group about some of the customs she had read in her library book.

She told them first about the different use of the snake symbol.

"That's true of many religions," the professor commented. "A few modern Native American tribes, influenced by Christianity, and the Judeo-Christian and Muslim traditions are the only exceptions."

Then she went on to tell about the face painting of the unmarried girls and laughed about how the males seemed to have no similar responsibility.

"Western males don't wear engagement rings either," the professor said.

"So you see, not much has changed over the millennia." She laughed again.

Brandon chuckled. "Quite true, dear girl. Quite true. Please do go on. I find this stuff most interesting."

She took another bite of the cornbread and, when she could, continued. "I read about a troubling ritual last night. In some New Guinean tribes, a newly married bride and groom were dressed like gods and led to a house of heavy logs, built especially for the nuptial consummation. The tribe danced and sang around the structure containing the couple, smoking their pipe, and then, while the couple did its, you know, consummating, the side beams were dropped, and the heavy logs above crushed the couple below."

"Holy cow," Mark gasped.

"And they knew it would happen. The couple died willingly, happy to become gods, honored to make such a sacrifice. They did it to new mothers, too."

"Yes, I've read about that. The practice continued as recently as 1970," the professor said. "Interesting."

Brandon pressed his handkerchief to his forehead. "Indeed."

"That's not all," she continued. "Their bodies were then fished out of the logs, roasted over a fire, and eaten by the entire tribe. Their bones were made into ornaments and weapons."

"Excuse me," Brandon said, rising from his chair and limping from the room.

"Oh no." Samantha covered her mouth after Brandon had gone. "I shouldn't have said that while we were eating."

"I wouldn't worry about it, Sam," Mark said.

The crew continued their meal, expecting their host to return, but he never did. Nor did he make his usual appearance in the study, where the professor waited, smoking his cigar, until he could no longer stay awake.

That night, as Samantha lay awake in her bed, hoping the music on her iPod might lull her to sleep, she saw her bedroom door open and a dim light spill into her room. She sat up and pulled the earplugs from her ears.

"Who's there?" she asked.

"It's me," Mark said, nearing her bed. "I've missed you."

"Geez. You scared me."

"I knocked. Is this a bad time?"

"Well, to be honest, I'm dead tired and stressed beyond stressed."

He sat on the edge of the bed. "Why are you so stressed? You got what you wanted, right?"

She couldn't reply.

"You know, if you're interested, I have a great remedy for stress. Doctors even recommend it. It causes natural opiates to relax the body. It's all natural and one hundred percent guaranteed." He looked at her mouth.

"That's a great offer. And it's tempting." She squirmed in the bed, realizing he meant sex. "But I think I ought to go to sleep. We've got another big day tomorrow."

"That didn't stop you before."

She shook her head. "I know. But it's all taking its toll on me. Having to put everything back."

"Yeah, I know." He stood up and went to the door. "Good night, Sam."

"Good night."

Samantha lay back on her bed and sighed. If only she wanted Mark, things wouldn't be so complicated.

The next morning, Samantha made her way down the front winding stairs toward the dining room for breakfast, after another sleepless night. Before she reached the table, her cell phone rang.

"Excuse me," she said to the professor and Mark, already seated. "Hello?"

"I saw your picture in the paper this morning," Dorothy Beck said to her daughter over the telephone. "And last night, you were on the evening news."

"Really? I didn't know it would air so soon."

She left the dining room and lingered in the foyer.

"Yes. I wish you would have said something to me."

"Well, luckily you didn't miss the coverage."

"I wish you would have told me you were conducting interviews already."

"I didn't know myself until the night before, when we arrived late Tuesday night. What does it matter?"

"Just don't say anything else to the press or publish any of your writings until we have a chance to talk."

"Why, Mama? What's wrong?"

"Are you coming for the Fourth of July?"

"I told you I'd be there."

"How early can you come home?"

"Thursday evening. Week from today. That okay?"

"I guess so. We'll talk more about it then. Have you gotten the DNA test results yet?"

"More about what? What are you talking about?"

"I don't want to get into it over the phone."

Jes beckoned to Samantha to follow him into the parlor, so she did. He motioned to the sofa. Samantha nodded her thanks and gave him a smile as she accepted a warm cup of coffee from him and sat down.

After he left the room, she said into the phone, "Now I'm worried. Tell me what's bothering you. Are you embarrassed by me?"

"What? What makes you think such a thing?"

"Tell me what's wrong, Mama. I won't hang up 'til you do."

Her mother was silent.

"Hello? Are you still there?" Samantha asked.

"I'm still here."

Samantha sipped at the coffee. "I'm waiting."

"Liebe Gott. Are you sitting down?"

"Yes."

"Ach, my sweet Liebling. I should have told you years ago!"

Samantha returned the cup and saucer to the coffee table and stood up. "Mama." She swallowed hard. "My God, Mama, tell me."

Ten minutes after her call with her mother had ended, Samantha was still sitting in complete shock in the parlor when the professor and Mark came to learn why she had never come to breakfast.

"It's time to get started, mija."

"Sam, you're shaking."

She looked up at them, vaguely aware someone was speaking to her. A bit of drool tickled her chin, so she wiped it away with the back of her hand.

"What's happened?" The professor stepped closer.

Samantha's eyes fixed above the mantel on a lovely portrait of a young woman, her long blonde curls cascading over the top of her bare shoulders. Her grey eyes looked up with wonder. She held a bouquet of jonquils in one hand and a fishing pole in the other and was standing in a field of daffodils, the hem of her white summer dress nearly hidden from view.

Samantha realized she was looking at another portrait of Tukihëla's mother, Rebecca.

"Sam?" Mark asked.

"I don't feel well, that's all."

The professor put his hand on her shoulder. "Do you want to stay behind today? Mark and I can go on without you while you get some rest."

She shook her head. "No. I'll be okay."

"We'll wait while you have your breakfast then, okay mija?"

"No. I'm not hungry."

"You're sure, Sam?"

"Huh?" She looked over at Mark. "Yes. Yes. I'm sure."

Photographing the rest of the site and its collection had taken all of the previous afternoon and evening and most of Thursday morning. The team took several more shots of each item, to ensure good results. Although they had revealed their findings to the press and had allowed the journalists to take a few pictures, the archaeologists would also give television interviews and would eventually write and publish their findings in academic and trade journals and, finally, a book. And as they would have no further access to the excavation site and its contents, it was important they be thorough in documenting everything now.

Mark took most of the pictures, with both his digital and his 35-millimeter cameras, as Samantha added to the notes she had already taken on each item, making each description more precise and recording the shot numbers as Mark called them out to her. The writing took longer than the photos, even though the professor took great care in the presentation of each artifact before Mark shot it, repositioning it several times, especially the skeletons, and playing with the lighting. The writing provided a kind of therapy for Samantha, a distraction from the feeling of longing and abandonment gripping at her heart.

They took one break for fifteen minutes to eat the lunch Jes had sent with them before beginning the process of putting their findings back into the ground.

Over the past week, storms and wind had washed some of the top-soil back into the excavated areas where the artifacts had once lain, so before they could return their findings to the ground, they needed to clear out the soil.

Samantha felt sick over having to put the precious whisperings of a past culture beneath the dirt where they could no longer be seen or heard. Only the bandolier bag would remain above ground and in possession of the team. The weapon fragments, utensils, jewelry, pottery, and ornaments—even the infant wall carrier—would all be returned to the ground with the human remains.

To the Underworld and to the river of forgetfulness, Samantha thought.

Samantha sketched a map identifying the location of each artifact as it would now exist beneath the earth. By the end of the day, only the skeletons remained above ground.

As they organized their possessions inside the tent, packing up for the evening, the tears came over Samantha. She kept looking at the bones. It was like they had died all over again. She couldn't believe they weren't her ancestors, having already loved them for too many years, long before she knew for sure of their existence. The conversation with her mother earlier that morning must have been nothing but a bad dream. She adopted? It couldn't be true.

"It's a damned shame," the professor said in a low voice beside her, and for a moment she thought he must have telepathic powers. They stood looking over the skeletons, still wrapped in the protective plastic, which would be removed before they were repaired to the ground. "We could learn more about these people if only we had the chance. But I suppose we should be grateful, right? Grateful for the opportunity to meet them at all."

Later that evening, Samantha marched down the hill with her flashlight and unlit lantern and a pack strapped to her back.

How could she be adopted without knowing it? She would have felt something.

When she came to the boulder, she heaved it aside with the stick. Her light, discarded for the moment, cast against a nearby shrub. She listened to the silent wood nearby. Not even the crickets chirped.

Peering through the opening to the cavern, squatting in darkness, Samantha shined her flashlight for signs of life. Satisfied that no critters, or worse, humans, presently occupied the catacombs, she grabbed her lantern and climbed inside.

When she lit her lantern, she was once again struck by the magnificence of the catacombs.

As she made her way through the tombs, silently saying good-bye, she noticed a tunnel, about three feet in diameter, at the back, to the right of the record. She shined her light as far as she could, but she could not see where it ended, so, she crept inside.

Samantha felt faint inside what appeared to be a never-ending descent further into the ground. The humidity rose around her nostrils, making it difficult to breathe. The wall of the tunnel narrowed in one spot.

She backed away, on her knees, concentrating on her breathing, trying not to panic. She hadn't backed up far when she thought she saw an opening at the end. She crept forward again.

On her hands and knees, she crawled through the hole, with her flashlight in one hand and the lantern in the other. She stopped every few feet to shine her flashlight ahead of her.

When, at last, she came to the end, she crawled from the tunnel, and lifted her lantern in front of her.

"Holy Mary, Mother of God!" she cried.

She set down the lantern and stood there, gazing at the magnificent chamber. Such places existed in the southwestern parts of the country, but this kind of geology was rare in the north. On top of that were the exquisite artifacts and preserved remains surrounding her. In disbelief, she lay on the damp sloped ground of the enormous cavern, flat on her back, facing the deeper end of the chamber, her hands laced behind her, and wept, as she gazed around her, at the most incredible find in modern times.

More primitive tombs surrounded the circumference of the room, which wasn't level, but sloped down at about a twenty-degree angle so the highest part of the cavern was at least sixty feet above the lowest. Stalactite and stalagmites abounded, some thin like straws, others thick, resembling miniature mountains. One cluster of such mountains divided the room in half, providing a focal point nearly dead center in the room. A cluster of tombs, half-wedged in the center rock formation, were barely visible.

At the deepest end of the cavern, a large cliff stretched out, like a balcony seat in an opera house, about twenty feet, and it housed a rough pile of a hundred or more skeletons, without tombs, many of them wedged into rock formations.

Surely the world should know of such a place. She wouldn't go to her professor behind Tuki's back, but she had to convince Tuki, somehow. The world deserved to know, and the people here, in this catacomb, deserved to be heard.

They were her people, she had decided. Blood didn't matter. She had loved them all her life, these ancestors she knew she would find. Their voices had called to her from their graves. They had chosen her to find them, after all. Luck chose her. The cosmos. Spirits?

Who the hell knew? She wanted to believe in something. But all seemed lost. She was lost, shattered into a million fragments spread out over the sea, over the river of forgetfulness.

Lying on her back among the ancient spirits, gently weeping in a pool of longing and confusion, she turned on her side, like a fetus, tucked her hands, palms together, beneath her cheek like a pillow, closed her eyes, and went to sleep.

Samantha lay on a table. Her belly was swollen, so she could not see her feet. The old woman beside her spoke in a language she did not understand, but her voice was soothing.

The pain between her legs magnified, so she pushed. The woman's eyes opened wide with fright. She shook her head, shouting.

Then she felt a rip, like a knife between her legs and the sound of a baby crying. The old woman took the baby and cried out, "Attac-ullakulla!"

Samantha felt herself growing weaker, weaker, unable to stay awake. She closed her eyes.

"Beck! Wake up! Tukihëla! Please! Tukihëla!"

She opened them and closed them again. She could not keep them opened. But they were opened long enough for her to see Tuki looking down on her, his face half black and half red, the bearskin rough against her arm.

"Her blood!" he cried to the old woman as Samantha drifted, drifted, drifted.

She could hear, far away, the sound of a baby's cries, and she smiled.

"Wake up! Hello? Samantha? Wake up!"

Samantha opened her eyes and saw an angel bending over her, a halo of light behind her against the upper part of the cavern.

"Am I dead?"

"What? No, silly. Did you sleep here all night?"

Samantha sat up to find Sister Claire on her knees beside her in the deeper chamber of the ancient catacombs.

"When I came in this morning to collect some things for my craft show, I saw your light. I've been trying to wake you up for almost five minutes now. You had me worried."

"I was having the most bizarre, most real dream."

"Have you really been down here all night?"

"Yes. I guess so. I just closed my eyes for a minute. I must have been really tired. But I'll tell you what, I had my best sleep last night, until just now, with the dream."

"Maybe you should try sleeping on a damp hard floor more often," the sister laughed.

Samantha smiled. "The funny thing is, the dream was better this time. There wasn't the same fear. It was different."

"So, you've had this dream before?"

"Yeah. Ever since I arrived here."

"I'm Claire, by the way. Tuki's told me about you. I hear you're our long-lost cousin."

Samantha gave a weak smile to the pretty woman, young like she, wearing baggy jeans, tennis shoes without socks, and a long-sleeved button-down shirt, untucked and loose. Her almost black hair was tied back in a ponytail in the same style sometimes worn by her brother. Samantha wasn't ready to explain just yet about their not being cousins. "It's nice to finally meet you."

"Likewise. I want to thank you from the bottom of my heart for what you're doing—keeping our secret, I mean. We're really fortunate that you're one of us and that you can understand our point of view."

Samantha avoided her eyes. "I wish I had the opportunity to learn more about this place."

"What do you want to know? I know just about everything there is to know about it."

Samantha's eyes widened. "What? Really? Like how ancient it is?"

"Our tribal legends trace our presence in this place back to 700 A.D. Beyond that, we aren't sure."

"Oh my gosh! That's amazing!"

"Some stories mention crossing a land of ice, which supports modern theories claiming we came across the Bering Straight, but that far back we just don't know."

"Seven hundred A.D.? That's incredible. Can you identify any of these tombs, or any of these people?"

"The education of a Unikwëti begins at a young age, and it begins with the stories of Mother Earth and Father Sky and continues with the first Grandfathers. Our teachers used wooden sticks banded together illustrated with symbols—unfortunately not exact dates and numbers, but enough information for us to piece together a general picture. I'm sure an archaeologist could add a great deal to our piecemeal body of knowledge, but before you came along, we couldn't risk jeopardizing our current way of life."

"Current way of life?"

Claire stood up. "Twice a year, once in the spring and once in the fall, the descendants of these great spirits meet for a traditional pow-wow. It's not open to the public like those of registered tribes, for obvious reasons. For one, Brandon Gellermann is unaware of them."

"Traditional powwows? Here?"

"They give us an opportunity to reinforce our connection to one another and to educate the younger among us in the ways of our ancestors."

Samantha now also stood, dusting the back of her jeans. "I sure wish I could attend one of those."

"You can. You're one of us. After all this blows over, and the rest are gone, after there's no more threat of archaeologists imposing rights to search the land, then you come back for a visit, okay? And we'll tell you everything. The fall powwow will be in September, Saturday the twenty-seventh."

"That's the weekend right after my birthday."

"Then you must come, as a present to yourself.

CHAPTER SIXTEEN

Seven Clans

Vendors, bearing their wares in little booths set up for the craft fair, covered the two acres on the northernmost part of the Gellermann land surrounding the church and convent grounds. Claire had a booth in which she displayed her brother's dream catchers in addition to Native American jewelry she handcrafted herself. Claire had told Sam that the craft vendor's entrance fees and ten percent of sales went directly to a local orphanage sponsored by the nuns. She had invited Samantha to come shopping and to keep her company for an hour or two. So, in the afternoon, after spending a few hours at the dig, Samantha asked Jes to drop her at the convent.

Wearing a bright red short set and a little purse not much bigger than her hand, hair fastened up in a high ponytail, Sam walked around the many booths. She hadn't had lunch, so the first thing she did was purchase a corndog and soft drink.

At least a hundred other people walked the grounds with her, some obviously tourists with their "I love Pennsylvania" t-shirts and cameras strapped around their necks. Two nuns, dressed in full habit, walked past, licking caramel apples on sticks. A dozen or so children were present, half of whom ran wild among the grounds, another constantly pulling on his mother's arm, another strapped in a sack to her father's back, and two or three pushing awkwardly through the long-cut grass in strollers, slowing down the pedestrian traffic around them.

She saw many beautiful works of art as she searched for Sister Claire—paintings, sculptures, wind chimes, ceramic and wooden figurines, jewelry, tie-dyed shirts and dresses, handcrafted wooden furniture, leather belts and purses, and hand-painted birdhouses. After she finished her lunch, she chucked her stick and empty soda can into the garbage and stopped to look at the birdhouses. She was drawn to one resembling a little church.

"That one's twenty-five," the tiny old woman sitting in a lawn chair said suddenly.

Samantha hadn't noticed her, hunched and sipping her lemonade through a straw, occasionally clicking her false teeth together.

"Did you make these?" Samantha asked.

The woman nodded. "Yes. You want to know how? I find old, discarded barn and fence wood. That's right. My husband, he cuts the wood for me after I pencil on the patterns. I nail the pieces together, and then I paint them, and fix them up with different things I find at yard sales and such. The glass doorknob there for the perch on that one there you're holding came from my mother's house. It's at least a hundred years old. Probably older."

"Did your mother live around here?"

"Oh, yes. My family has been here for centuries."

"This one is lovely. They all are, but I think I'd like this one." She carried the little church to the table to pay.

Claire was thrilled with Samantha's find. "That's so pretty. You should display it inside, on a mantle, as a showpiece."

Samantha plopped down on the empty chair across from her. "No, I think I'll hang it in my backyard from one of the oaks outside our kitchen window. It'll make a nice home for the hummingbirds that come to the feeder."

"It'll make a lovely home for them."

Samantha looked over the birdhouse a moment longer, feeling satisfied, pleased. The house made her happy; she couldn't explain why. She set it down on the grass beside her chair, nearly under the chair so it would be out of the way of shoppers.

"Oh, how gorgeous," Samantha said looking over the pieces of jewelry displayed on the table. "You really made these pieces?"

Claire nodded. "I put a lot of love into them. It's difficult to part with them, but it's for a good cause."

"This one's beautiful." Samantha pointed to a necklace, a kind of choker made of thin black wire. Smaller pieces of wire attached seven silver Concho shells across the band, and glued to each Concho was a flat, round deep blue stone thinly streaked with gold. "These aren't turquoise, are they?"

"No. They're lapis lazuli. The gold streaks are called pyrite, or fool's gold. I mined them myself, down in some of the other caverns. I shape them into flat circles using an ancient rock rubbing technique, and then I polish them in a modern electronic tumbler. The silver pieces are from a dismantled Concho belt, and the wire I got at a local craft store, but the stones I found, shaped, and polished myself."

"Other caverns?"

"Oh, yes. There are three other places on the Gellermann property." Samantha's eyes widened. "None with tombs. They were inhabited, but not used as catacombs, by our ancestors."

"Do they contain artwork? Pictographs on the walls?"

"Yes. I'll have to give you a tour sometime." Then she whispered, "Maybe when you come for the powwow?"

Samantha nodded.

"And these seven stones represent the seven clans of our tribe."

"Seven clans? What are they?" Samantha's grandmother had never mentioned anything about clans.

"They are Bear, Wind, Earth, Hawk, Fish, Wolf, and Turtle."

"Turtle?"

"Each clan is responsible for carrying out a specific duty for the tribe." Claire pointed to the first stone. "The Bears are the medicine men and women. Children born of this clan learn how to use plants and herbs to heal sores and illnesses. They become our doctors and nurses and such." She moved her finger to the second blue stone. "Those born of Wind learn to speak other languages, so they can communicate with other tribes and people of other races. They become diplomats. Those who signed treaties with the early settlers were of the Wind." She moved her finger again. "Those born of Earth oversee the farming and harvesting. Earth children study agriculture from the very beginning, and Earth adults make decisions about when to plant and where." Claire moved her finger to the next stone of lapis lazuli. "Hawks oversee hunting. Hawk children learn all about game animals, tracking, and making and using weapons. Hawks are also responsible for making weapons for battle." Claire looked up at Samantha. "Am I boring you?"

"No, not at all. Oh my gosh, please continue."

But a man came to the booth to ask about a dream catcher. Samantha couldn't resist sharing the fact that she owned one and that, when she hung it over her at night, she slept free of nightmares. "Whether or not the dream catcher has anything to do with it, I can't say," she added.

The man bought it. "You never know," he said, leaving.

"Hmm, you're pretty good! Maybe you should come to my craft fairs more often!"

Samantha laughed.

"Now where was I?"

"The hawks oversaw the hunting and making of weapons."

"Oh, yes. But you speak in past tense. Modern-day hawks still do that."

"Really?"

"Oh, yes. Some members of our tribe go on organized hunts throughout the year, depending on the season. And the meat is always used, never wasted."

"Does the Mësingw still visit beforehand?"

Claire smiled. "Misink? Absolutely." She lowered her voice. "You'll meet him at the powwow, if you come."

Samantha shivered, not so sure she wanted to meet him.

Claire placed her finger on the fifth stone. "Now, let's see. The Fish make decisions about travel and relocating. In the old days, the Fish were much more important than they are now, but even today, we usually call one of the Fish for travel advice before making a long journey. Modern-day Fish become meteorologists, travel agents, tour guides, geographers, surveyors, and map makers. As a matter of fact, Tuki conferred with a Fish before going to Texas to see you and your colleagues."

Samantha's mouth dropped open. "Really? So is that why he drove?"

Claire nodded.

Samantha thought for a moment. "How many are there, today, in the tribe?"

"Just over two hundred."

"No kidding? That's amazing! I had no idea!"

"Yeah. Up until the mid-eighties, the tribe lived on the Gellermann land in the caverns and wigwams as they had for centuries. I don't think most of them were even legal citizens of the U.S. They didn't integrate into American society until they were forced to. Now we're all spread out across New England."

Samantha shook her head. "Wow. How interesting. Okay, what about this one?" She pointed to the sixth stone.

"That's for the Wolf. Those born of the Wolf organize sports and games. Children born of the Wolf almost always become athletes, coaches, and referees. The Wolves are in charge of organizing the games we play when we meet bi-annually as a tribe. My and Tuki's grandmother was a Wolf, so we have a little of the athletic tendencies in us."

"But you aren't Wolves?"

She shook her head. "We're Turtles."

"This last stone, right? What do Turtles do?"

"They are the overall leaders—the dudas, sachems, and chiefs. Dudas are women leaders and sachems are men. They are like the congress. The Turtles also bear the future chiefs of the tribe. You and Tuki and I are of the Turtle."

This explained the turtle symbols she found on some of the artifacts. "How do you determine your clan? It's not through the mother or father?"

"It's through the mother except when it comes to the Turtle. When someone marries into the Turtle clan, their children are always Turtles. Being of Turtle blood is kind of like being born of royalty, but unlike the European concept. And Turtles are the only of the seven clans who are permitted to marry another from the same clan."

"Brothers and sisters?"

"Oh, no. There is a certain distance required. I can't remember. And it is always for the Bear to decide, for, in addition to medicine, the Bear is responsible for marriages, births, and deaths, when possible."

Samantha's brows lifted the instant the idea had come to her. "Would a Bear have been present at Tuki's birth?"

"Of course."

"Would he or she still be alive?"

"I don't know. I can find out. Why?"

"I'm hoping to learn more about the death of Tuki's mother."

"She died in childbirth. I'm not sure what else there is to know." She shifted in her chair—uncomfortably, Samantha thought—and turned her attention to rearranging the dream catchers.

In the end, Samantha bought the elegant choker, paying twice what Claire asked, reminding her it was for a good cause. She fingered the stones now, her arms against a sea of troubles, pretty sure she wouldn't be sleeping much tonight.

They all dined together that evening for the first time in the nearly two weeks her team had been restoring the site. Mark said something about fate, about how knowing more about the lost tribe "just wasn't meant to be," especially when the DNA test had proved disappointing, though they said they knew Samantha couldn't be related to every member of the Unikwëti.

Samantha replied sharply, "Democritus once said that fate is mostly but the echo of our character and passions, our mistakes and weaknesses."

Tuki then said, much to her surprise, "But Epictetus warned us to remember that we are only actors in a play, which the *manager* directs."

Samantha's eyes bore into his as she, red-faced, added, "He also said not to tie a ship to a single anchor, nor life to a single hope. I'm afraid I've been guilty of doing that." She immediately looked away, realizing the others were feeling uncomfortable.

Luckily, Brandon changed the subject and put everyone back at ease—everyone except she and Tuki.

So, after mulling for hours over what she might say or do to bring some kind of resolution to the bitter exchange between them, she finally left her bedroom, still wearing her white dinner dress and choker of lapis lazuli, and headed down the balcony corridor, her hand rubbing along the smooth cherry wood balustrade, toward Tukihëla's room to say goodbye.

She approached his bedroom door, still unsure of herself. It was nearly ten o'clock. He might be asleep. This was a mistake, she thought. She was about to leave when his door opened.

Tuki took a step back when he saw her. "I didn't hear you knock."

"Did I catch you at a bad time?" She asked bravely.

He was wearing his blue cotton pajamas and no slippers. "I was just going downstairs to play."

"To play?"

"Piano. It calms me."

"Oh, well then…alright then…goodnight." She turned back toward her room and then stopped, her heart pounding madly. "Can I come?" Heat spread through her as she realized she had spoken out loud.

"Um, that might reverse the calming effects."

"Oh. Right. Sorry. Goodnight then." She turned away once more biting into her bottom lip, staying back tears.

"Well, alright."

She stopped and waited for him, without looking at him. He was letting her come out of charity, which hurt her feelings, but not enough to prevent her from following him down the stairs and into the conservatory. As they neared the end of the stairs, she asked, "Did you study Epictetus?"

"Greeks and Romans 101. All Harvard students have to take it."

"Oh. I had an eighth grade English teacher, Mr. Griffin, who liked to quote the Greeks a lot. Epictetus was his favorite." She followed him into the room. "Where should I sit?" she asked after he had turned on a dim lamp near the entrance.

"Anywhere. It doesn't matter."

The grand piano was situated at the far end of the room, facing out of the corner toward the center. Ornamental chairs of carved cherry wood with red velvet upholstered seats lined all four taupe walls except for a red chenille couch in front of the great window on the right wall and a taupe velvet chaise lounge sofa, directly in front of the piano.

She crossed the hardwood floor to a chaise lounge in front of the piano, where she'd be out of Tuki's view as he played.

He clicked on another light in the corner of the room, behind the piano, to illuminate the keys.

She closed her eyes as he struck the piano abruptly and went directly into some kind of adagio. Samantha did not recognize the slow-moving piece, but she relished its sound as she lay back, pushing her white pumps off her feet so she could stretch across the chaise lounge.

The notes started low, and then lifted up the scale, only to dance down and up again, slowly, like a graceful skater over the ice. The melody then shifted down again, lower than it had begun, into sadness, deep melancholy, turning over and over, circling, like a leaf down a whirlpool. A staccato sprint up the scale resonated in a long, drawn-out chord, a high note, exhilarating. Several slow chords followed, peaceful now, like a spring morning.

Samantha lay on a table. She could not open her eyes as the old woman spoke beside her. "No!"

The pain between her legs magnified. She could not prevent herself from pushing.

"No!" the old woman shouted again.

Then the knife ripped her flesh between her legs and she felt the bath of blood wash over her as the sound of a baby cried.

"Attacullakulla!" The woman cried.

Samantha could barely open her eyes. She opened and closed them, opened and closed them. The Mësingw stood over her, shaking her, screaming at her. "Beck! Tukihëla!" he cried. "Wake up!"

She could not open her eyes. "Attie!" she muttered.

"Beck? What did you say?"

Attie knelt over her, shaking her. "Wake up!" He slapped her cheek.

"Attie!"

Her eyes opened.

Tuki knelt over her, shaking her. He slapped her face.

She blinked.

"Were you dreaming?"

She put her hand to her burning cheek. "What's wrong with you?"

"Don't mess with me, Beck. I hope you're not playing games."

Her eyes narrowed at him. "Why would I be playing games?"

"How do you know my father's name?"

"What? Your father's name? Why are you asking me that? You told me, remember? Attacullakulla. Geez. How do you forget a name like that?"

"His nickname. How did you know his nickname? Did Claire tell you?"

"His nickname?" She sat up and put her face in her hands for a minute. "I don't know your father's nickname. Why are you asking me all this?"

"Because just now, you shouted my father's name. His nickname. Attie."

"Yes! He was in my dream. Only I thought it was you. But it was Attie. His name was Attie. And he was dressed as Misink. And he was calling me Beck. And I was having a baby, but I couldn't stay awake. There was this terrible pain, and blood, and he was shaking me."

Tukihëla stood up. "It's all that stupid mythology and cultural rituals you've been reading about. That's what's giving you nightmares."

With her heart pounding, Samantha climbed from the chaise lounge and ran across the conservatory and foyer into the parlor. She felt around in the darkness for a switch. She found it, and the light poured from a fixture hanging from the center of the room.

Her heart racing in her chest, she went and stood before the mantle looking up at the portrait of Rebecca in her white dress, surrounded by flowers, fishing pole in hand. Tuki came and stood just inside the doorway.

"What are you doing?"

Samantha didn't answer right away. A foggy aura surrounded her, and she felt light-headed. After a few seconds passed, she blinked and focused again on the painting. "You're trying to tell me something, aren't you?" she said softly to those deep grey eyes.

Tuki shook his head. "It was just a dream, brought on by all your fantastic ideas. Believe me, my mother is not trying to speak to you from the grave. She's not trying to let the world know my father murdered her. He never would have done such a thing, or would have allowed such a thing to happen. Besides, I thought you didn't believe in spirits."

He angrily walked out, leaving Samantha alone with the portrait.

<u>CHAPTER SEVENTEEN</u>

Beloved Bones

Samantha sat at the breakfast nook with her parents eating ice cream. She knew they were upset about something.

"Just tell me," she finally said. "What's going on?"

Luther pushed his empty bowl away from him. He had eaten it so fast, Samantha expected him to yell, "Brain freeze," like he used to when she was little and eating ice cream was a weekly event. He leaned toward her, elbows on the table.

"Your mama wants to tell you who your biological mother is."

Samantha nearly choked. "You, you know her identity?"

Dorothy nodded without looking at Samantha. "She was a friend of mine in trouble. She wanted to go to school and have a career, and I was desperate for a baby. My first husband had just died, and the baby we were trying to adopt was taken away from me. So when my best friend's sister turned up pregnant…"

"Your best friend's sister?" Samantha felt the blood rush from her face. "Do you mean Josie? Josephina Schmidt?"

Dorothy glanced at Samantha, then nodded.

Samantha sat back in her seat, stunned. She played back the few times she had spoken to Josie, looking for some clue, some indication that Josie cared a scrap for her.

"Josie doesn't know," her mother said.

"What? How can she not know?"

"Well," her mother started. "She might have an idea, but Maggie and I tried to hide it from her. I was worried she might later change her mind, and I couldn't stand to lose another baby."

"I don't understand."

"I helped Josie secretly deliver you in New Braunfels, at my opa and oma's old house, which my parents hadn't been able to sell. Josie was scared to death of her mother finding out. I told her I would put you up for adoption. Maggie told her you were a boy. Then, a few months later, when she came back to Fredericksburg and learned I had adopted a baby, she suspected what we had done, but Maggie and I denied it. Ach, I don't know what Josie thinks."

"What about my father?"

"Some college boy. I never knew."

Samantha smelled a strong, bitter scent penetrating the kitchen. "What's that smell?"

"What smell?" Luther asked.

The smell was followed by the beating of drums and a strange chant of hidden voices: "He-ya, he-ya. Unikwëti hach ki? He-ya, he-ya. Unikwëti hach ki?"

Sam collapsed onto the table.

The next day, Sam's mother came to see her in the hospital.

"No one will know," Dorothy assured her as she pressed a cool rag to Sam's forehead. "We've told no one and we plan to tell no one, so you don't have to worry."

Samantha lay on the pillow looking up at the white ceiling, unmoved by and indifferent to her mother's words.

"It's just for a week or two, until you're better. The doctor says you've experienced too much stress, and your body needs time to process all that's been going on." Dorothy sat down in the chair beside the hospital bed, placing the wet cloth back into the bowl on the nightstand.

"Your father and I will come to see you every day, and we'll bring you home just as soon as the doctor says you're better."

Samantha sat up, started to say please don't and then didn't. She pushed the button on the rail to raise the head of the bed. Then she repositioned herself as her mother turned on the television.

"*General Hospital* is about to come on," Dorothy said.

Samantha sat against the pillow with her eyes closed. Did she come to see me, or to watch her soap? "Why don't you go home, Mama? I'm fine. I'm sure I'll be out of here tomorrow. I just need to go back on medication."

Dorothy raised her brows and looked at her daughter. "Liebling, the doctor doesn't think it was a grand mal. Epilepsy doesn't cause people to chant strange songs in a foreign language and then go comatose for twenty minutes."

"I really think I've been having seizures again."

Her mother shrugged. "I suppose it's possible, but that doesn't explain what happened last night."

"There was a funny smell. It made me nauseous, that's all. I passed out from the smell."

"But, sweetheart, that's my point. Neither your father nor I could smell it."

Samantha closed her eyes. "That's because you're used to the smell, and Dad doesn't smell anything, not even sulfur or skunk anymore. He's lost the use of his olfactory nerves entirely." She opened her eyes and saw her mother rolling hers. "You had just told me Josie was my mother. What did you expect?"

Her mother gave her a hurt look.

"Why did you tell me, anyway?"

"I was afraid you'd find out on your own one day and accuse me of making a fool of you."

"What?"

"Those articles about your long-lost relatives."

"Oh. But how could I possibly find out?"

"Those DNA tests. They won't ever match yours. They'll match your father's and your grandmother's but not yours." Then she added, "And I was afraid Josie would tell you, now that you're getting to be famous."

"She must be a horrible woman."

Dorothy didn't say otherwise. "I'll let you get some rest now." She leaned over, kissed her daughter's forehead, and left, closing the door behind her.

Samantha turned off the television and lay with her eyes closed thinking, yes, perhaps she had gone mad. That wouldn't be so bad, would it? Going mad?

She could still hear the chant ringing in her head: "He-ya, he-ya. Unikwëti hach ki? He-ya, he-ya. Unikwëti hach ki?"

Rubbish. Just a bunch of gibberish. She wasn't going mad.

Just because you hear voices in your head, just because you decide to break out in song with those voices, suddenly, while eating ice cream in your parent's—not biological parent's—kitchen, that doesn't make you mad.

She had asked her mother to bring her backpack filled with a few of her things—her Algonquian book, a notepad and pen, her iPod, her micro-recorder, and her cell phone. She may as well work while she's locked up—metaphorically locked up, of course. She could walk out if she wanted, she supposed.

The nurse had warned, in her happy, merry, high-pitched voice, "Nothing that might excite you, okay Hon'?"

Hon'. She had been reduced to a Hon'.

Hun, an ancient, warlike people who, led by Attila, attacked the Roman Empire in 400 A.D.

Perhaps she would grow into one of those old eccentric women that people respected and feared, that people admired though seldom wished to be. She might like that, living somewhere in a big ghastly house, with stacks of old newspapers, several cats—no she was allergic to cats—

then several dogs, maybe a guinea pig or a parakeet. Maybe she'd become a yellowed old academic instead and lecture abroad, frighten people with her strange ways, but intrigue them enough to want to hear about the lost tribe of Unikwëti—the part she was allowed to tell, not the real part, not the description of the seven clans, the bi-annual pow-wows in the ancient catacombs, the tradition of consulting a Fish before traveling on long journeys.

She rubbed the seven polished stones around her neck.

Eventually, Tuki and Claire must know the truth. She couldn't keep her secret from them forever. She had to be honest in her articles, in her interviews. She couldn't lie to the editors of the goddamn *Time Magazine*. (Look, now she had stooped to cursing. She never cursed. But it's okay. It's only cursing in the mind. And why was she so afraid to curse? It had no inherent meaning. An arbitrary assignment of significance to certain words by a culture.) Maybe she would wait, just a little longer, before divulging her secret to the Nishas, until the week after her birthday, the week after she attended the fall powwow and learned as much as she could—not to publish, right? Did she or did she not intend to betray the Unikwëti of Lenni-Lenape? No. Right? She did not.

Two weeks later, Samantha sat with her father in a little courtyard outside of St. Mark the Evangelist Catholic Church waiting on Dorothy, who had stopped to talk to someone.

"Is it true that a bone once belonging to St. Mark is encased in the altar of this church?" she asked him.

"Yes. A fingerbone. All Catholic churches built before Vatican II were required to possess a holy relic from a saint. It's not required anymore, though I do remember reading that if a relic is used, it must be an entire bone and not blood or hair or fragments of bone. Too many fraudulent claims."

Samantha licked her dry lips, and asked, "Has Grandma ever mentioned anything to you about bone relics among the Lenape?"

He shook his head. "Why?"

Samantha shrugged. "No reason."

Samantha woke up one morning to her mother standing over her bed.

Anna Gold Schmidt, her biological grandmother, had died.

Her mother drove her to Fredericksburg on Tuesday morning, so she could attend the funeral, but Dorothy did not go in with her.

"It'll upset Maggie too much to see me. She's so sour about my telling you, you know, about Josie. I'll go back to Opa Stehling's and pick you up in an hour. Okay?"

"Mama, I'm sure Maggie would want you there."

"You don't have to go if you don't want to."

"I want to." No wonder I'm crazy, she thought, climbing from the Suburban. Even the doctor had said as much. He hadn't wanted to put her back on her epilepsy medicine without further proof she had been having seizures. A twenty-four-hour EEG had revealed nothing.

She sat in the back pew and felt surprisingly peaceful. She thought of her little birdhouse hanging from the big oak in her backyard and smiled. That was the nice thing about churches. They made good homes.

She participated in the funeral mass without having to think. The familiar words flowed from her lips. She stood when it was time to stand, she knelt when it was time to kneel, and she shook hands with those around her when it was time to give the sign of peace.

When it was time to view the body, she went.

As she gazed down at the body of her biological grandmother, she said silently, "You'll go to your grave without knowing me, but here I am, your granddaughter, the shame everyone kept from you."

As she turned from the casket and that awkward, stony grin, she caught sight of Josephina Schmidt kneeling in the first pew, watching her. Samantha looked away and walked past, back to the safety of her seat. A few pews ahead of her on the backside of a pillar hung a life-size statue of Jesus. She went down on her knees and stared up at the Christ nailed to the crucifix, his eyes entreating her.

Who are you? he asked.

Samantha ignored the question, looking now behind her at the doors, wondering if Dorothy might be looking for her, though barely half an hour had passed. Upon seeing no one but the usher, she turned back around, and her eyes, against her will, went upward.

Who are you?

She clenched her teeth together and replied in a whisper, "I have no idea."

She allowed herself to stare at his eyes, at his suffering, at the blood. He had died willingly. This is my body. This is my blood. I give it up for you.

Suddenly the face of Rebecca looked down at her from the face of Jesus.

What?

Rebecca smiled.

Sam looked around her, to make sure no one could tell she was having this strange conversation with a statue. You died willingly, didn't you? You sacrificed yourself for your people! You weren't killed against your will! It wouldn't have been the same if you had been!

"It had to be a willing sacrifice!" she cried aloud.

The people nearby looked at her, then shifted in their seats. The usher approached, asking if she was okay.

She smiled at him as she stood from her seat. She nearly kissed the man as she went past him, through the doors, and out to the front of the church. When she didn't see her mother waiting in the parking lot, she started walking, then running, toward her opa's house.

She avoided her mother's look of surprise, her opa's snort, when she walked inside, breathless and soaked in sweat. She went directly to the spare bedroom for her purse and took out her cell phone.

Samantha trembled as she dialed. She had spent two weeks in the hospital and two more sunning by her pool, watching the hummingbirds take up residence in the little house she had bought, and the first person she was calling wasn't the professor, wasn't Mark, wasn't Grandma Beck.

"One moment, Miss Beck."

After several minutes, "Hello?"

"Tuki, it's Beck."

"Did Claire get a hold of you?"

"I've been away. It's a long story."

"I heard. The Bahamas. I trust you had a good time?"

"What?" No not the Bahamas. Did she want him to know the truth? "Oh, well, I have to tell you about it later. Listen. I know this sounds crazy."

"Well?"

"I just wanted you to know—even though you could probably care less what I think—anyway, I just wanted to tell you that I don't think your father, or any of your, of our, ancestors murdered your mother."

He was quiet on the other end.

"That's all. I won't keep you."

"What changed your mind?"

"Well, according to my book, the couple and the new mothers always died willingly. As humans, they couldn't have ascended to the level of god or goddess without making a noble sacrifice."

"Great. So now you're saying my mother allowed herself to be killed? Some kind of assisted suicide? Isn't that still murder? Look, I don't see the good of all this speculation. We can never know what happened."

"Why not? Isn't there anyone who was living then who could tell us?"

"No. The medicine woman who delivered me died years ago."

"But someone else might know, especially if this was a custom still being practiced when you were born. Was a Bear present who might still be alive?"

"Why can't you just drop this? Why do you have to know?"

"Why don't you want to know? Are you afraid of what you'll learn?"

The loud crash on the other end of the line caused Samantha to pull the phone from her ear. It sounded as though he had smashed his phone on a hard surface. After a second, she nestled hers back in place. "Tuki? Are you there?"

Nothing.

A week after the funeral of Ana Gold Schmidt, Samantha received a manila envelope in the mail with Tuki's return address. She opened the envelope and found a letter enclosed, but it was addressed to Tuki.

Dear Mr. Nisha:

After several studies, we at Forensic Anthropology Labs, Inc. believe the four specimens you sent to us to be the phalanges—second, third, fourth, and fifth from the same hand—of a human adult female who died in the range of fifteen to forty years ago.

Samantha gasped, her hand flying to her mouth. She'd been right.

Heart pounding, she continued reading the letter:

We believe the specimens to be human due to the circular and oblong patterns of trabeculae in the spongy bone of the shafts. This is usually more dense or granular and often homogenous in animal bones, without the pattern seen in human bones. Additionally, your specimens lack a sharp line or border between the spongy midshaft and the internal aspect of the bone. That is almost always present in animal specimens.

Please note the rate of correct species identification using this method to be between 82-87%.

Our belief that the specimens are from an adult female is based on measurements taken of the bones and used in a time-proven formula trusted by forensic pathologists for nearly a century. Two formulas were used on your specimens. First, we measured the length of each bone and divided it by the diameters of both their midshafts and the rounded ends. Second, we took the diameter of the midshafts and divided them by the diameters of the rounded ends. Using both formulas, and applied to all four specimens, we concluded them to be adult and female.

Please note the rate of correct adult/child identification using these methods to be in the order of 88-90%, and the rate of correct gender identification to be 76%.

Our belief that the postmortem age of the specimens ranges from fifteen to forty years is based on our observations of the condition of the bones, using a bone-weathering grid, used by forensic pathologists for over sixty years, and including the following: The lack of grease, soft tissue, and marrow suggests the specimens are older than one year. The slightly moderate longitudinal cracking places the specimens in the 4-20 year range. The moderate flaking of the outer surface of each bone puts the specimens in the 10-30 year range. The coarse, rough, and fibrous texture of the surface of each bone, along with the presence of splintering on each specimen, places them in the 20-40 year range. One such splinter completely detached during our observation, but it did not cause a crack or penetrate to the inner cavity, which would have suggested an even older specimen. The intact structures and the lack of heavy fragmentation, exfoliating powder residues, and open cracks suggest the specimens are not older than forty years (postmortem).

Please note that postmortem time range estimates are usually large, encompassing twenty to fifty years, and so the correct time range estimate consequently has a higher success rate, usually in the order of 96-98%.

We concluded the bones came from the same hand because the circular and oblong patterns of trabeculae in the spongy bone of the shafts of one bone precisely matched the patterns in the other three.

We hope our services have been helpful to you. Please contact us if you have any questions or are in need of further services. We have enclosed our bill and an envelope for your convenience, along with your four bone specimens, wrapped per our specifications.

Cordially,

Carl Fromme, Senior Forensic Anthropologist

Samantha read the letter again to be sure she had understood it correctly. Then she paced around the room, wondering what to do.

Later that evening, she decided to write a brief note and send it back to Tuki with the forensics letter. She wrote:

Please call me if you want to talk about it. Thanks for sharing the letter.

The following morning, after she mailed the letter, she sat in her little Ford Mustang convertible, the one her parents had given her as a college graduation gift years ago, and wept.

She decided to keep driving, past her street, further south, down San Pedro, near Woodlawn, and onto Craig Street, to her old school, Keystone. As it was a late August Monday afternoon, school had not yet started. It usually began right after the Labor Day Weekend, but the teachers and administrators were there, organizing, planning, and attending workshops. Samantha pulled into the parking lot, walked to the front office, wondering if the same secretary, Mrs. Holsbrooke, would be there to greet her. As she rounded the corner, she could see through the glass window from the foyer that it wasn't Mrs. Holsbrooke, but someone else, someone she did not recognize.

She went inside and asked if Mr. Griffin, her favorite English teacher, was still there, the one who had danced for the eighth graders a linking verb dance with two fingers clasped, first in front, then behind: Jane is president; President is Jane. The one who quoted Greeks, especially Epictetus. The one who had made her the editor of their school newspaper.

No, the unfamiliar secretary said, Mr. Griffin retired two years ago, and then four months ago, passed away from colon cancer. Samantha's mouth dropped open. The secretary asked if she were one of his old students, and Samantha nodded. She stood up and took Samantha out of the office and down the hall.

"This bulletin board is a memorial to him. Maybe you'd like to see it."

She nodded and thanked the woman and then was left there, standing alone, to gaze at all the pictures of him through the years, notes from students, pictures they had made him, awards he had won, and a beautiful description, written by the headmaster, describing his contributions to the school. Samantha was about to leave when she noticed an inconspicuous note in juvenile writing on the lower left-hand side, a flower made of construction paper glued in the corner of an index card. The note read:

Dear Mr. Griffin,

I'll never forget you.

Love Always,

Samantha

The memory of making it flashed into her head. It had been the end of her eighth-grade school year. As she looked at her young writing, the flower she had cut and pasted, and tasted those memories of being a little girl, so young and unaware of the world and its complexities, so sheltered and safe, so loved by all in her life, Samantha began to sob— not weep as she had in the car, where the tears just sort of slid down her cheeks as her nose sniffled, but fully sob, shoulders shaking, face scrunched, mouth open, bottom lip quivering, total, uncontrollable sob.

The secretary must have heard her, or seen her as she conducted some errand, for the woman came back to Samantha and gave her a wad of tissue.

"Are you okay, Hon'?"

In between sobs, she said, "Hun, an ancient, warlike people who, led by Attila, attacked the Roman Empire in 400 A.D."

"Miss, are you mocking me?"

Samantha looked at the woman, startled by the question. "No, m'am. Not at all. I'm just upset. Excuse me." Then she ran past the perplexed woman, out the school doors, and into the parking lot where she sat in her car for half an hour before returning home.

Later that evening, Tuki called.

"Are you still planning on attending our fall gathering?"

"If I'm still welcome."

"You understand it was as our cousin and not as an archaeologist that we invited you?"

"We?"

"You know what I mean."

"Yes. I understand," she said, a bit curtly.

"Beck?"

She softened. "Yes?"

"I have a huge favor to ask of you."

"Anything." She swallowed the lump in her throat.

"Can you come this weekend?"

Her mouth dropped open and her heart raced. A smile crossed her face in spite of the fear and the incredulity. "What? I thought we weren't going to do this. It would wear on you after a while, Tuki. I would go on and on. As it is, even from this distance, I will probably continue to try to persuade you, covertly of course. But it would be unethical for me to do so while dating you. I just couldn't."

"I'm not asking you to come for a date."

"Oh." Her face burned. She felt like a fool.

"I need your help."

"You need my help? What can I do?"

"I want to find out if my grandfather knows anything about the bones. I have an uncle I will go see, but I'm not sure I can trust him. I don't know what to think anymore."

"What is it you want me to do?"

"Come this Labor Day weekend and ask my grandfather what happened. See if you can persuade him to tell you the truth. I'm afraid he won't tell me or Claire. I think he thinks we can't take the truth. But I want to know. I need to know. And he likes you—he's even said you remind him of my mother—and I think that if he's going to tell what he knows to anyone, he will tell you."

"He might not know anything."

"I know. But we may as well ask. Maybe you could tell him that you think the bones I once wore around my neck are human. You don't have to tell him what we know from the lab. Don't tell him we suspect the bones belonged to my mother."

"Did you stop wearing them?"

"Yeah. For now. It's funny, though. I'm not really grossed out. It's nice having a part of her. That may sound strange."

"I'll come."

"You will? That's great. I'll have Jes make the arrangements."

CHAPTER EIGHTEEN

Jeannie's Story

When Samantha arrived at the airport in Lebanon, she was disappointed to see Jes, and not Tuki, waiting for her.

Jes drove her to Gellermann Manor in the black Mercedes coupe. As Brandon was in the middle of conducting business over the telephone in his study when they arrived, Samantha found herself alone for a while. Jes offered her refreshment, but she kindly refused. He helped her carry her things up to her room, and after looking around it, absorbing the familiar furniture and paintings like a dry sponge, she decided to head down to the conservatory to try her hand at the piano.

Her mother had wanted her to become an accomplished pianist like most of her classmates, but Samantha lacked the patience to practice. She preferred to read or play tennis, yet she had taken just enough piano lessons that she could squeak her way through the one Beethoven piece she had memorized.

She started over five times before the notes came back to her, flooding her memory, and attached to those memories came other images, wonderful images of her childhood. She felt transported in time, a little girl at the keys, preparing for the recital at the end of the year, after which she would be free to do what she wanted. She recalled some of her favorite birthday parties—pony rides, tea parties, and roller-skating. She remembered riding on her father's shoulders at the Fourth of July parades and fairs in Fredericksburg and eating funnel cakes. She remembered Opa Stehling's homemade peach ice cream, Grandma Beck scratching her back while they watched television, her mother's perfume, Chanel Number 5, always Chanel Number 5.

She was almost twenty-six, but she sometimes felt like a little girl. Was she ready to be anything else?

Upon her final note came unexpected applause.

"It's amazing how much your playing reminds me of my daughter's."

Samantha turned to see Brandon standing in the entryway of the conservatory. "She must have been much better."

Brandon chuckled. "No. Much worse. She preferred the outdoors."

Samantha smiled and wiped her cheeks with the back of her hand.

"I say, are you all right, dear girl?"

She nodded. "Tell me more about your daughter. She's so beautiful in the portraits I've seen around the house."

Brandon Gellermann pulled one of the carved cherry wood chairs from against the wall, setting it at an angle so he could sit and face Samantha at the piano.

"It would please me to talk about my Rebecca. She was such a vibrant character, always running around doing things, sometimes getting into mischief. I remember once when she was still quite young—two or three years old—we didn't realize she had left the house. We searched all over, in such a state of frenzy and panic like you've never seen. We finally found her out in one of the fields. It took a helicopter to do it, but we found her."

"How scary."

"Yes. We found out later she had followed her new puppy, little red dachshund, into the fields. We found him romping around there the next day."

"Thank goodness."

Brandon told a few more stories, aware perhaps of his own self-indulgence, but feeling perhaps it wasn't too much to ask of his guest. Eventually he moved from his daughter's toddler years, apparently forgetting he had a listener, into her childhood. He spoke of her academic achievements in boarding school, her love of fishing, her fascination with plants and animals. "Rebecca grew up to be such an intelligent girl, more like her mother."

"You're too modest."

"Should we move into the parlor?"

"I'm fine here, if you are."

He smiled. "Yes, just fine. And might I say what a lovely necklace you have on. Is that lapis lazuli?"

Samantha nodded, fingering the stones. "Thanks. I bought it from Claire at the craft fair."

"It's just beautiful. But no, it's not modesty to say Rebecca inherited her brains from my wife Jeannie. And her beauty. Jeannie was so beautiful—more beautiful and more intelligent than most. People probably thought she married me for my money, but I knew otherwise. You can tell when you're loved. I was lucky and still feel grateful to have had her in my life, even though it wasn't long enough. Both of them."

"How long ago did your wife pass away?"

"When Charles was about twelve, I think."

"Were you serious when you said the Unikwëti killed her?"

"Charles doesn't know about it."

"But that explains so much, Brandon. That explains why you seem uncomfortable with that part of Tuki's heritage."

"Uncomfortable is putting it mildly. You speak with the diplomacy of a queen, my dear. The truth is I despise them. I'm sorry, dear. I know they are your family, too. But they took my family away from me, you see? A man never gets over that."

Samantha caught a glimpse of Tuki standing quietly in the foyer, with an urgent look on his face.

"What happened, Brandon? What was the dispute?"

Just then, Jes entered the foyer beside Tuki. "Why Mr. Nisha, welcome home. May I, what?"

Tuki frantically tried to signal to the old butler not to reveal his presence, but Jes didn't comprehend.

"Charles?" Brandon stood and turned, painfully, from the chair, his hip always causing the transition to be slower than it is for most people, and hobbled over toward the foyer.

"Hello, Grandfather. Samantha." Tuki entered the conservatory as though he had just arrived home. "What a day. I'm ready for a drink. Will you two join me before dinner?"

Samantha was invited to join Brandon and Tukihëla after dinner to watch television in the third-floor media room. As she entered, she was immediately impressed by the large oak media unit lining the right wall from the doorway, from floor to ceiling and as wide as the room. Although the lower cabinets and drawers were made of wood, the doors on a few of the uppermost cabinets were glass and were lighted from the back.

With a flip of a switch on the wall, Brandon caused the doors of the large cabinet in the center to mechanically separate, as those of an elevator, revealing the largest television screen Samantha had ever seen.

Brandon took up the remote and changed the channel. "Ah, more coverage on the war in Iraq."

"No thanks," Tuki said.

"Or we can watch the ball game," Brandon said.

"That was on this afternoon," Tuki said.

"I know, my boy, but I taped it. Care to watch?"

"Naw. The Pirates lost. It was a terrible game."

"Thanks." Brandon said. "I suppose there's no point in watching it now."

"Sorry." Then, as Samantha took a seat on the brown chenille couch across from the screen, Tuki added, "I think I'll go ahead and turn in. It was a long day at work today, and I'm tired."

"Are you sure, my boy? Why not sit and have one drink with us?"

"Tomorrow night, Grandfather. You two go on without me."

"Good night," Samantha said, giving a knowing wave. "See you in the morning."

"Good night."

"So, my dear. What shall it be? A game for which we already know the disappointing ending, bits of the news—oh, look at that. There's more on Hurricane Katrina."

"Oh, I can't look at any more of that. It's too sad. All those people. I'd actually prefer to visit. You started to tell me something before dinner, about the death of your wife. I've been so curious ever since you first mentioned it but didn't want to bring it up in front of Tuki, since you said he didn't know about it."

Brandon turned off the television. "I had a feeling I had piqued your curiosity. That, of course, was not my intention."

"I'm sorry. Let's talk about something else."

He sat down in the brown chenille loveseat, which was positioned at a right angle to the couch where she sat.

His eyes rested on a painting above the fireplace to the left of the room, behind Samantha. She turned to look as well. The short blonde hair curled under at the nape of the woman's neck and along her jaw line. Her blue eyes glistened, looking up, as though asking the artist, "Is this right? You want me like this?" Her full lips were almost puckered, though less for a kiss than for retrieving a thought from the back of the mind. Her high cheekbones resembled those in the portraits of Rebecca, and Samantha now realized, upon seeing the adult version of them, those of Tukihëla.

"That purple blouse Jeannie's wearing was her favorite. She was buried in it."

"It looks lovely on her. She was beautiful, just as you said."

"Yes. And she was a pleasant woman, which doesn't always come with beauty."

"Has it gotten any easier?" She turned to face him.

"Yes. Yes, it has. If you had known me before, you'd see the difference. Time does heal, as they say."

"Are the Native Americans really to blame for her death?"

"They don't think so. It depends on whom you ask," Brandon said.

"What do you think?" Samantha asked.

"I know the Indians are to blame."

Samantha sat forward on the couch. "Can you talk about it? Or is it still too difficult?"

Brandon shrugged, lifting his palms up. "I haven't tried to discuss it. Ever."

"I'm sorry. You don't have to now. Unless you want to."

He looked up again at the portrait. "Jeannie was never the same after Rebecca's death."

"How did Rebecca die?"

"The Indians said she died while giving birth to Charles. They said Charles was breech, and Rebecca pushed too hard. The mid-wife hadn't yet got into position, hadn't found a leg. He presented his backside. My daughter ripped herself up pushing him out. She lost so much blood so quickly, that there was nothing anyone could do."

"I'm so sorry."

Images of her dream flitted through her head.

"Charles had to be rushed to the hospital. He wasn't breathing well on his own. Fluids were trapped in his little lungs. Jeannie went with Attie and the baby to the emergency room while I went looking for Rebecca. I found her in the Indian house on a table surrounded by a group of them. They had covered her body—all but her face, which was painted, her head crowned. Her face was cold. I knew instantly I had lost her. I lifted the blanket to find a white silk robe on her body, and…and…the Indians had, they had cut off the fingers of Rebecca's left hand. Dear Lord, excuse me." He cleared his throat.

"Why did they do that, do you think?"

"The sachem explained it to me this way. He said it was customary for family members to keep some part of the deceased loved one, typically a finger bone and locks of hair. I was shocked when I first saw, under the blanket, her body, it was," he paused, "terrible. But after a while, I accepted and respected their beliefs. I related it to my own belief that the bones of saints hold special powers."

"Then what caused the dispute?"

"That happened years later, after Attie died."

"Tuki's father?"

Brandon nodded. "He died of pneumonia. It was awful, just awful. I had him brought into Rebecca's old room. I hired the best physician in the state, but evidently it was too late to do much good. Charles was permitted brief visits, with a mask over his mouth and nose. The poor boy was only eight years old, he had no mother, and he had to watch his father slowly die."

Samantha shook her head. "That must have been difficult for you as well."

"Oh, yes. And Jeannie. I think that's when she really began to lose it."

"What do you mean?" Samantha asked.

Brandon took a handkerchief from his trouser pocket, leaning over as he did so, and he dabbed his face with it.

"Are you okay?"

"Dear me. Look at this." He held out his hand, which was trembling. "Perhaps we can finish our discussion some time tomorrow. I think I need to settle myself down. At my age, I have to watch out for a heart attack, you know."

"Of course. I'm so sorry if I—"

"No, no, no. Please don't apologize. This is good for me. Cathartic. Like going to confession. I just can't do it all in one night, you see."

"Why don't we both call it a night?" She stood, holding a helping hand out to her host.

He shook his head. "No, my dear. I won't be able to sleep right away. I'll just catch some of the evening news while having a drink or two to calm my nerves." He reached over to the end table between them and pushed a button on the intercom system. "Jes, would you please bring me a drink, my good man?"

"Right away, sir," the butler's voice rang out over the speaker box.

"You sure you don't want one?" Brandon asked Sam.

"No, thank you. I'm tired from the travel. But thank you again for the delicious dinner."

"You're quite welcome."

"I can't do this," Samantha said to Tuki when she entered her room and found him waiting there. "That poor man is falling apart! I'm falling apart!"

Tuki closed the door behind them. "Come sit down. You heard what he said. It's cathartic for him. And he hasn't yet explained how my grandmother was killed. You can't stop now."

She sat on the bed, he opposite her in the chair. "I can't lie to him. I need to ask him if he will tell the both of us. I can't take this deception."

"He knows I'm listening."

"What?"

"He saw my reflection in the French door. I thought he'd turn and ask me to come in for a drink, but he understood immediately. This is the only way we can get through this, Beck. He can't tell me to my face, and I can't hear it with his eyes looking into mine. You have to be our intermediary. Don't you see?"

She sighed and closed her eyes but nodded.

"But you aren't agreeing to act as this intermediary on condition. You won't ask something of me regarding the catacombs?"

She shook her head, a bit peeved. "No. This is an entirely separate matter, as far as I'm concerned."

He sat back in the chair and studied her. Looking her over from head to toe. "Then why are you helping me?"

"I suppose I'm curious to know the answers myself. I want to know why your grandfather hates your—our—people. I want to know more about our ancestors."

"I see. Okay. Fair enough." He stood to go.

"Wait a minute." She also stood. "What do you want me to say?"

He glanced down at her. After a minute, he said, "Are you and Mark involved?"

She opened her eyes with surprise.

"I want the truth," he said.

"We were. But it was nothing. I never loved him like…" she dropped off.

"Like what?"

"We've been through this already, haven't we? Tuki, wait. Wait. Don't go, please."

He faced her again with his back against the bedroom door, his arms crossed. "It seems wrong that two people, two spirits—yes, I said spirits—should find one another, only to…and, it just seems wrong."

She stood about three feet away. "What's the answer then?"

"We quit fighting our destiny."

She raised her palms to the ceiling, as Brandon had done earlier. "How do we know what that is?"

"Look inward." His eyes bore into hers for a brief second, then he turned, opened the door, and left.

She dropped on the bed, exasperated.

Look inward? How did one do that?

CHAPTER NINETEEN

Kukna's Womb

Samantha became dimly aware, as, on Saturday morning, Sister Claire led her down a gravelly descent on the eastern end of the Gellermann property, that maybe, subconsciously, she had, all along, been searching for her mother's womb.

"Watch your step," Claire warned from below her.

As soon as they were underground, they each turned on their lights.

"You'll be able to see better in a minute. Watch it. It narrows here, and then there's a steep drop. Are you okay?"

Samantha didn't mind heights, darkness, or deep water, but tightly closed in spaces gave her the creeps. "A bit claustrophobic, but okay." Her blue jeans and long sleeves protected her legs from getting scraped, but they also made her warm.

"It gets really humid down here, too. Sometimes, especially in summertime, it's hard to breathe." Claire said.

"This is really narrow. I bet not all can fit through here. Can Tuki fit?"

Claire laughed. "Yes, believe it or not."

Samantha stopped.

Claire shined her light back toward her. "You okay?"

"I don't think I can do this."

"Yes, you can."

"I don't know. It's so narrow. I can hardly breathe."

"Here's the drop. We're almost there."

Samantha heard a rush of gravel.

"Come on! I'm in. It's great! Just sit on your bottom and slide down."

Samantha sat on her bottom with her eyes closed to the rock closing in around her and slid the rest of the way through the narrow tunnel. "Ahhh!"

She landed on her feet on the bottom of a large cavern. It was about fifty feet wide and thirty feet high. Stalagmites and stalactites joined together in various rock formations throughout the cavern, so the room wasn't nearly as open as the major chamber of the catacombs. A hazy light came in through crevices above them, making it possible to see beyond their flashlights.

A rush of bats exited above them. Samantha shuddered.

She was relieved to be in the open space, out of the tunnel. "This is where you found the lapis lazuli?"

"Yes. Look along here."

Claire pointed her light to mounds of rock, dirt, and gravel along the back walls of the cavern.

"That's a lot of dirt and gravel. I bet it takes you quite a long time."

"You have to sift through it all. I haul out bags of this stuff and then put it through a sifting pan. Sometimes I come up empty, but often I find something."

"Sounds like a lot of work." Samantha looked around the ground of the cavern.

"Yes. It's probably a lot like the work you do. It's painstaking but exciting, right? Kind of like fishing. You never know when you'll get a bite."

Samantha laughed. "That's true."

Claire pointed her flashlight in the opposite direction, back toward the tunnel through which they had just entered. "You can understand the pictures best by standing here and looking all around."

Samantha looked at the opening, then she turned and pointed her light up and behind her, realizing she was looking into two black eyes. "It's one big painting."

"Carving. It's a painted carving."

"It's the Mother Goddess? Behind us, up there, that's her face?" The two black eyes were framed with lashes and thin, arched brows. Long black hair was painted all along the top of the cave, like a rim in a giant bowl, and over the eyes on top of the black hair was a jeweled crown.

"And these are her arms all along here." Claire said, moving her light along both sides of the cavern.

All around the arms were painted in green and orange the heads and tails of snakes wrapped around and around so it was difficult to tell where one snake started and another ended.

"Up above us, and beginning there where we entered, are her legs, can you see that?"

"So, we came in between her legs?"

"Yes. We are in the womb of Mother Earth."

"Wow. How interesting. It's beautiful artwork. They must have stood on rock formations while they worked." She studied the walls, flashing her light around them. "What was this cavern used for?"

"Different religious ceremonies. You see, our people believe that all of earth is the body of Kukna, Mother Earth. She's not really a separate entity from the world. She is the world. That's why each time our ancestors ate a meal together, it was a religious ceremony. They gave thanks to Mother Earth for allowing them to consume that certain part of her.

"The difference between Christians and the Unikwëti is that Christians see God's creation as something separate from God; whereas the Unikwëti believe they are one and the same. The world is the god. This also explains why Christians often tend to suppress the natural parts of themselves and to view nature as an evil temptation, as a fallen state with God ruling above it. Our people see everything natural and of nature as an aspect of God, as a manifestation of God."

"That's interesting," Sam said.

"The human body isn't covered up in shame, for example. Animals and plants aren't killed needlessly and wasted. There has never been a problem among our people with pollution. In our eyes, to pollute is sacrilegious. Also, there is no such thing, among our people, of hunting purely for sport."

"Do you ever have to choose between a Unikwëti and a Christian belief?"

She shook her head. "No. I see Christ as the clarifier of all things. He came to make clear the ancient teachings. But human beings twist his words, even though they are written. People misunderstand and forget his message of love. They become judges, caught up in their own righteousness, not realizing they, in their prideful hate, have fallen furthest from the tree of life. They would do well to remember God is present in each of us, and that is a Unikwëti concept I am thankful to have had handed down to me."

Samantha began to feel faint. "I can't breathe too well down here, unlike in the catacombs. I wonder why."

"The air doesn't circulate as well in here. It's not as large. The catacombs have more than one entrance, so the air flows."

Samantha's eyes widened. "Really?"

"You'll see when you come in a few weeks for the powwow. You know, the Unikwëti also teach that staying in Mother Earth too long away from Father Sky will make you sick. So why don't we head out?"

The hardest part was getting back up the steep drop. A large boulder against the wall of the cavern helped them to climb the steepest part of the path. After that, they no longer had to use their hands, but could walk upright the rest of the way.

As they ascended, Claire spoke. "I remember an uncle telling me once if you spend all your time looking to the past, you can't live. The past must always die, as does the future, so the present can exist. Just like parents: as soon as they beget and bear children, they begin to die. One generation must die so the new generation can exist."

Samantha laughed. "Is that why you became a nun?"

Claire also laughed. "Of course." Then she added, "The sad thing is my body won't live on through progeny, so if I want to continue to live on earth, I'll have to be eaten."

"What?"

"Look. Here we are. Back to the light of day."

When they were finally above ground, Samantha asked Claire, as they turned off their lights and caught their breaths, "Are you trying to tell me something?"

Claire gazed at the white clouds overhead. "I think it's wonderful that you want to know about your ancestors. It's important to know. As I said before, we keep records so that our past won't be forgotten." She looked at Samantha. "But don't let your search for your past stop you from moving forward, from living your life."

"You think I'm obsessed?" Samantha dusted off her blue jeans as she waited for Claire's reply. She had been expecting a different message, one about cannibalism.

"You really want to know what I think? There's a thin line between passion and obsession. I think you're standing on that line. You remember the story of Lot and his wife? When God destroys the cities of Sodom and Gomorrah, he tells Lot and his family not to look back, but Lot's wife does, and she turns into a pillar of salt?"

Samantha nodded.

"Don't live your life looking back. You'll sacrifice your future."

"But sometimes something from the past prevents you from living forward, like with Tuki and his grandfather."

"In that case, you should consider looking back and fixing it, because you could die either way. But only then." As they neared Claire's old jeep, the nun added, "So that's why you've come? To help Tuki?"

Samantha shrugged. "I'll give it a try."

Back at Gellermann Manor, after taking a warm shower and putting on a fresh set of clothes, Samantha found Tuki outside of her bedroom door leaning on the cherry wood balustrade waiting for her.

"My uncle was gone all morning, but I just got a hold of him. He's agreed to meet with us."

"Us?"

"That alright with you?"

"Sure. But I'm starving. What about lunch?"

"Let's pick something up on the way."

"Like old times?" She started to laugh but then didn't when she saw his weak smile. No. Not at all like old times.

She followed him down the winding stairs and through the foyer.

"I've already let Jes know we'll be out for a while," he said as he led her under the giant sycamore and then opened his truck door for her to climb in.

Without thinking twice, she slid to the middle and buckled herself in, as had been her custom when riding with Tuki, but as he scooted in beside her, he said, "I had the other belt fixed, if you'd be more comfortable over there."

"Oh, okay. Thanks." Samantha slid across the seat to the passenger side and re-buckled herself in. As she looked at him from across this new distance, she wanted to cry.

He started the engine. "Look, if you want to sit next to me, then sit next to me."

"I don't want to sit next to you."

"Fine, but then why the long face?"

"Where are we going? Where does your uncle live?"

"New Jersey."

"New Jersey? How long will it take us to get there?"

"About two hours."

"I wish you would have mentioned that when you asked me to come along."

"If you don't want to go, don't go."

"I want to go, I just didn't expect…I want to go. I want to meet your uncle."

He pulled from the circular drive onto the paved road and drove half a mile, to where the paved road ended, and the dirt road began. He stopped the truck.

"What's the matter?" Samantha asked.

"This is agonizing. I can't take this, this silence, this distance. I thought it would be easier with you over there, but it's not."

She undid the seatbelt and moved beside him and belted herself in again. She gave him a smile, a sad smile, a smile that said she understood and yes, it was agonizing.

He stepped on the gas and drove onward, putting his hand on her knee. "Thanks."

She wrapped her arms around his arm and leaned her head against his shoulder. "What are we going to do?"

"I don't know.

CHAPTER TWENTY

The Sacred Ritual

After getting sandwiches from a drive-through restaurant, Tuki and Samantha took the Pennsylvania Turnpike and then eventually turned off toward the Ben Franklin Bridge. During the entire trip, Samantha had begun to feel like a deceiver. She had previously justified not mentioning what her mother had revealed to her about her ancestry by telling herself she needed to wait until she confronted her birth parents before talking to anyone else about it. Then she hadn't expected to see Tuki until the powwow. Now, there seemed to be no easy excuse for keeping her secret.

"You know, there's something I've wanted to tell you for a while now."

"Yeah?" he smiled.

She sensed he was expecting her to confess her feelings to him. Dear God. This was going to hurt. "It has to do with my search for my grandmother's ancestors."

"Oh. What about it?" He sucked on the straw in his now empty cup of cola, bringing up air. Balancing the steering wheel, he removed the plastic cup and straw, tossed them onto the passenger side floorboard, and tilted the cup to his mouth, catching the squares of ice.

Samantha watched him crunching on the ice, as she teetered on the verge of confessing. She feared he may not take the news well, and he may not allow her to attend the powwow. Then the Benjamin Franklin

Bridge came into view, and its beauty momentarily distracted her. "Wow!"

"How'd you like to have this view every day going back and forth from work?"

"I'd love it."

"We should be there soon. Another thirty minutes. My uncle lives in a house in a suburb on the outskirts of the city. Now, what were you saying before?"

"Oh, nothing really. Tell me about your uncle."

"Okay. Let's see." He spit ice back into his cup. "He's currently the chief of the UniKwëti. And he's an attorney. Environmental law. He also teaches part-time as an adjunct at Rutgers School of Law in Camden. He's serving his fourth term as a state representative in the general assembly. Democrat. Let's see, I guess that just about does it."

"Is he married? Does he have children?"

"Oh, yeah. He's married and has three children—a daughter by his first wife and two sons. His daughters about fifteen, I think, a sophomore in high school. His sons are fourteen and thirteen. You won't get to meet them, though, because they went to the coast for the Labor Day weekend with friends. Only Wëli and Donna will be there."

"And what's Donna like?"

"She's a schoolteacher. High school algebra. Man, I haven't seen my aunt and uncle since before I left for Iraq, at a powwow before I graduated from college. I remember her being a nice lady. She's tall and thin, just like he is, and black. The boys are tall and thin, too. Only the girl is small, like her mother was."

"Was? What happened to her mother?"

"She died in childbirth."

Samantha gave him a suspicious glance, but he didn't see it. She wondered now if the uncle might be able to explain all the deaths the women in the Nisha clan had suffered. "Well, I can't wait to meet your aunt and uncle."

It was nearly two o'clock in the afternoon when Tuki pulled his truck into the drive of Wëli and Donna Nisha's house, a brown brick home of modest size, single story, probably seventeen hundred square feet. It was surprisingly smaller than Samantha had anticipated after hearing the uncle's résumé. The lots seemed smaller than those of two other suburbs they had driven past, and the lawns weren't as well manicured. About every tenth house looked like a dumping ground.

Chain-link fencing divided the backyards, and Samantha could see, as she climbed from the passenger side of the truck, a German shepherd in the uncle's yard barking at her.

"It's okay, boy," she said.

"How do you know it's a boy?" He called from the other side of the driveway.

She walked around the cab of the truck. "Oh, trust me. It's obvious."

He laughed as they approached the front door together and rang the bell.

"I'm nervous," he said.

"So am I."

Wëli Nisha, an older version of Tuki except for the darker complexion, the lower cheekbones, and the more almond shape of the eyes, came to the door with arms outstretched and gave each of the visitors a tight embrace. "Well, well, well. You're finally here."

"We stopped for some grub on the way over," Tuki explained.

In a lower voice Wëli said, "Oh, no. Donna's in the kitchen now throwing something together. Just act like you're starving, okay? She made a special trip out to the store and all." Then, aloud, he said, "Come in, come in."

As they entered, they walked right into the living room, decorated in earth tones—a brown shag carpet, brown fabric sofas and a matching recliner, oak coffee table and end tables, and a set of lamps with orange shades and brass bases. Orange and beige pillows were neatly tucked in the corners of each of the two couches, and several copies of *Sports Illustrated* and *The Ladies' Home Journal* were fanned out on the coffee table. The television console sat on the floor before the front windows, which were draped in heavy plaids of earth tones. A bookcase full of law books, biographies, and romance paperbacks sat against the left wall. All the walls were covered in wood paneling, except for the kitchen, which was brightly decorated with yellow floral wallpaper, visible through a small window bar at the back of the living room.

Donna poked her head through the small opening between the kitchen and the living area. She wore short, neat braids and thin gold hoops in her ears. "Hello, there! Let me come and get a look at you."

She rushed around the corner and entered the room, with her hands at her cheeks in surprise, "Oh my goodness. I haven't seen you since you were in college. Why, you a man now. Look at you, all thick and muscular. You were just a pole about two years ago."

"Mama, war will do that to you," Wëli said.

"I didn't fight in the war," Tuki objected.

"Just look at you. Give your auntie a hug." She wore a cream silky blouse with a cowl neckline and black slacks and platform sandals. A yellow ruffled apron was tied around her waist. "Aren't you gonna introduce me to your friend?"

"This is Samantha Beck. Like I told Wëli, she's a cousin of ours and found us recently. She's an archaeology student at Trinity University in San Antonio."

Donna extended her hand. "It's so nice to meet you."

Samantha shook the lady's hand. "Likewise. Thank you so much for letting us pop in on you like this."

"We're glad to have you. Now tell me the truth. Are you hungry? Because if you're not, I can let the food simmer for a couple of hours, and we can eat an early supper."

Tuki glanced at his uncle for a sign.

Wëli said, "They just ate, Mama, so why don't we visit for a while first, and then eat?"

"Sounds fine. I'm making my specialty, Chicken Parmesan, and the sauce can simmer nice and slow, so all the flavors are fully absorbed. I got the meat wrapped in foil in the oven, and I can make the noodles and salad later, whenever we want to eat. Is that okay with you all?"

"Of course," Tuki said.

"But for now, what can I get you all to drink?" She named a list of choices and then rushed off to the kitchen to get glasses of lemonade.

Samantha noticed a family portrait on one of the end tables and picked it up to inspect the three children: the oldest, but most petite, light brown girl with straight brown hair pinned to the side with a barrette, and the two tall boys—the younger slightly darker than the older and with kinky hair. After Donna returned with the drinks, they talked at length about Tuki's cousins, the schools they attended, and their extracurricular activities. Then Wëli talked about legislation he and some of his colleagues were trying to get passed in the state assembly.

"So many of the cities in New Jersey are in trouble and have been since the fifties. Our neighborhoods are in a state of decline, our cities are overpopulated, and we don't have enough money to support the growing number of disabled and elderly. And we need to do something to regulate the toxic wastes polluting our beautiful rivers and streams and the air over our cities. I'm concerned about our environment, especially here in New Jersey where we seem to have more factories than we do trees." He took a sip of his tea. "You've seen the Delaware Bridge in Trenton, haven't you? 'Trenton makes, the world takes?' That could be said of the whole state. Manufacturing plants everywhere."

"Honey, these people didn't come here to learn all about the state of New Jersey and its socio-economic problems! Come on, let's let them talk some, too." They heard a low buzzing sound. "That's my timer. Excuse me."

Wëli blushed. "I feel strongly about these things. So many of our people resent the government, but they don't do anything to try and change things. We Native Americans must get involved and make this country ours, too."

The buzzing sound stopped.

"I agree," Tuki said. "Wholeheartedly."

"So, when are you running for office?" Samantha teased.

Tuki smiled. "One day, maybe. It is my destiny, you know. And yours, too."

"Because we are of the Turtle," Samantha said with a tentative smile, wishing she had told the truth so her lies could finally end.

"Exactly," Wëli chimed.

Donna came in from around the corner. "You all won't mind if I work a little in the kitchen, will you? I want to whip up a cake for after our meal. I bought one at the store earlier, but now I know I have the time, I'd rather bake one."

"Please don't go to any trouble," Samantha said.

"Store bought is fine with us," Tuki added.

"Oh, no, no, no. You wouldn't think so if you had ever tasted Donna's red velvet cake. Is that what you're making, Mama?"

She nodded. "Mmm-hmm. Excuse me for a while. You three go on and visit, and just holler at me through that window if you need more lemonade or anything."

After Tuki answered his uncle's questions about his employment at an engineering firm in Myerstown, and after Samantha described her archaeological projects, particularly this latest discovery and what it meant for her grandmother and her career, Tuki finally broached the subject he and Samantha were anxious to discuss.

Tuki pulled out his necklace from beneath his shirt, the four bones reattached with the leather ties that had originally knotted them on either side of Misink. "Wëli, certain factors have led me to believe these bones belonged to my mother. Do you know anything about that?"

"Yes. I saw your father make that necklace, and I'm sure they were your mother's."

Tuki sat in silence. He moved one of the bones to his lips.

"Mr. Nisha—"

"Please. Wëli."

"Wëli, I've been studying ancient Native American rituals, and well, one in particular. You see, we were wondering. Hmm, how can I put this? I couldn't help but wonder about all the women in our family who have died in childbirth. Your first wife, Tuki's mother, his grandmother, your grandmother. Can you explain all these deaths?"

"Yes, I can, but brace yourselves. People outside of the tribe have a hard time understanding. And Tuki's been away from us most of his life."

"Don't worry about me," Samantha said. "I am an archaeologist."

"First of all, Tuki's mother's death isn't related to the others. She died accidentally, during childbirth. Her death was a sad time for the entire tribe. It was especially hard on Attie."

"What do you mean 'she died accidentally'? You mean the others didn't?" Tuki asked.

"Now this may be hard for you to understand."

"Just tell me," Tuki said.

"The others sacrificed themselves."

"What?" Tuki's face paled.

"Now listen. When your grandfather took you away and raised you Catholic, you lost a great deal of Unikwëti culture and understanding, and even when you rejoined us while you were at Harvard, it was so infrequent, the bi-annual powwows, it's been difficult to pass all we need on to you. Then you went straight from your graduate program to Iraq. This is a delicate matter and most of the Turtle didn't think you could handle it. We also thought your grandfather may have told you things, turned you in some ways against us. Perhaps I have no choice today but to tell you the truth. Yes, I'm glad you came today. There is much you need to know. Even Claire understands more than you."

"How can she know more? She's a nun in a frigging convent for Christ's sake."

"But she's been visiting with us and joining us at the powwows since she was fifteen or sixteen. She chooses to worship the Christian God, as many of our people have, but she can still understand our beliefs, especially the old ones I am now going to tell you about. This might shock you."

Samantha nodded. "Believe me, as an archaeologist, I completely understand what you're saying."

"I'm saying this for Tuki's sake."

"Just tell me how they died," Tuki insisted.

"The ancient Unikwëti always said birth and death are one and the same, and birth and death are holy events. Although we always view every meal as a sacred sacrifice, the sacrifice of a woman who has just given birth renews all of us who eat of her flesh and drink of her blood with the spirit of Mother Earth and Father Sky joined together in the one body, death and birth combined. A woman must feel called for this, though. She must feel as though she has been chosen by Father Sky to be, in that moment, Mother Earth. And believe me, it was an honor many young girls aspired to possess."

"Wait, did you say *eat*? *Eat* of her flesh and *drink* of her blood?" Tuki asked. "She sacrificed herself and then you *ate* her?"

"Not all of her. Only the flesh from her fingers and hands. And just a small amount—enough for her spirit to enter us. I can't tell you how spiritual this was for us, of the tears and the peace and the love. You look at me with that look of disgust but remember—and Claire told me this years ago—that right before Christ's passion and after the Last Supper, he sang a song. He sang, 'Let us dance,' and his followers shouted 'Amen!' and then he sang, 'Glory be to the Father. Glory be to the Word. I would be born and I would bear. I would eat and I would be eaten!' So even he saw consuming flesh as a natural way to absorb the divinity of the thing eaten."

Samantha narrowed her eyes. She couldn't recall that particular passage from the Bible, but she hadn't memorized it. "Isn't it possible Jesus spoke symbolically?"

"Is transubstantiation a mere symbol to a Catholic?" Wëli asked. When she didn't reply, he continued, "You must remember the ancient UniKwëti perceived both animals and humans as people. In fact, all were Lenape, and we distinguished ourselves from other animals when we began referring to ourselves as Lenni-Lenape, or genuine people. So eating human flesh was not so different from eating the flesh of other animals until recently, when attitudes among our people began to be more heavily influenced by ideas on the outside.

"Our people tell a story that happened long ago, when the animals completely disappeared from our land. When the sachems sent their best Wind to learn what had happened, the Wind men and women returned to explain that all the animals had been imprisoned by Giants, but they weren't eager to be rescued by humans because of the way we treated them. The Wind returned with a message saying at least once a year we should eat of our own flesh to demonstrate our respect to the animals we eat. Otherwise, we will offend them, and they would no longer sacrifice themselves for us. This story held power over our people for many years."

Tukihëla shook his head and looked to the shag carpet. "I come from a long line of cannibals? I don't know what to say. This is disgusting."

Wëli spoke, "Tuki, all modern people are descendants of cannibals, even though they might not like to admit it. I've actually done quite a bit of research on this. The numerous references in Chinese literature to cannibalism suggest the ancients there practiced it. The Europeans are known to have eaten humans during times of great famine in the Middle Ages. Aztecs have a well-known record of eating their enemies. The Old

Testament indicates cannibalism may have been done by early Semites. Prisoners of War were eaten by both sides during World War II.

"Some people ate out of necessity, and others ate for spiritual reasons. Our ancestors did both. It's a natural thing, present in most of the Animal Kingdom, especially among pigs and rodents in captivity, spiders, and chimpanzees.

"A special herb was always given to the goddess to numb her to any pain. After the logs were dropped on her—"

"Logs were dropped on her?" Tuki asked with disgust.

"The herb was what killed her. The logs were part of the sacred ritual. The women never suffered pain."

"Were you always sure of that?" Tuki asked.

Wëli frowned and bent his brows, sat up, and pointed at Tuki, "I knew by faith, young man. Some things must be accepted by faith alone."

"What happened next, Uncle?"

Wëli crossed his arms and scratched his face. "The Bear confirmed the sacrifice was finished. Afterward, the Unikwëti ate the flesh of Mother Earth's fingers, and then we kept the finger bones and made ornaments to give to her child, to be presented to the child at the age of wisdom, seven years. Quit looking at me like that, Tuki."

"Did you also eat the flesh from my mother's fingers?"

He hesitated. "Yes. But her death was accidental. We wanted the bones to give to you. We did this with all our loved ones who passed away. And we wanted her spirit to live on in you. Your grandparents did not believe us about the death. They did at first. But years later, they wrongly concluded that we murdered their daughter."

"If her death was accidental, why did she wear the robe of corn silk and the crown of jewels? Wasn't that reserved for the Earth goddesses?" Samantha asked.

"The tribe dressed her in those items after her death, because we decided Father Sky had chosen her, that she had indeed become Mother Earth. This was the part your white grandfather could not accept."

"So my grandfather knows about this? But our people continued to live on the Gellermann land for years after my mother's death."

"Your grandparents didn't know about our ritual sacrifice until later, fifteen years ago, when my first wife became Mother Earth. That's when Gellermann banished us."

"What happened?" Tuki asked.

Wëli shifted on the couch, took several swallows of his tea. Then he shook his head. "I think you should ask your grandfather about that. What happened that night should come from him, not me."

"Please, Uncle. He won't talk about it."

Wëli shook his head. "He told me to never speak of it. I doubt his threats would hold up in court today, but I promised then, and I'll keep my word now, even though it was a promise made out of fear."

Samantha cleared her throat. "Do our people, do we, does the tribe continue to practice this ritual even today?"

Wëli shook his head again. "It's a terrible shame in my view, but no, we no longer do. My first wife was the last of the chosen ones. After that, we had no safe meeting place except for the ancient catacombs. Then, too, it became risky to continue a practice shunned by the rest of the country. Gellermann's knowledge of our ways made us nervous. Also, many of us had become secularized, and many had become Christians, and our youth rebelled against these traditions. We discontinued the holy sacrifice rather than risk fragmentation. At our powwows, we do a symbolic communion, but it's only symbolic, so it lacks the significance of the old way. Imagine a Catholic without transubstantiation. But it's an attempt to show the animal spirits our respect, and to provide the feeling of absorbing the spirit of Mother Earth and Father Sky."

Tuki nodded. "The Rite of the Misink."

"That's right."

"Does Donna know about all this?" Tuki asked.

"Yes. Leyla still wears something similar to that around her neck," he pointed to Tuki's necklace, "with her mother's finger bones. Donna has specified in her will the same be done for the boys when she dies, because she sees how much Leyla treasures hers. Even more than a photograph or a vague memory, they help the living remember their dead, treasure their dead, and touch them with tenderness even after their spirits have gone on."

Tukihëla fingered his mother's bones.

Donna re-entered the room. "How are you all doing with your drinks? Anybody need more?"

"Mama, we're doing fine. Will you just come on and sit down now?"

Donna crossed the room and sat next to her husband. "We haven't had company in a long time. It feels so nice. The cake's in the oven baking now. It's gonna be good! Do you two play Scrabble?"

Tuki couldn't reply, perhaps still trying to process the stark truth of his people and their ways and feeling the absurdity of it all juxtaposed with a Saturday afternoon visit, Chicken Parmesan and red velvet cake, and a game of Scrabble in the living room of an ordinary middle class suburban home with his aunt and uncle.

Samantha nodded, not wishing to appear impolite.

"Are you okay?" Samantha finally asked sitting beside Tuki in his truck as they drove the Pennsylvania Turnpike toward Lebanon.

He nodded. "Still shocked."

"I know."

"But you aren't." He looked at her. "You knew all along." He turned back to the road.

"I didn't know. I suspected. There's a big difference. I'm shocked, too."

"All those women who died needlessly at such a young age, who would never get the chance to meet their babies, watch them grow up.

The possible pain of being crushed to death by logs if the herb didn't, you know. I wonder if…it seems crazy."

"I know."

"I'd feel even worse if my mother," his voice dropped off. "I don't know what to think."

Samantha patted his thigh. "The women in your family died for a cause they believed in. I know it seems crazy, but people still do this all the time. Think of the Pakistani suicide bombers."

"Wasted lives."

"Think of the soldiers in Iraq."

He shot her a look. "You can't equate—"

"Just wait. I'm saying people throughout history and even today continue to die willingly for causes they believe in. The women in your family felt good about what they did. And they brought about a positive result for their community, for the whole tribe. They helped to unify them and make them strong spiritually so they could be productive and successful in their lives. They didn't die needlessly—at least, not from the perspective of the Unikwëti."

Tuki shook his head. "I see what you're saying, but I just don't know. I've had so much pride in who I am, and I just don't know. They were cannibals."

She squared herself to him. "Please, Tuki. It makes me so sad to hear you say that. Please think about this. Remember, that day I mentioned the Crusades and the Inquisition? You said all cultures have their skeletons, remember? I was so impressed with that statement. I haven't forgotten it. I thought, how true. We're human beings and we have so much in common as human beings, but our ideas and our ways can also be so different. What's good and bad in one civilization is not so in another. In Japan, it was considered noble for a person to take his life to avoid shame. Here in the Western world, suicide has always been viewed as a weakness, as a medical illness, as a cry for help. Please don't judge your ancestors using a set of standards that come from a different culture. You'll throw away so much of the good. Think of how peaceful your people were. Think of how much they helped other tribes and even the European settlers, all they taught them, all they tolerated from them. Think of how well they took care of the land and all of its inhabitants, including one another. They were a great people. Please remember that."

"They indoctrinated young women into sacrificing themselves for spirits who don't require it."

"How do you know what the spirits require?"

"Are you saying you think a benevolent maker would…"

"I have no earthly idea."

He nodded again but remained silent. Then he said, "Now that we know they were cannibals, what used to be *our* people has become *my* people. Did you realize what you were saying? 'Tuki, *your* people.'"

"No. But that's not what I meant." She knew this was not a good time to reveal the truth, while he was bothered by another, more disturbing one.

"But you're doing the same thing. Already distancing yourself from them."

"Believe me. That's not what I'm doing," she insisted.

"You still plan to attend the powwow?"

"Absolutely. Don't you?"

"I don't know." Then he added, "I can't believe Claire never told me about any of this."

"We should go see her and talk to her. Maybe she's available tonight."

"No. I want you to get the truth from my grandfather about what happened the night the Unikwëti were banished. I want to know tonight."

"Okay. I'll try my best to get your grandfather to tell me."

When they arrived at Gellermann Manor, they were both surprised to learn Brandon was not at home. The butler said an opportunity to acquire a rare work of art had suddenly come up and Mr. Gellermann would not be returning until late Sunday night.

"But my flight leaves Monday morning," Samantha said, turning to Tuki once the butler had left the foyer.

He closed his eyes and sighed.

"Should we call Claire to see if she can meet us tonight?"

Tuki looked at his watch. Eight o'clock wasn't too late. He turned on the light in the parlor and went to the phone, dialing from the couch, but when he asked for his sister, he was told she was participating in a bible study and would not be available for the rest of the evening. Tuki hung up the phone and passed the news on to Samantha.

"Maybe we can see her tomorrow." She stood over him.

"Yeah. Maybe so. I'm just so damned anxious for some answers." He looked at the grey eyes in the portrait above the mantel.

"Do you believe your uncle when he says your mother's death was an accident?"

Tuki shrugged. "I don't know what to think anymore. I guess I'll know more after I speak with Claire and my grandfather."

"Are you going to confront him, then? Are you going to talk to him without me?"

"I don't know if I can. I just don't know. I suppose so. If I can't do it, you'll be back in three weeks, right?"

She nodded.

He stood from the couch and embraced Samantha.

"Shh, don't say anything," he said before she could object. "Just shut up and kiss me."

She closed her eyes and obliged him.

Grandma's Stories

Samantha sat between her father and grandmother in an airplane on the way to Lebanon, Pennsylvania, and, in her hands, she held the already opened and thrice read birthday card sent to her from Josephina Schmidt.

She had received the card in the mail, a day late, just as she and her father were leaving their house to pick up Grandma Beck on their way to the airport.

It had been Tuki's idea to include Luther and Grandma Beck in the annual powwow, and Samantha had been glad when both had eagerly accepted the invitation, pleased, like she had once been, for the opportunity to learn more about their heritage and relatives. Dorothy, her mother, had been invited as well, but she could not cancel a prior commitment to work in their parish festival, and so had insisted they go without her.

Although Samantha had hoped to sleep during the flight—the dream of Misink had returned in spite of her hanging the dream catcher again—she could not stop pondering over the meaning behind Josephina's words in the juvenile card she had sent.

The outside of the card pictured a hot air balloon rising before white clouds, with a rainbow in back and yellow letters saying, "Here's hoping all your dreams come true." On the inside, the printed card read, "Happy Birthday!" In blue ink, in tiny cursive script, Josephina had written a letter, beginning on the left side of the opened card, continuing on the right, and ending on a piece of stationary inserted inside:

Dear Samantha,

Dorothy called and told me the truth, and said she told you as well. This letter is difficult to write, so please bear with me. I had a better card picked out, but I messed up my message and had to start over, and I happened to have this card on hand.

I'd start over now if I had another card, but I don't, and I'm afraid if I don't send this today, I never will.

I suppose I suspected, when you were little, you might be the baby I had twenty-six years ago, but your mother and my sister denied it, and I decided to believe them. You looked so much like me, but my sister Maggie told me I had given birth to a boy. So, even though the suspicions occasionally haunted me when I would see you at holidays, I decided to believe Maggie, since she had sacrificed so much to help me have my baby secretly, and I worked hard at burying those suspicions and keeping them dead.

This is embarrassing for me, having to face this now, even with both my parents gone. Everyone seems to think of me as the smart one in the family, and what I did twenty-six years ago was not smart at all.

But you aren't to blame. And I don't have any hard feelings toward you. And I am, now that I've been forced to think of you, curious to know what you're like. Part of me is afraid to go any further than this card, though. I feel so vulnerable to pain right now after working hard for so long to avoid it.

So I'm sending you this birthday card, and I want you to know that every year since you were born, I've thought of you on this day, even though I always imagined you as a boy. I've tried not to think of you, but always on this day, it would hit me like a truck, and I'd sink into the deepest depression.

Please give me time. I will write again, or call, perhaps, when I'm stronger. Remember that my pain is not about you, the person you are. It is about a secret I carried for twenty-six years that I had rather hoped I would never have to tell.

Sincerely,

Josie

Samantha tucked the stationary insert inside the card and put the card back in the envelope. Her father was looking at her, but she avoided his eyes. She didn't want to talk about it, didn't know how she felt about it, and wished she had never been told the truth.

She slipped the card into her purse and stuffed the purse beneath her seat.

A little while later, Grandma Beck, who had the window seat, exclaimed, just as Samantha had closed her eyes and was about to doze off, "Look at that. How beautiful."

A crisp afternoon sunbeam broke through the clouds in a postcard-like magnificence.

"That's Father Sky kissing the face of Mother Earth," Grandma Beck said.

Samantha's eyes widened. "You know about Father Sky and Mother Earth, Grandma?"

"Of course, dear."

"But you never mentioned them before."

"I did when you were younger, but then your mother asked me to stop. She didn't want me telling you all those old stories. Like I said the other day, she was afraid you'd get confused, question your Christian beliefs."

"I really liked the story about Misink. Will you tell me another one now?"

She looked past Samantha at her son, waiting for his approval.

He shrugged. "Sure. Go ahead." He turned back to his hunting magazine.

"Hello? Guys? I am a grown woman, you know."

Gale smiled, the wrinkles in her face deepening around her mouth and deep brown eyes. Her white hair was knotted on her head in a tight bun. For eighty-seven years of age, she had remarkable energy and stamina. "Yes you are. And I'd love to tell you a story, even though it's not yet winter, and Grandfather always said to save storytelling for winter, when there is nothing else to do."

"Did he say the bugs would bite otherwise?"

The old woman laughed with surprise. "That's right. Oh, my Grandma Kexi said nothing would really happen, but it was wise to save storytelling for winter and to keep your mind on work in the spring, summer, and fall, during planting and harvest time."

Samantha sat back in her seat and listened to her grandmother's stories.

The following morning at breakfast after their first night at Gellermann Manor, Samantha sat beside her father and across from Tuki and her grandmother at Brandon's table, with Brandon seated at the head, as usual. After Jes served their breakfast, and after her father and grandmother told Brandon and Tuki a little about themselves, they somehow got on the subject of language.

"Lots of common English words have Algonquian origins," Samantha was saying. "For example, 'Mississippi' comes from the Ojibwe misi-izibi, which means 'great river.'"

"I didn't know that," her grandmother replied.

"There's tons of place names, but also everyday words. Moose comes from the Narragansett's moos, opossum from Powhata apasum, spelled A-P-A-S-U-M, and pecan from the Objibwe's bagaan."

Luther said. "I didn't realize."

"There's tons more. I can't remember them all. The most surprising one to me was caucus, which comes from the Powhatan caucauasu—C-A-U-C-A-U-A-S-U——which means 'counselor.'"

"I knew that one," Tuki said.

Samantha then convinced her Grandma Beck to share the story she had recently told her on the plane about First Man and First Woman, so, after blushing slightly, Grandma agreed.

"A long time ago, when the world was brand new, First Man and First Woman were walking around discussing things, and First Man said it was time to decide how things will be. First Woman agreed. First Man said since it was his idea to decide things, he should have the first say in everything. First Woman agreed, adding as long as she had the last say.

"So, they continued walking and looking over creation when First Man said men should be hunters and the animals should come to the men when they are called. First Woman agreed men should be hunters, but she said hunting should not be so easy, that it would make men smarter and stronger if the animals ran away and were difficult to kill. First Man said, 'You have the last say.'

"So, they walked around some more when First Man said people should have eyes on one side of their faces and their mouths on the other. The mouths should go straight up and down, and they should have ten fingers on each hand. First Woman agreed that their eyes and mouths should be on their faces, but the eyes, she said, should be on the top and their mouths on the bottom, straight across. She said she agreed their fingers should be on their hands, but they should be five on each because ten would make them too clumsy. 'You have the last say,' First Man said again.

"Then after a while, as they were walking by the river, First Man said it was time to decide about death. He said he would throw a buffalo chip into the river, and if it would float, when people died, they would come back to life on earth after four days to live forever. First Woman agreed they should decide by throwing something into the river, but not a buffalo chip. She chose, instead, a stone. She said if it would float, it would be as First Man had said, but if it would sink, people would not come back to life on earth after they died. So she threw the stone into the water and, of course, it sank.

"First Woman said it was good, for if people lived forever, the land would become too crowded and there wouldn't be enough food. Death would create sympathy in the world between people. First Man said nothing.

"After a while, First Woman had her First Child, whom she and First Man loved very much, but, one day, First Child became sick and died. First Woman went to First Man and said, 'Let us decide again about death,' but First Man said, 'No, you had the last say.'"

Samantha shook her head. "Golly, it's always the woman's fault. Eve with the apple, First Woman and death. What's the deal?"

Gale laughed. "Well of course it's always the woman's fault when the men are the storytellers!"

Everyone laughed.

Gale added, "You know, my Grandma Kexi taught me that women were revered by our people because of their ability to give new life. They were seen almost like goddesses, up above men in some ways, especially when they were pregnant."

Brandon took the cloth napkin from his lap and patted his forehead. "Are you sure of that, Mrs. Beck?"

"Oh, yes. They were a spiritual people. I know from my grandmother's stories they were a civilized and spiritual people, an organized people, and an educated people. They knew how to take care of themselves and the land. They had no problems for centuries upon centuries until the European migration to this country. They were a brilliant, intuitive, loving people who took a great deal of mistreatment."

Face flushed, bottom lip slightly quivering, Brandon stood from the table, slowly due to his hip, and tossed his napkin onto his half-eaten plate of food. "Excuse me, everyone. I'm suddenly feeling rather ill."

After breakfast, the group piled into Tuki's pickup and headed for the powwow.

"Where are you going?" Samantha asked Tuki from the backseat of the pickup. She leaned close to her Grandma, who sat in the middle of the front seat, between Tuki and her father. "Why are you going this way?"

They had just left the excavation site, where there hadn't been much to see. They had stood over the earth, and Gale had said a few words to her great grandparents and the uncle, only a baby, buried with them.

Now Tuki drove even further south, in the opposite direction of the catacombs.

"We'll take a left up ahead and curve around to a different entrance. It's easier access and the one used by the others. That entrance is completely out of view from anyone who might be wandering out across the creek. Not that my grandfather ever wanders far from his house. It's also furthest away from the view of the neighboring ranchers who might otherwise see our smoke and get suspicious."

"That sounds risky, if you ask me," Luther said. "It seems sooner or later, someone would see the smoke."

"Someone called my grandfather once, and I said I had been burning garbage. But I don't know of any other times. I guess we've been lucky so far. Maybe the spirits are on our side." He glanced at Samantha in the rearview mirror.

Tuki pulled from the gravel road beside four other vehicles parked near a copse of sycamores. Except for the clearing and the road, they were surrounded by dense wood and brush. Nestled into the sycamores were two portable restrooms.

"Jack brought those last night," Claire said of the portables after the party had climbed from the truck. "And he's got two tables he needs help unloading. Sorry. Hello. I'm Sister Claire." She wore a beaded dress, the earth tone beads making a geometrical design similar to the one Samantha saw in the smaller chamber on some of the tombs. It was belted with a thick string of beads, and on her head was a band with a single white feather. She wore sandals on her feet, and her neck and wrists were adorned with jewelry.

"You look great," Samantha said to her.

"Thanks."

Samantha introduced both her father and grandmother to the young nun and then Tuki and Luther offered her their help. Claire seemed flustered and nervous over having to set up for the big gathering.

Claire directed the two men to another pickup truck, where Jack, a tribe member, but no relation (part of the Bear clan and currently attending medical school, Claire said), heaved two long buffet tables from the bed of his truck and set them on their sides to lean against a tree. Instead of traditional Native American clothing, he wore blue jeans and a long-sleeved western shirt and boots, which put the Becks a bit more at ease as they had no special clothing of their own. Jack's long hair fell in a single braid down his back.

After introductions, he said, "We'll have to carry these down one at a time."

Samantha asked Claire if she could help with anything, and Claire gave her an enthusiastic nod. "There's plenty still to do before the others arrive. Come with me."

The two Beck women followed Claire through the brush about ten feet to a small opening in the side of the hill. A cardboard box full of flashlights sat on the ground outside of the cave. The nun handed them each a light. "I've got lanterns set up throughout the main chamber, but you'll need one of these for the path down."

They followed Claire, having to stoop slightly, as they climbed down the stone steps that wound through a narrow passage, about four to five feet wide—not as narrow as the path between the legs of Mother Earth, but not expansive enough for two people to comfortably walk side by side.

"You okay, Grandma?" Samantha asked after they had walked about twenty yards.

"A bit winded."

"Put your hands on my shoulders. There. That better?"

"Yes. Don't worry. I'm okay."

After descending down a gradual slope of about twenty to thirty degrees the distance of fifty yards, they eventually arrived at an opening that Samantha soon realized came directly behind the long shelf of rock that had appeared to her like a balcony seat at the opera, the one with the large pile of skeletons. They stepped out onto the shelf and crossed past the skeletons to where the shelf sloped down and led them to the floor of the great cavern.

"Oh, my word!" Gale exclaimed. "I've never seen anything like this in all my life!"

Samantha looked around in similar wonder as Claire and some of the others set up the cavern for the special occasion. The lanterns alone made the chamber appear grander than she remembered it.

The thick rock formation in the center of the cavern that had reminded Samantha of a mini cluster of mountains divided the chamber into two areas. The first area they came to from this back entrance at the deepest end of the cave had a pile of cedar logs in the center surrounded by stones that Samantha guessed never left the chamber. Four drums made of barrels and elk or deerskin circled the pile of logs, and a few metal chairs were arranged at the outskirts of the room. Claire explained the chairs were for the elderly and those unable to sit "Indian style." She said Gale might be more comfortable in one, and Gale agreed.

On the other side of the mini cluster of mountains, in the second area of the cavern, were several tables, three near the shallowest end of the cavern, and three off to another side. The tables off to the side held papers or documents of some kind. After the women dropped their flashlights into another cardboard box, they walked over to this second group of tables. Jack led Tuki and Luther with another table off to the opposite side.

"Right there is good," Claire said to the men regarding the tables. Then she turned to Samantha. "These tables hold our family trees, for each of the seven clans. We display them for people to look at and remember, but also so people can pencil in recent births and deaths. You'll have to be sure and add your names onto the Kishku tree."

Samantha gave her a weak smile, avoiding her grandmother's raised brows, fearful she might give her secret away.

"Over here are blank sheets of paper and pencils so tribesmen can report any news, like degrees earned, awards won, offices held, or whatever, so they can be included in our annual newsletter, which has become another record of our tribe.

"This table with the candles is our remembrance table." The votive candles appeared to be those Samantha had discovered months ago near the statue of Mother Earth at the other entrance to the smaller chamber. "We light a candle and keep it burning throughout the day for those who have died within the past five years. And this place beside the candles is for people to display photographs they want to share with the others. These here are pictures I took at the last powwow, back in April."

Gale and Samantha looked over the fifteen or so photographs. "This is going to be a really big event," Gale commented.

"You're telling me!" Claire said. "Those tables Jack, Tuki, and Luther are setting up will hold all the food. In fact, would you mind helping me with the tablecloths?"

"Not at all."

"Of course."

A woman walked up from behind with a tray of crafts, and Claire introduced her as Kennie, explaining that the three furthest tables displayed the art of various tribe members, available for others to purchase. "Some of my jewelry is over there, and Kennie's beautiful wind chimes and wampum belts, and Stacey's turkey feather capes. Stacey should be here soon."

"Here I am," a voice called out as a short woman hidden by a pile of feathers appeared.

Claire introduced them to others as more people arrived, some with sandwiches and finger foods, turkey legs, corn on the cob, baskets of fresh fruit and vegetables, salads, desserts, water and tea dispensers, ice chests full of drinks, paper products, instruments (a flute and rattles), and other items to be used in the celebration.

One new arrival set up a case of plexi-glass on the table near the family trees. He explained that the case contained the sticks banded together with the first records of their people, dating back to 700 A.D.

"Oh my God!" Samantha inspected the long chains of sticks comprising several rows and bearing images and symbols she could not understand.

"You understand them better with the stories," the man explained.

"Samantha!" a woman's voice called from behind.

Donna and Wëli Nisha, followed by their three children, and all dressed in Native American clothing, crossed the chamber to greet her and to meet her father and grandmother.

After another two hours of setting up, as more and more people gradually arrived, the moment had arrived for the powwow to officially begin.

CHAPTER TWENTY-TWO

The Rite of Misink

Four teenagers sat behind the water drums on the four corners of the pile of logs and began a cadence, soft at first, for people had not yet taken their places in the outer ring. Some of the younger children had to be fetched and forced onto the laps of their parents. Hushing and shushing ensued. A few late arrivals straggled in and hurried to their places after dropping photographs on the remembrance table in the other half of the chamber. One late arrival, slow and elderly, leaning heavily on his cane, went to the remembrance table and lit a candle and then somberly sat in one of the metal chairs. All of this movement and settling down took at least half an hour, as the drums played, gradually building in volume, until everyone in the cavern was at last still and silent.

Claire got up from where she had been sitting beside Tuki and Samantha, crossed over to the pile of logs, and, as the drumbeat softened, announced to all, "Kàles'ta! Listen. Please welcome Chief Wëli."

The drums grew louder with the applause as Wëli took the center next to the pile of cedar.

"Wanish. Thank you, Wisawtayas. We begin, as always, with the story of creation and the lighting of the fire. Please welcome our tribal storyteller, our Lachimo, Kent Wisawta."

The drums and applause filled the cavern and then quieted as Kent, an old man with a missing tooth, took his place near the pile of logs. Wëli returned to his seat beside Donna on the floor.

The drumbeat softened as Kent cried, "Kàles'ta. Listen. Kunakwat, lowat, nuchink, a long, long time ago, in the beginning, nothing existed but an endless space. There lived Kishelamàkânk, the Creator, also known as Father Sky.

"From the dust of his stars appeared Kukna, or Mother Earth.

"According to his vision, Father Sky first created the Keepers of Creation, the four powerful spirit beings from the four ends of Mother Earth: Grandfather North, the spirit of rock; Grandfather East, the spirit of wind; Grandmother South, the spirit of fire; and Grandfather West, the spirit of water." After naming each of the four spirits, the storyteller pulled out a feather from his robe, so that he now held four feathers in his hand.

"The Creator instructed these spirits to come together to help him infuse living beings onto Mother Earth. Grandfather North gave form to all life, Grandfather East gave the breath of life, Grandmother South gave inner fire, and Grandfather West provided life's blood and also mortality.

"First came the plant beings, then the animals, and finally, the humans.

"Kishelamàkânk weaved many laws into his creation for harmony and balance, governing the powers of rock, wind, fire, and water, the circle of life, birth, growth, and death.

"Grandfather North has provided us with these logs and rocks. Grandfather East sends wind through the upper openings of the cavern to feed the fire Grandmother South will now provide as I light this match." Kent took a box of matches from his robe, struck one against the box, and put it to the kindling beneath the pile of logs. Another man stood up and fanned the fire with a piece of cardboard as the sound of the drums increased. Kent then added, "We will call upon Grandfather West to provide us with water to put out the fire at the end of our celebration. Wanishi. Thank you."

The drums and applause roared as Kent returned to his seat and Wëli got up and stood near the fire. The drumbeat softened, and the applause ended.

"Now it is time for the lighting and passing of the hupa'kàn." Donna brought him a small ceramic bowl with a hollow stem and flat mouthpiece. He patted the tobacco with his fingers, then with a thin stick, took fire from the kindling, and put the stick to the tobacco. He sucked on the mouthpiece to draw the air through and get the pipe smoking. Then he gave the pipe to Donna who returned to her seat in the outer ring and breathed in from the pipe. As she passed it to her daughter, who passed it on around the circle, Wëli spoke.

"I tell you now how the pipe came to the Unikwëti of Lenni-Lenape. A long time ago when Mother Earth was young and the people were all one, a disagreement came about over a sacred medicine derived from the tooth of a certain bear. The Council fire burned for many moons. No agreement could be reached. So the people divided into groups and went their separate ways.

"Over time, the language and ways of each group changed. Nanapush, a spirit helper to Father Sky, became concerned. He went to Father Sky and reminded him of the pipe once offered to him by Grandfather West, symbolizing their reconciliation. Nanapush asked Father Sky if a similar pipe could be made and given to the Lenape.

"So Nanapush made a great signal fire, calling all the different groups of Lenape back together again to Council. As they circled around the sacred fire of peace, Nanapush fashioned a pipe from stone, filled it with sweetgrass, blessed it, and lit the pipe from the fire of peace. As he smoked, he spoke with the Lenape, and their hearts were filled with peace and understanding. Nanapush instructed them to take the pipe as a gift, to fill it with a certain tobacco plant, and to smoke it as he had done that day whenever they were in Council, so their thoughts would rise with the smoke up to Father Sky, the Creator, and peace and order would be restored among them."

The pipe continued to make its way around the ring of nearly two hundred people sitting on the floor, crossed legged, side by side. All those past the age of wisdom, which was seven years, smoked, including the elderly on the metal chairs. As the pipe made its round, Kent returned to the fire of peace to tell another story. Wëli went back beside Donna.

This time he brought with him a birdcage, and inside on a small perch stood a black crow. Kent held the cage up for all to see. Then he asked, "Who knows what creature this is?"

Several children raised their hands in earnest, and Kent pointed to a young girl, age five or six.

"It's a bird."

"What kind of bird?"

More children raised their hands, and Kent chose a young boy, about seven.

"It's a crow!"

"That's right. And now I will tell you the story about our friend Crow, who wasn't always black. A long, long time ago, when Mother Earth was young, Crow had feathers of many colors, but in saving the other animals from the Great Snow, his feathers became sooty, and his once magnificent voice was reduced to an annoying caw."

Samantha whispered to her grandmother, "This isn't the same story about crow you told me last year."

Grandma Beck shook her head. "No, you're right."

The storyteller continued, "One day, after he had turned the color of soot, he found four colorful feathers on his side." Kent pulled the feathers he had held before from his robe and held them up again now in his other hand. Still holding the bird cage in the other, he walked around the fire of peace and the soft-beating drums so all in the circle could see and hear.

"Confused, Crow flew to Father Sky and asked him what this meant. Father Sky, our Creator, replied that Crow was very special in that not only had he saved the four-legged creatures from the Great Snow, but now he had an opportunity to save the two-legged as well. Crow asked how he was to accomplish this. Father Sky said it was for him to find out. He told Crow to fly back down to Mother Earth and listen to her heartbeat and then he would find his answer."

Samantha shifted where she sat on the cold floor thinking to herself that she too should listen to the heartbeat of Mother Earth and maybe she would know what to do.

"But Crow had no idea where to find the heartbeat of Mother Earth, so he flew around hoping to find it. Then one day, he heard the beat of a drum. He circled above it, listening. As he neared the source of the beat, he saw it came from the two-legged creatures, and he realized their drums were the heartbeat of Mother Earth.

"He followed the people as they danced around the circle, feeling peace and tranquility, and suddenly the meaning of the four feathers came to him. They represented the four corners of the Earth and were a reminder to him and to the two-legged creatures that the circle of life depends upon all the people to care for Mother Earth. For, without her, there is no future. Crow realized the Creator had given him this sign so he could save the two-legged creatures as he had once saved the four."

After the applause and hoots of appreciation, Kent invited other members of the tribe to come to the fire of peace and share stories they remembered from long, long ago.

Three others shared their tales—Muni, the oldest of the Earth, who was tall and wiry even beneath his deerskin suit; Harley Dan, a middle-aged biker and a Wolf who taught tennis lessons in Chester, and was not bad looking, Samantha thought; and Patty, a large woman and the oldest of the Fish. In between their stories, Samantha begged her grandmother to tell the story about First Man and First Woman. After much begging and pleading from her son and granddaughter, and then from others nearby who heard the pleas, Gale Beck finally stood up from the metal chair and went to the center to share her story.

"My Grandmother, Kexi Kishku Smith, told me this story many times when I was a little girl. I have told this story to my son, and also to my granddaughter, and now they wish me to tell it to you. It concerns First Man and First Woman and their decisions about how things would be."

Gale related the story exactly as she had first on the plane and then again at breakfast that morning, bringing enthusiastic applause from the crowd when she finished and nods of recognition from three or four of the older among them.

Before Gale left the center of the ring, Tuki stood and introduced her.

Gale added, "Being here tonight makes me wish my grandmother had never left the Unikwëti."

Then Tuki asked Luther and Samantha to come to the center as well, to meet the entire tribe. "Many of you met them before we began, but I wanted to be sure you all had a chance to learn who they are and why they are here. This is the line of Kexi Kishku, daughter of Chief Wëli Kishku."

Samantha gave Tuki a grateful, nervous smile as they sat back down in the outer ring.

What an imposter I am. How can I tell anyone the truth now that I've gone this far?

After a few other stories, Wëli announced they would now have their remembrance ceremony, if those who had not yet lit their candles would please do so. He said the candles represented those who had died in the past five years, but it was traditional to name all those members of the tribe who had died within the past fifty years and all of the chiefs from the beginning of time. The drums beat softly as one woman crossed the ring to the other area and lit a candle at the far table next to about ten others, already with flames.

Wëli then read from index cards the names of the people the candles represented, the years in which they lived, which clans they belonged to, their professions, and their surviving family members. Then he began a list of names that sounded like a chant, a song, an auctioneer even. Samantha recognized Tuki's father and mother among them. She glanced at him, and he gave her a smile.

Very rapidly, Wëli named the chiefs from the beginning of time, which Tuki had told Samantha took them back to 700 B.C. He recited them from memory, like a student of geography naming the countries of Europe or a student of science the elements in the Periodic Table. "Selàkhatin, Pahapema, Ahanikula, Masënulei…" The sounds flowed together and were also song-like and, to Samantha, hypnotic. She swayed slightly as she sat there and listened to the leaders of the centuries. The entire ceremony took about twenty minutes.

Then those in the outer ring held hands as a woman of the Wind led the group in prayer. She said, "Heavenly Creator, fill our hearts with gladness as we remember these loved ones who have joined your spirit world. Help us to know they are still with us even though we can no longer see them."

The sound of the drums grew louder as the people paused for a moment, all silent, and then, Wëli spoke again. "Before we break for our first meal and for some free time for visiting and games, I want to remind you to be back in this formation by four o'clock, which gives you two and a half hours. As always, we will begin with announcements of personal achievement or interest, then we will discuss any business and concerns pertaining to the tribe, and then any concerns people have about the nation or world at large. Following this tribal meeting, which usually takes thirty minutes, we will dance three traditional dances. This time they are the Grass Dance, the Duck Dance, and the very popular Stirrup Dance, so you might want to grab a beer to get you in the mood. He paused for their laughter. "After the dancing comes the Rite of the Misink, so we need a young woman of childbearing age and a man of the Turtle to volunteer. No one has yet stepped forward. Samantha and Tuki, maybe you would consider the honor?"

The group clapped and hooted as they broke up and headed toward the serving line. Samantha's face paled. She hadn't expected this. Could she really represent Mother Earth in the Rite of the Misink if she weren't a true descendant of the Unikwëti of Lenni-Lenape?

Samantha's father and grandmother enjoyed eating flatbread, roasted corn on the cob, a number of salads and fresh fruit, and roasted turkey legs while they visited with other members of the tribe. But Samantha couldn't eat. She was too anxious about the ceremony. Surely, she could get out of it?

They also watched the games taking place around the fire. The younger children competed against one another first, then the men, and finally, the women. After Samantha laughed at Jack for falling down during a jumping contest, he challenged her to compete with the women. She at first refused the challenge, much too nervous to play, but everyone around her pressured her until she, at last gave in. She ended up feeling glad for the distraction and relaxed a little in spite of her fear. Tuki, Gale, and Luther looked on with amusement as she hopped across the chalk lines and the referees marked her position with small stones.

"Not bad," Tuki said.

She laughed but inwardly thought, if only he knew just how bad I am. I should tell him the truth, now, before the ceremony.

They went to another area and watched a dice game.

Later, after they had eaten their lunch and the games had all ended, the drums, with their heartbeat cadence, notified the tribe it was time to reform the outer ring.

Announcements were made around the circles from individuals, mostly parents concerning the latest accomplishments of their children, followed, each time, by enthusiastic applause and hoots and requests for the child to speak. Most of the children were too shy, but some of them, including a four-year-old girl, said a few words to the group.

The four-year-old stood and said, "I did a good job on my dance recital." She chewed nervously on the end of a beaded string.

The mother said softly, "Say when it was and what kind of dance."

"It was in the summer, and I did ballet."

The circle of people clapped and cheered as the little girl sat down.

When it came time to discuss tribal matters, Wëli asked Samantha, Luther, and Gale to step into the center near the fire. With a rattle made out of a turtle shell, he touched each of them, giving them a name. "Gale will be known as Chawachto, which means dear, or precious, because she is like a lost pearl we have recovered from the ocean's depths. Luther will be called Zelozelos, meaning cricket, because he is light on his feet, has a grainy voice, and has a round face and eyes. Samantha will be called Wulik Etchilhillat, which means beautiful mediator, for she has come to help Tukihëla reunite with his white grandfather after all these years."

Applause ensued, the three returned to their places, and the tribal meeting moved on to other matters, including a collection to help the recent Hurricane Katrina victims.

Soon the drums resounded more loudly, and a flute and rattles made of gourds joined them as Wëli called the men forth for the Grass Dance.

Tuki encouraged Luther to join in, even though he stood there, bewildered and late in catching what it was he was supposed to do. The other men, moving in a circle counterclockwise around the fire, shook themselves and stomped their feet, with their arms straight against their sides and their heads lifted up. Donna leaned over and explained that they represented the preparing of the field for planting with their stomping and the grass blowing in the wind with their swaying upper bodies. The dancers made several revolutions around the fire to the flute, the rattles, and the drums before they began to shout to the rhythm of the heartbeat, "Kwëti, nisha, naxa, newa. Kwëti, nisha, naxa, newa," which Donna said meant "One, two, three, four. One, two, three, four."

"It's a way of teaching some basic language to the children," she added.

The drums roared and the flute and rattles stopped as the spectators clapped vigorously. The men returned to their places in the outer ring and the women and children stood now, forming a circle around the fire holding hands. Claire and Donna coaxed Gale and Samantha into joining the group.

Wëli announced, "Let the Duck Dance begin!"

The flute and rattles rejoined the drums as the dancers dropped their hands and then made quacking motions with their fingers, dancing around the fire, counterclockwise like the men, for one revolution. Samantha and Gale did their best to imitate the others. Then, during their second lap, the dancers flapped their elbows and wiggled their hips while the men hooted and cawed, and the children laughed at one another.

Samantha also laughed, especially when she caught Tuki smiling at her.

After alternating these motions for two more laps, the women and children began to sing as they continued with the dance: "Xami, xami, ng-a-tup-wi! Xami, xami, ng-a-tup-wi!" which Tuki later translated as "Feed me, feed me, I am hungry! Feed me, feed me, I am hungry!"

When Samantha took her seat beside Tuki, he put his arm around her shoulders and whispered in her ear, "You make a fine duck."

She flashed him a brilliant smile as they broke out in laughter. Then they returned their attention to Wëli, who now announced the Stirrup Dance.

"Come on!" Tuki said, jumping to his feet and pulling Samantha up. "This is the craziest one yet!"

"I don't know."

"Hey, I agreed to the *Grand March*, didn't I? You owe me!"

Samantha laughed and followed him to a place in the ring.

The men formed an outer circle, and the women faced the men in an inner circle closer to the fire. First, they stood and clapped their hands to the beat of the drum as the flute and rattles joined them. The younger children, unattended, ran in circles around the outside of the men.

Then each man bent his right knee up in front and took the hands of a woman across from him. Tuki had made sure Samantha stood opposite him. Luther and Gale stood on one side of them and Wëli and Donna on the other. The women then mirrored the men, each placing her left foot over her partner's right foot, as though on the strap of a stirrup. Now, guided by the men, as the drums played louder, the couples hopped counterclockwise around the fire, trying to maintain the position. When two partners lost their balance, so the lifted feet touched the floor, they returned to their sitting position in the outer ring.

Grandma Beck was too old to last for more than a few seconds, so she and Luther sat down in the outer ring.

Gradually one couple after another dropped out of the dance until there were only five remaining, including Samantha and Tuki. The people seated on the outer ring then began a chant to the beat of the drums: "Heya, heya. Unikwëti hach ki. Heya, heya. Unikwëti hach ki."

Samantha recognized the sound of the voices that had rung in her head just before she had passed out and entered a coma in San Antonio. They sounded the same now. Her mouth dropped open, her eyes widened, and Tuki looked at her, perplexed.

"What's wrong?" he asked.

But she gave no answer, for her eyes rolled in the back of her head, her body stiffened, and she suddenly fell in his hands.

Samantha frowned and wrinkled her brow. When she opened her eyes, she saw Tuki scowling at her. "What happened?"

"I'll let your father explain. Excuse me."

But before Tuki could leave her side, Wëli congratulated the winners of the Stirrup Dance. He and Donna had won second place to Jack and his wife. Then he called Tuki and Samantha to the center of the ring to begin the Rite of the Misink.

"Sam, are you sure?" her father called out to her, to which she shrugged, and then, hesitantly, nodded.

Before Tuki could object, the mask of Misink was painted onto his face and a bear skin hide draped over his shoulders. Wëli gave him the turtle shell rattle. At the same time Tuki was being outfitted, Samantha was wrapped in a white robe of corn silk, and a bronze tiara with turquoise, lapis lazuli, and ancient coral was placed on her head. Someone then smeared white paint on one of her cheeks and blue paint on the other, and a snakeskin belt was fastened around her waist.

"Wëli," Tuki said. "You ought to know that…" His voice was drowned by the crescendo of drumbeats.

The sound of the drums beat louder as the helpers returned to the outer ring, leaving Tuki, Samantha, and Wëli in the center with the drummers. Wëli took a pocketknife from his robe, opened the blade, and held it to the fire.

"Brothers and sisters, we are in the midst of two great spirit beings, Kukna, or Mother Earth, and Misink, the guardian spirit of game animals. Please welcome them."

Samantha wondered what was going on as Tuki tried once again to whisper his urgent message into the chief's ear. Wëli brushed him off as the crowd applauded and he hastened the ceremony onward.

Reluctantly at first, and then with fierce anger, Misink danced around the fire as the crowd chanted to the beat of the drum, "He-ya, he-ya. He-ya, he-ya," until Wëli lifted his hands and silenced them.

Samantha felt her knees go weak.

"As a sign to Misink and all the animals who sacrifice themselves for us, particularly the turkey who honors us today, we draw blood from one of our own, touch the blood to our fingertips, and taste it with our tongues. This will enable us not only to pay homage to the animals whom we taste, but also to share in communion with Mother Earth and one another."

Samantha looked nervously at Tuki's eyes, but she found no sympathy there. He seemed to transform behind the painted mask into an angry spirit.

"Oh, Misink, I present to you the knife, so that you may cut into the flesh of humans as we do in the animals you guard. Our sacrifice will then transform into Kukna."

Did he say cut? Samantha glanced nervously at her father, whose expression had also changed from happy to concern.

Tuki abruptly grabbed Samantha's hand and pulled her toward him, causing a cry to escape from her lips. He dragged her in a circle around the fire to the beat of the drums.

Then, Tuki cut through the skin at the tip of her index finger.

"Ow!" she cried. "That hurt!"

"You okay, Sam?" her father called to her.

She frowned but nodded as the voices began to chant: "He-ya, he-ya. Unikwëti hach ki? He-ya, he-ya. Unikwëti hach ki?"

"What does that mean?" she whispered to Wëli.

"Hey there, hey there, are you Unikwëti?"

Her head spun and she could barely maintain consciousness. Tuki held her finger high in the air, holding her up and keeping her from falling. The men formed a circle around them, and one by one, they put their fingers to hers and licked her blood from their own. The women went next, Tuki squeezing the finger to draw the blood, and then the children, all the while chanting that song: "He-ya, he-ya. Unikwëti hach ki? He-ya, he-ya. Unikwëti hach ki?"

At one point, Tuki burned his eyes into hers and then uttered, loud enough for Wëli to hear, "Getschihillalowet!"

She blinked and fought to keep from passing out, her head dizzy, her knees weak. "What did you say? What?"

"Why do you say that?" Wëli asked.

Samantha turned to Wëli as her finger remained stretched out from her body, held by Tuki, and the children, one by one, touched theirs to hers. "What does it mean?"

"Traitor," the chief replied. "What are you talking about, Tuki? Why would you say such a thing of Wulik Etchilhillat?"

Neither Tuki nor Samantha replied.

After the last of the food and decorations had been carried above ground and packed away in various vehicles, Tuki pulled Samantha aside on the gravelly parking lot just as she came from the portable toilet.

"So, your father says you were adopted. I never, in a million years, would have pegged you for a liar. Talk about broken hearts." He walked away, leaving her standing there with her mouth open.

In the backseat of the truck Samantha sat, arms folded, wishing she could scream.

Gale and Luther also remained silent during the ride down the gravelly road toward Gellermann Manor.

As they passed the old excavation site, Samantha tried to pinch back the tears by squeezing her eyes shut, but they dropped down her cheeks against her will. She knew there was little she could say to make things right again.

When Tuki pulled into the circular drive under the great sycamore, Luther and Gale thanked him for including them.

"I can't tell you how much it all means to me," Gale added.

Tuki nodded and muttered, "Of course," as they climbed from the truck and entered the double oak doors of the manor.

They entered the foyer to find it abandoned, without Jes's welcoming presence and offer of food and drink.

"I think I'll turn in," Luther said.

"Me, too," Gale agreed.

"It is late," Tuki said.

Samantha looked down at the red carpet and followed her father and grandma to the foot of the stairs.

As they all four ascended the stairs, with Tuki taking the rear, Gale and Luther spoke of the evening to one another sharing their exhilaration. On the second floor, the three Becks wished one another goodnight once again with hugs and kisses as Tukihëla turned the corner toward the west wing. When he was out of their sight, Luther and Gale asked Samantha what had happened.

"I hadn't told him yet about, you know, being adopted," she explained. "I had been meaning to, but I was still getting used to the idea myself. And then, well, I wanted to go to the powwow. I was afraid I wouldn't be allowed if they all knew the truth."

"Oh no," Gale said, patting her granddaughter's shoulder. "Don't you worry another minute about it. Once you explain that you've just learned the truth yourself, he'll come around."

"I don't know if he'll give me the chance. Besides, I've known for months now."

Luther patted his daughter on the back. "I'm sorry, Sam. I spilled the beans. I didn't know you hadn't told him. When you were having a seizure, I thanked him for including you even though, you know."

"It's not your fault, Dad."

"It'll work itself out, okay sweetheart?" Grandma Beck said.

Her dad added, "Just apologize. Say you're sorry. It's the only way."

"Okay, Dad. Well, goodnight."

She watched as they circled the cherry wood balustrade to the west wing and to the rooms that had once been occupied by the professor and Mark. They waved back at her and then disappeared behind their doors.

She stood there in the hallway feeling restless, knowing good and well she would not be able to fall asleep. She decided to creep up to the third floor, to the media room, to see if she could figure out how to turn on Brandon's television.

She thought how strange it was that she had heard those voices before she knew the meaning of the words. How was that possible? Perhaps she had read the words in her Algonquian book and had forgotten about them, and then somewhere in her subconscious they had reemerged. She knew there had to be a logical explanation.

When she walked through the open door of the media room, she found the television already on. She walked further into what she thought was an unoccupied room, wondering if Brandon had stepped out for a moment or had forgotten to turn off the television. Then she noticed him lying on the couch, asleep. The back of the couch had hidden him from her view. She was about to step out when he opened his eyes and saw her standing over him.

"Oh heavens, my dear girl, you startled me. For a moment there I thought, with that paint on your face, oh never mind. So you're back then from the visits with the other Indians?" He sat up and unruffled himself, beckoning to her to come and have a seat.

"Yes, we just got back." She took a tissue from a box on an end table and walked around and sat on the other couch. She rubbed at the paint with the tissue, having thought she had already gotten most of it off earlier.

"Looks like you did more than visit, huh?"

She nodded. "Tuki's uncle showed me a few of the traditions."

"I apologize for leaving the breakfast table so abruptly this morning."

"You? Apologize? That's not necessary. You've been so gracious, allowing us to stay here, feeding us."

"I'm ready to tell you what happened the night I kicked off the Indians."

"Now? Tonight?"

"Are you up for it, my dear girl?"

Samantha glanced toward the French doors leading to the balcony outside, and her heart nearly stopped. In the pane on the door, she could see the reflection of Tukihëla. She turned, catching sight of a movement out in the hallway. Then she looked at Brandon, whose back was to the interior door, but whose facial expression hinted at understanding as he eyed the French doors across from him.

"Yes. Of course."

CHAPTER TWENTY-THREE

Grandfather's Story

"Yes. It's time to tell," Brandon said, turning off the television.

Samantha sat up from the back of the couch, clasping her hands in her lap. Her knuckles turned white.

"Well, my dear, after Rebecca died, the whole ordeal took a terrible toll on Jeannie, especially the business concerning the fingers, which gave Jeannie nightmares. Neither of us harbored any resentment toward the Indians, you understand; we were simply disconcerted by the practice, but respectful, nonetheless. When they came to us the morning after she died to talk to us about their practice of keeping small bones of loved ones close by, we cringed at first, but then, over time, could understand how possessing a bone relic might be a comforting practice."

"So, you've known all along about Tuki's necklace?"

Brandon nodded. "I assumed he did, too, though we never talked about it."

Samantha glanced at the pale image in the glass French door.

"But Jeannie became very preoccupied with the idea of the bones. One day, before Attie gave the necklace to Charles, she determined to discover where they were. We used to, both of us, go down fairly often, by foot, to visit Charles and Attie at the cottage, and sometimes, too, we would drive up further northeast to the wigwams. We'd watch Charles playing with his cousins, and we would speak with them, making sure Charles learned his English and offering them gifts of food. They would give us gifts in return.

"One day, I saw Jeannie asking a boy of, I don't know, fourteen, perhaps, what people usually did with the bones of the dead. He wouldn't answer at first, probably unable to understand the English, but then, when she held up her fingers, making a cutting motion, he nodded and seemed to understand. He pointed to the necklace of a passerby on which hung two small bones. Then the boy did something quite curious. He put his own fingers to his mouth and performed an eating motion.

"'You eat the fingers?' she asked, imitating his motion.

"The boy nodded.

"She asked Attie about this as soon as possible. He said they only ate spirit beings. Mother Earth, or some such nonsense. Jeannie kept after him to explain. Did they or did they not eat the flesh of humans. Attie said some, not all.

"Confused and horrified, she came to me and told me what she had learned. At the time, I was acquainted with a professor of anthropology, and so I decide one day to pay him a visit. He told me cannibalism was more often practiced than most people realized. He told me about many different instances, including the ritual you described to me from your library book.

"I shared this information with Jeannie, which I will regret for the rest of my life. She became obsessed, convinced that our daughter had been killed and eaten. She secretly watched the Indians, all day long, well into nightfall. It wore her out, you know. She had been undergoing chemotherapy. Anyway, all her charity work fell to the wayside, as did her other interests. She didn't touch the piano for years.

"When Attie was dying, she tried to get him to admit what had happened. To his death, he continued to claim Rebecca had died of natural causes. Jeannie would scream at him to tell the truth, and I would have to pull her from the room with brute force to make her stop."

Samantha glanced at the French door and saw the bent, forlorn reflection.

"Then one late afternoon, a couple of years after Attie died, Jeannie came running into my study screaming I had to come see, that they were doing it again. 'Just like Rebecca! They're doing the same thing now they did to Rebecca! Bring your gun! They're going to kill this poor girl!'

"So, I grabbed my rifle from the gun case upstairs—oh how I regret that impulsive decision—and drove us up to the northeast end of the land. She made me park several yards out so they wouldn't hear us coming. Then she led me through the thick brush to a hiding spot near the Indian grounds.

"Charles had been living with us some of the time, but I allowed him to be with the Indians whenever he wanted, and because he had cousins his age to run around and play with, he spent most of his time with them. We didn't fight it. We made sure he came home and spent time with us several nights out of the week. We wanted him to have two people he could know he could depend on to be there for him. And we wanted him to learn English.

"Anyway, we could see Charles running and dancing among them, around a small fire. A young pregnant woman, Charles's aunt we later learned, was standing at the center of the ring, next to the fire. A pipe was being passed around and smoked by young and old alike. They were chanting a song, some kind of gibberish.

"Off to the side we saw a short house of logs that had been recently built. The pregnant woman was led into the house. She appeared to be drugged, with a peculiar smile on her face in spite of the labor pains she must have been experiencing. Her face was painted white and blue. She wore a white gown and had a crown on her head. Just as I had seen my Becky appear the night that I found her dead. Anyway, two other people went inside with the pregnant woman, one with his face painted in different colors.

"The tribe sang songs and performed dances for at least an hour with no sign of the people in the log house. Eventually, the man with the painted face came out holding up a baby girl, still covered in blood.

We could hear her little cries. Then the other person left the log house and fell to his knees. The drums stopped and then started again at a slower cadence. Several men went to the house and dropped the side beams, causing the heavy logs to collapse on the woman inside. Jeannie screamed, but I covered her mouth, and no one seemed to hear her over the drums.

"She told me we had to do something, to save the poor mother, but I told her it was too late, that surely the pile of heavy logs had crushed her. I told her to be silent so we might learn what had really happened to our Rebecca.

"I'm sorry, I haven't offered you anything to drink. Are you thirsty, my dear?"

"No, no. Not at all. Thank you."

He looked at his watch. "I suppose I shan't wake up Jes at this late hour. It's nearly midnight. But, if you wouldn't mind, over there on the sideboard is a bit of brandy. The glasses are in the cabinet below. Would you be so kind as to, I say this hip of mine..."

"Positively. Please, don't get up." Samantha walked across the room to the sideboard and poured the brandy, stealing another glance at the pane in the French door.

Tuki's reflection was still there.

"Please go on. You have me on pins and needles." She handed him the glass.

"Thank you, my dear." He took a drink. "Now, yes, where was I? Oh, yes. The logs.

"The men moved the logs while the women and children sang. Charles was there among them, apparently oblivious, like the other children, to the terrible crime committed by his people. Jeannie cringed and hid her face in my chest as the fingers of the dead woman were brought from the logs, impaled on a stick, and roasted over the fire. The man with the painted face recovered the rest of the body and lay it gently down on a table, covering all but the face with a heavy blanket, apparently handmade, and bearing peculiar symbols, just like that covering the body of our dear Becky, who lay on a similar table, wearing a similar crown and robe, face painted blue and white.

"We watched as the roasted flesh of the hand and fingers was evenly distributed throughout the tribe. Before they ate it, the painted man danced around the fire. Then all of them, including the painted man, ate.

"Jeannie and I were so disgusted, we were both sick there in the woods, and before I had fully recovered, without quite seeing it coming, Jeannie grabbed my rifle and charged the ring of Indians, firing shots into the air like a mad woman, without ever having fired a rifle before. The rifle kept kicking her back, so she didn't realize when she hit a young woman, Claire's mother, and killed her instantly. As the Indians scrambled and fled, the women grabbing their children and running away, the men charged Jeannie. Just as Jeannie fired another shot, killing one of the men, the circle of others fell upon her and turned the rifle on her."

"Oh my God." She glanced at the door. Tuki's reflection was no longer in it.

"I yelled at them to stop, but they must have thought I was attacking them as well, because a few of them ran in my direction bearing the rifle. Dusk had just fallen, making it difficult to see, so I hid in the shrubs, frightened for my life and praying to God Jeannie would live and that Charles hadn't been harmed.

"They found me there, lying face down, waiting. They saw I had no weapon. A few of them kicked me, I guess to see if I was alive, or to see if I had weapons. I don't know, maybe they kicked me out of anger. Anyway, I winced, and so they pulled me up to my feet. One of them spoke in English.

"He asked why we had done this, but I couldn't answer the question. I couldn't say because you're nothing but a bunch of barbaric savages. I begged him to let me go to Jeannie. And so we all went. But she was already gone. The bullet had pierced her heart.

"I fell on my knees and shook her, begging her not to die. But it was too late.

"The Indians left me there to check on their own dead. I remember seeing little Claire, only five years old, pulling on her mother's arm. That was the worst day of my life. Absolutely the worst day of my life." He put his head in his hands and sobbed.

Samantha didn't know what to say. She sought Tuki's image and saw nothing.

Where has he gone?

"Excuse me, my dear." Brandon took a few swallows of the brandy.

"Of course. Please, take your time."

"Well, that's really all. I told the one who spoke English they would have to go. I told them they had two days, and I would call the police. I told them it was against our laws to kill and eat a woman, and they would be put in jail if they didn't run and hide. They claimed they hadn't killed Jeannie. They said the gun went off accidentally in the struggle. They tried to change my mind, defending their ways, but I had no ears for them. Two days, I told them. That was the time it would take me to bury Jeannie.

"I took Charles and his sister with me, against the will of some of them. But Charles listened to me. I told him his grandmother was sick and needed help as I carried her in my arms, and he convinced Claire to come, too. I didn't want to split them up. I intended to keep them both with me. But, I didn't know how to teach a girl what a mother would, and I felt I was doing her a disservice, and so, after a few months, I took her to the convent, even though I knew it would be hard on both of them to be separated.

"I took Charles often to visit, and we brought her back here for holidays and such. In fact, she spent a good deal of her childhood here. I made sure of that. I could have sent her to a boarding school, but I wanted her nearby, for Charles's sake as well as her own. She all but lived here until Charles went to college. But I felt better knowing the Sisters of St. Matthew were ultimately responsible for her upbringing.

"I realized later the Indians could have killed me. They still held the rifle when I told them to leave. I'm not sure why they spared me my life." He took another drink.

"After I buried Jeannie, I went looking all over my land for the Indians, and I found no evidence of them, so I never called the police to report what had happened. Perhaps I should have, but I was afraid I wouldn't be able to prove what they had done to the young mother, that the Indians would call Jeannie a murderer, and that the newspapers and such would smear the Gellermann name.

"I kept my eyes out for the Indians, worried they'd sneak back onto the land, and once I did catch a child running around the northeast corner, but when I tried to find out where her parents were, she ran off. I tried to follow, but I never found her.

"I fretted over what would become of the children, since their parents would now have to find a source of income and a place to live. I knew none of them were legal citizens, and I worried over what they would do. The children were innocent. They had no control over the barbaric ways of their parents. But I didn't do anything to help them.

"It wasn't worth it for me to hire workers to keep the fields planted, so I leased out areas to neighboring cattle ranchers.

"Charles asked about his cousins and aunts and uncles often, but I told him they had to move away, and we'd never see them again. That was hard for a boy who had lost his father only two years before. I didn't know what else to do. I didn't want him to become a savage. No offense to you, my dear." He swallowed down what was left in his glass and set the cup on the end table.

"Would you like me to get you more?"

"Thank you, my dear. That's kind. Yes, if you wouldn't mind. This is all so difficult you know, and the brandy is going down smooth."

Samantha crossed the room with his glass and refilled it, tempted to pour herself a drink, but she decided she needed complete control of her faculties for what she was about to say.

"I know this will sound strange to you," she started. "It sounds strange to me." She handed him the cup and returned to her seat on the couch. "But I feel I have to tell you this."

"Please do." He drank the brandy.

"Ever since I first arrived here back in June, I've had this weird but vivid dream. Before I go on, though, I want you to keep in mind the ritual you witnessed seemed barbaric and uncivilized to you and Jeannie because you weren't aware of its cultural significance." She told him the Unikwëti story about when all the animals had been imprisoned by giants, their reactions to the humans trying to save them, and the request they made, through Misink. She also told him about birth and death, Father Sky and Mother Earth. She talked about Jesus and god-eating in other cultures, the idea of absorption through eating of the divine and powerful.

Although Brandon listened politely to all she said, when she finished, he commented, "You defend your people very well, but you must admit a bias."

"That's something else I need to tell you." She hoped Tuki could hear her, wherever he was. "You see, I truly believed Luther and Dorothy Beck were my biological parents for twenty-eight years. But while here, at Gellermann Manor, making reparations, after our press conference, my mother called to tell me to stop talking to the press about my ancestors, because they were, in fact, not my ancestors. I was adopted."

"Is that right? All these years you thought...how very disappointing for you, I can imagine."

"I was devastated. I spent my whole life believing I had Native American blood. I chose a career that would enable me to find my ancestors. And then I found them, much to the surprise of my parents and grandmother, only to learn they aren't mine after all."

"I'm sorry for you. But you must admit a sense of relief knowing you aren't descended from cannibals after all."

"Some would argue we are all descended from cannibals. But back to my dream. It's strange, because, as you know, I find it difficult to believe in anything supernatural, as hard as I try. But the dream feels like something supernatural almost. I don't know. I'm lying on a low table, like a bed. A painted man is beside me, yelling at me to wake up. I call him Attie. I scream his name—this dream happened before I knew Tuki's father's nickname. I then feel an excruciating pain between my legs, and I bear down as hard as I can. Then I feel my body ripping and a bath of blood wash over me. An old woman is standing beside me screaming in words I don't understand. I remember her shouting 'No!' Anyway, the painted man, who looks like Tuki, and whom I'm calling Attie, shakes me and tells me to wake up, but I can't open my eyes. I feel too weak."

"My dear, if this is an attempt of yours to get me to believe the Indians are innocent regarding my Becky—I'm sorry, I just find this hard to believe. You must understand."

"Of course, but I promise I'm telling the truth." She shook her head, her face blushing at the accusation. "I'm sorry. This was a mistake. It doesn't make sense to me either. If I were you, I wouldn't believe me. Spirits don't talk to people from their graves. But there were these voices, a song…never mind. Listen. It's late. I should go to bed now." She stood up. "Thank you for telling me what happened. I know it will help Tuki to finally know the truth."

"Wait a minute, my dear girl. I want you to know I'm not too blockheaded to understand what you were saying about cultural significance. We eventually accepted the business about Becky's fingers. But even if the young woman years later died willingly—"

"Like Jesus?"

"Hold on. Jesus was the Son of God. You can't compare what Jeannie and I witnessed that night to the crucifixion."

"Why not?"

"Because that young woman was not God."

"To them, to the Unikwëti, she was, though in a different sense."

"Listen, my dear, this conversation won't get us anywhere in terms of progress, so perhaps we should call it a night. You're right. It's late."

"I didn't mean to offend you. Thank you again for your hospitality and for sharing that difficult story. Good night."

"Good night."

Samantha left the room upset over the way the conversation had ended and feeling the hurt of Brandon's rejection.

When she entered the hallway, she expected to find Tuki there, but he was nowhere in sight.

She went downstairs and tapped on his bedroom door, but he did not come. Heart pumping madly, she turned the knob and walked in, looked at his bed and the sitting area, but he wasn't there. She even knocked on the bathroom door, opened it, and found it empty. She went to her own room, thinking he might be waiting for her there, but she was wrong. She decided to try the conservatory—perhaps he needed to play. This would definitely be one of those times he needed to play. But, when she got there and turned on the lamp near the entrance, he wasn't there either. She searched all the rooms on the bottom floor, the kitchen last, and then, standing there in the dark by the back door, she decided to try the creek.

She rummaged through the kitchen drawers for a flashlight, quietly so as not to awaken Jes. Finding one, she checked to make sure it worked and headed out the back door down the steppingstones to the creek. She went to the rock by the leaning tree and shined her light all around.

"Tuki?" She walked to the spot he had occupied that first night. "Tuki, are you there?"

She went to her rock by the leaning tree, looked up at the stars, and wept.

CHAPTER TWENTY-FOUR

Goodbyes

Samantha lay on a table. Beneath her a dog whined. The nostrils of a horse flared. The pain between her legs magnified and she pushed.

Her flesh ripped from end to end and a pool of blood spilled from between her legs.

"No!" she heard someone say.

"Wake up!" she heard another say.

Tuki's painted face leaned over hers.

"I love you," she said.

"Don't leave me," he begged.

A ringing far off in the distance made her smile.

What ringing?

Samantha awoke, the cell phone beneath the Tiffany on the nightstand ringing its familiar wail.

"Hello?" she said into it.

"Hi, pumpkin. It's Dad. The rest of us are downstairs at breakfast and were wondering whether we should wait for you. Are you coming?"

"What time is it?"

"After nine. Are we still going to mass at eleven?"

Samantha looked around the room, trying to get her bearings. Her eyes fixed on the portrait of Rebecca holding her Dachshund beneath cracked glass.

Her stomach cramped when she recalled her fight with Tuki.

She had no time for self-pity. "Start without me. I'm on my way."

She sprang from the bed and into the shower and a few minutes later, joined the others in the dining room.

All but Tuki.

"I'm so sorry I overslept," she said while taking a muffin from the center tray. She smiled and winked at her Grandma as tears welled in her eyes.

I will not cry. She bit the inside of her lip.

Just as the tears rolled down her cheeks, Tuki entered the room.

"Sorry I'm late."

Samantha choked down the bite of muffin and quickly sipped at her coffee. She dabbed her cheeks to hide the evidence of tears.

"Charles, good morning," Brandon said. "No worries. We're in no hurry. After all, Samantha only beat you by a few seconds at the most, wouldn't you say, Luther?"

Luther smiled and nodded. "Long night last night."

Grandma added, "And the old don't need as much sleep as the young."

Samantha could feel her face blazing red at the memory of their fight last night, but she forced herself to smile at Tuki. She knew he despised her for betraying him all these months, but she also knew he was hurting.

Her gaze was not returned. Tuki filled his plate and talked about getting a round of golf in while everyone else went to church.

"You're not going?" Brandon asked.

"Do I ever?"

"I just thought, well, as these are your guests, I just…"

Gale interrupted, "No, Brandon. Tuki doesn't need to go to mass on our account. Please, Tuki, do go play golf. We'll have to head directly to the airport from the church, anyway, so no need to spoil your afternoon."

"Absolutely," Luther agreed. "You've already done so much for us. Besides, Claire will be there to hold our hand if we need it."

"Brandon, you'll be joining us, won't you?" Samantha asked.

Brandon paused, as though he might say no, and Samantha knew if he did say no, she would break down. She had never felt sadder, a sweeping gloom that threatened to overwhelm her into hysterics. She hated she would be leaving today to never come back. She would miss this old mansion, the catacombs, the creek. She would miss Brandon and Jes and Claire. She would miss Tuki!

Brandon must have seen the desperation in Samantha's face, for he leaned toward her, looked closely into her eyes, and said, "Well, I was going to go this evening, but I think I'll change my mind and go with you, if that's alright."

Samantha nearly shouted. "Of course." She reached across the table and touched the old man's hand. "We'd be pleased."

She glanced at Tuki, who finally looked at her, but she panicked and averted her eyes to her plate holding the half-eaten muffin she couldn't finish.

Samantha breathed in the crisp fall air and closed her sweater tightly about her, holding it in place with folded arms. Her heels dug into the grassy hill until she reached the steppingstones. The wind hurled her long blue dress against her legs and lifted her hair away from her face. She had a half hour before they would leave for church, so she went to the leaning tree by the creek to say goodbye.

Not wanting to dirty her church clothes, Samantha did not take her usual seat on the flat rock by the leaning tree; rather, she stood over the water, arms folded, watching the leaves float aimlessly downstream.

She would miss this place most of all.

The trees whispered their sympathy as a gust of wind lifted through their golden leaves and carried them off, far off in the distance. The sound of a flute floated above the hemlocks and oaks.

Must be the wind.

She looked up and smiled as the tears streamed down her cheeks.

If only Tuki and she had met at some other time, in some other place.

No, she was glad it was there.

She heard a splash in the water below, but when she looked at the creek, she couldn't find its source. As she peered down at her own reflection, her heart nearly stopped beating. For just a second, but long enough to recognize it, Samantha saw, not her face, but the face of Rebecca Nisha looking up at her.

She leaned closer to the water, holding on to the tree, bending so that she nearly touched her toes.

"Come back," Samantha whispered. "I know it's you. I know it now."

"Who are you talking to," Tuki called behind her.

Before she could answer, she lost her balance, and toppled forward into the creek.

"Ahh! It's cold! It's cold!" she screamed.

She held onto the rocks on the bank so she wouldn't drift downstream.

Before she knew what had happened, Tuki had jumped in and grabbed her out, pulling her onto the flat rock. And now, he lifted her in his arms and ran up the hill, to the house, and into the warm kitchen.

"I'm so stupid!" she muttered her apology.

"Take off your clothes."

She looked up at him.

"In there." He pointed to a bathroom off of the kitchen. "I'll bring you a robe."

"What about you? You're shivering."

"Don't worry about me."

She looked again into his eyes, her jaw chattering with chill. She didn't care. She was just happy to be talking to him again.

"But I do, Tuki. I can't help it."

He clenched his jaw and closed his eyes. "I'll be back with a robe," he muttered as he walked away, leaving her there, dripping on the tile.

Samantha stripped out of her soaking dress and underwear. She doubted she could change and be ready for mass on time. Everyone would now be late because of her.

She found a thick towel in the bathroom cabinet and wrapped it around her shivering body. The icy water had numbed her.

I can't get warm, she thought as she rubbed her arms and hugged the towel around her.

At the tap on the door, she stuck out her arm for the robe. When she found nothing but air, she peered through the crack in the door. "Tuki?"

Wearing a robe and carrying another, he opened the door, entered the bathroom, closed the door, and locked it.

"What are you doing?"

He took the thick towel from her shivering body and wrapped her in the warm robe, warm from the heat of his own body. Then he folded his arms around her, holding her close, making her tremble, but not from cold.

She held on for dear life.

She leaned her head against his chest as she clutched his robe in her fists. "Please forgive me!"

"Kiss me."

She sought his eyes, to be sure she had heard correctly, but before she had lifted her face, he covered her mouth with his.

He opened the robes and pressed their bodies against one another, skin to skin, no longer numb from the icy creek, but hot and aroused.

"Where are the others?" Samantha whispered.

"In the parlor waiting for you."

"I should go. I don't want to. God, I don't want to." She kissed his lips, his cheeks, his hands.

"Go to church with them but come back." He licked her neck, caressed her breasts.

"But my flight."

"Cancel your flight." He kissed her mouth and looked into her eyes. "Stay behind another day, or a week, if you can."

"What?"

"I want to talk to my grandfather about last night, about his story, and I'd like you to be with me. I'm going to call a council meeting to get at the bottom of this once and for all."

"Are you serious?"

"Will you stay?"

That would be suicide.

"I, I don't know. This is so hard, being with you and knowing I can't have you. It's torture."

His jaw tightened. "Look, you haven't publicized the catacombs. Why do you have to make this so difficult? I want you and you want me. What's stopping us from being together?"

"So, you've forgiven me?"

He narrowed his eyes. "I didn't intend to."

She smiled. "Listen, Tuki. I haven't publicized the catacombs. That's true. But it's wrong not to. Those catacombs are ancient, filled with important history—important for this country, this continent, hell, the whole world. I'm not going to stop trying to convince you. In fact, I've already started drafting a letter to Wëli."

"You're going behind my back?" He stepped away from her.

"Calm down. I was going to tell you before I sent it. But this is what I'm talking about. We won't ever be happy together because we'll never agree on this. I won't give in."

"You care about the catacombs more than you do me," he said dryly.

"And you care about them more than you do me."

He rubbed his forehead and gritted his teeth. "Okay. I give up. You're right. Happy?"

"No." Then she stepped closer to him. "But I will help you. I'll stay a few more days and help you find out what really happened. And maybe then, if we think we can handle it, we'll say our goodbyes properly."

He gave her the saddest smile she'd ever seen.

That evening after a quiet dinner, Brandon asked Samantha and Tuki what they'd like to do—smoke cigars in the study, watch television in the media room, play piano in the conservatory.

"I want to talk to you, Grandfather. About what you told Beck. About my mother and grandmother and their deaths."

Brandon's face paled. "Oh, my. That again."

"Please," Tuki said. "I need to get at the bottom of this."

"Well, then, this requires brandy. Why don't we go to the study and have brandy. And, I dare say, a cigar would help matters, too."

Samantha and Tuki followed Brandon across the foyer to the study, each taking chairs beneath the huge elk head. Jes brought them drinks, and though Samantha didn't smoke, she decided to join the men and try a cigar. After one puff, she snubbed it out, coughing uncontrollably.

"Sorry," she said.

"Actually, my dear, it is I who owe you an apology," Brandon said, taking a large gulp of brandy.

"What do you mean?"

"For years now, I have been having a dream similar to the one you described last night, but when you told me about it, I immediately got defensive. It was easier, you see, than considering an alternative, which is that there might be some purpose to the dream."

At that moment, the framed photograph of Rebecca and Jeannie on the beach at Ocean City fell back on the hearth and made all three in the room jump with surprise.

Brandon reached from his chair and set the frame right again, as though he had done it a hundred times.

"What I am trying to say," he continued, "is I believe your dream, and I'm sorry I accused you of trying to trick me."

Samantha blushed. "What happens in your dream?"

He cleared his throat and leaned one hand on the mantle. "I'm standing beside Becky and she's having the baby, and suddenly I'm covered in blood and a painted man is screaming at me. Although it's not perfectly clear whether someone kills her or not, the dream has the feeling of accident, of Becky dying in childbirth, but I was never able to accept it until after we spoke last night."

Tuki leaned forward. "So you believe it was an accident?"

"I don't know. I've spent so many years believing otherwise. But I've come up with a plan that might help me put all this to rest."

"What plan?" Tuki asked.

"I've decided to have your mother exhumed."

CHAPTER TWENTY-FIVE

Return to Mother Earth

Monday night, Brandon, Tuki, and Samantha followed the doctor down the corridor, which was cold and musty and smelled of formaldehyde, to his basement laboratory at Weidner College in Chester.

Tuki whispered to Samantha, "It's pretty strange to be meeting my mother for the first time tonight."

She squeezed his hand. "I know."

"It's just a bit further down this hallway," Dr. Chase said.

"Thanks for giving this top priority on such short notice," Brandon said to the doctor.

"You've made it worth my while, Mr. Gellermann."

The cold, medicinal-smelling room was dark except for a dim light on a desk at the back and a brighter light from the lamp overhanging an empty table. Beside the table was a closed white coffin made of marble.

The doctor, his assistant, and the three visitors were the only living people in the room, though there were others present. Four tables, exactly like the one near the coffin, were spread with human cadavers covered in blue cotton cloths.

"You might want to wait and let me look at her first," Dr. Chase said.

Brandon shifted his weight from his cane and touched the doctor's arm. "You're sure about using this facility? No conflict of interest I should be worried about?"

The fifty-ish doctor patted Brandon's hand until it dropped from his brawny arm. "Not to worry, Mr. Gellermann."

"And I have your word as to the privacy of your findings? No matter what you learn from this investigation? Isn't that right, Doctor?"

"You have my word."

"And your assistant here is trustworthy?" Brandon gestured toward the other man bent over the desk in the back of the room. He appeared younger but less muscular.

"Of course, Mr. Gellermann. Now please quit worrying and let's get started." Dr. Chase took the crowbar from the tiled floor beside the coffin and worked it beneath the lid.

Samantha's heart raced. She clutched Tuki's hand. This was all so bizarre. She felt like a character in a vampire movie, less the wooden stake for the heart.

The stake goes into my heart, she thought.

"Stand back and let me see how she is," the doctor said. "People don't always realize what a shock this can be. Robert? A hand, please?"

Robert stood from the desk where he had been writing. He passed the four cadavers as he came toward them, and then wedged the fingers of both hands at the seam beneath the lid of the coffin. Dr. Chase worked the crowbar through the seam, jamming it in until the seal was at last broken and he could wedge the tool completely beneath the lid.

"Ready?" Dr. Chase said to his assistant.

Robert nodded and then the two of them pried open the coffin.

"Remarkable," Dr. Chase said as he peered inside the coffin. "Come see for yourself."

Brandon limped with his cane around to the front of the open casket, knees wobblier than usual, and peered inside.

Samantha and Tuki followed close behind. The three of them stood shoulder to shoulder, looking upon the body of Rebecca.

She lay on the white satin pillow with a serene smile on her beautiful face as though no time had passed since she was laid in the ground. Her blonde curls cascaded over her shoulders down by her hand, which held a black rosary. Her other hand was tucked at her side, beneath her powder blue dress.

"Oh, my." Brandon removed his handkerchief from the front pocket of his jacket and wiped his eyes. "Excuse me, Doctor. I didn't expect…" His voice dropped off.

Samantha recognized her. Even with her eyes closed, Rebecca's face was unmistakably the one Samantha had seen on the Christ and in the creek.

Rebecca's cheekbones were like Tuki's. Samantha had assumed Tuki looked more like his father, but as she gazed at his mother's face, she saw Tuki's there, too.

After a moment, Brandon asked. "She looks alive. How is this possible after thirty years?"

Dr. Chase turned to Robert, who also stood hovering over the beautiful woman. "Note the body was buried in a triple sealed, air-tight casket. Apparently no water leaks." Then he turned to Brandon. "Money can't buy immortality, not yet anyway, but it can preserve bodies beautifully. Full embalmment, triple-sealed casket. No water leaks, no air— until today. Decomposition hasn't had much of a chance."

Robert went to the desk in the back of the room and returned with a pen and clipboard. He scribbled down the notations the doctor made.

Tuki looked up at the doctor. "Can I touch her?"

The doctor nodded. "Yes. Of course."

Tuki rubbed his fingertips along his mother's brow, caressing her like a father might his child. He felt her hair, her cheek, her hand. Samantha reached out and stroked her forehead, surprised by how fleshy it felt— cold, but fleshy. Brandon stroked Rebecca's hair. Then Tuki took his mother's face in his two hands and leant down and kissed her forehead.

"I love you, Mother," he whispered.

Brandon wrapped his arms around Tuki from behind and said, "There, there, my boy."

Samantha watched the two men sob, bringing tears to her own eyes. She could see it was peace—not pain—that moved them. She had the serene feeling Tuki had at last made peace with his people—not the Unikwëti, but the Pennsylvania Dutch. They were his people, too.

The drive in the limousine back to Lebanon County was quiet. No one spoke even as Jes pulled under the giant sycamore in the front of the manor.

"The doctor will call in the morning with his analysis," Brandon finally said somberly as they entered the foyer, even though both his listeners had been present when the doctor had said he would call and so knew this already. "Perhaps after breakfast, we'll know something."

"I hope so." Samantha started up the winding stairs, with Tuki behind her.

"I think I'll have a nightcap in the study before bed." Brandon remained at the foot of the stairs. "Either of you care to join me?"

"No thanks, Grandfather. I'm bushed."

Samantha looked down at Brandon. "Are you okay? Do you need some company?"

"No, no. You've done enough. I won't be up but a few minutes anyway. Go on to bed."

"Are you sure?"

"Entirely."

Samantha climbed the stairs with Tuki, not sure what Brandon really wanted from her. As they reached the second floor, she asked, "What about you, Tuki? Do you need some company, or do you need to be alone?"

She held her breath as she waited for his reply.

"I want to hold you in my arms, Beck, but not tonight. Tonight, I've got my mother on my mind. I'm anxious to find out what the doctor says."

"Me, too."

He moved closer to her. "I'm grateful to you for being there for me. Thanks." He kissed her softly on the lips.

"So, I've redeemed myself, then?" she asked once he pulled his lips from hers.

"Not completely," he teased. "You're getting there. But there's still something else I want from you."

"But not tonight."

He grinned. "Hmm, maybe a distraction isn't a bad idea." Lifting her chin, he kissed her again, this time longer and more passionately. "Let's go to your room," he whispered. "We're less likely to be heard."

In the parlor after breakfast, after Brandon had talked on the phone to the doctor for at least a half hour in his study, Brandon told Tuki, Samantha, and Claire, who came at Brandon's request, what the doctor had concluded from his analysis of Rebecca's body. "He said he felt certain she had died of natural causes. I had to explain about the fingers, because he needed to know when they had been removed. He said it was clear she had died giving birth."

Tuki put his face in his hands.

"I still don't have one hundred percent assurance my daughter was not killed by the Indians, but the scales have significantly tipped in the direction against that having happened, so much so, I am willing to hear from any living eye witnesses their version of what took place the night my Becky died. Do any exist?"

Claire blinked her eyes with astonishment.

"What do you expect to happen in such a meeting?" Tuki asked.

"I've put a lot of thought into this. It was hard to accept the ritual that killed your aunt. She gave her life for religious reasons. It's hard to comprehend, even though Samantha compares it to Jesus giving his life to save us Christians. What do you think of that comparison, Claire?"

"Ooh, that's a tough one. There's more that's different than similar about those two sacrifices. The Unikwëti part of me can appreciate the comparison, though. A willing god gives his or her life so others can be saved. The Unikwëti believed the chosen women became gods and sacrificed themselves to Misink to maintain harmony with the other animals and to provide the people a chance to have communion with Mother Earth and Father Sky. I see it all as cultural mythology. I don't believe in the communion, so of course it's hard to make the jump and say it's anything like Christianity."

"At any rate," Brandon continued, "barring judgment on what happened to your aunt, if your people are innocent of Rebecca's death, my wife and I may have done them an injustice fifteen years ago. I consider myself a fair man of honor. I have always felt, just as my father and his father and his father before him, that there was some right of theirs ignored by our government. I have been thinking on this now for two days. I don't know if any of the remaining Indians would even be interested in returning here, to farm what can be salvaged of the fields, or to live as they once did in the eastern wood, but before I try to make peace with them, I need an honest explanation of what took place by a firsthand witness. Does one exist?"

The two siblings looked at one another.

"Yes," Claire said. "One does."

"Are you serious?" Tuki asked Claire in the foyer as they and Samantha left Brandon in his study.

She nodded. "Did you hear him in there? He recognizes that our people have always had some kind of claim to this land. He feels sympathy toward us even after all he went through with his family. If he knew how ancient our hold on this land really was, I think he'd respect our continued use of it for our powwows. Just think. We wouldn't have to hide anymore."

"We'd have to take the idea to council first."

"You called a meeting for tomorrow. That shouldn't be hard to do," Samantha interjected.

"You realize this could backfire," Tuki warned. "If he learns we've been trespassing on his land all these years, in the legal sense, his sympathy could very well be replaced with resentment."

"I don't think that's what will happen," Claire said as they reached the double oak doors.

"But you understand the risk?"

Claire nodded.

Samantha and Tuki lay together on the bed in Samantha's room at Gellermann Manor after making love. Samantha was propped on her side stroking Tuki's long dark hair and wondering about the thoughtful frown on his face.

"Quarter for your thoughts?" she said.

"Don't you mean penny?"

"Inflation."

They both smiled, but immediately the frown returned to Tuki's face.

"When my father was dying, I felt so helpless."

"You were just a boy. There wasn't anything anyone could do. Your grandfather said even the doctors couldn't help him." She stroked his forehead.

"I know. But I felt I had disappointed him in some way. I can't explain. He wasn't a very happy man. Now I understand why."

"Oh, Tuki." She kissed him, but the frown reappeared.

"My promise to him, to keep the catacombs safe and out of the hands of the government, that's the only thing he ever asked of me. Do you understand? I couldn't save his life. I took my own mother's life by being born…"

"But…"

"Just listen. This is the one thing I can do for him. For the both of them. Understand?"

She lay back on her pillow and squeezed her eyes closed. Tuki would never change his mind. "Yes." Tears tumbled down her cheeks.

"That's kind of you, Mr. Gellermann," Wëli said in his living room with Tuki, Claire, and Samantha and two Unikwëti councilmen—Kent and Muni—sitting on the couches and chairs around him. "I, too, apologize for our misunderstanding and for the end of a two-century long friendship between our families."

The tension unsettled Samantha. This was supposed to be a harmonious, healing moment, but it seemed intense and combative.

"Thank you for your personal account of what happened to Rebecca. I'm still disturbed, you understand, about your late wife. I don't think it was wrong of me or of my wife, Jeannie, to feel repulsed at the sight of your sacrificial ritual that night."

"Just a minute," Muni started to say, but Wëli raised his hand and silenced him.

Wëli's face turned red, and his eyebrows could not disguise his anger despite what followed from his mouth. "Not at all. It was perfectly natural for an outsider to feel repulsed," Wëli said. "Most religions are repulsed by the beliefs and actions of the others. Again, it's only natural. However, to kill in response to that emotion is most disturbing to me. Recall we lost two of ours that day."

Kent and Muni nodded their agreement.

"Three, if you count your late wife," Brandon said.

Wëli's face turned a deeper red and he did not respond.

"You can't compare cold-blooded murder to a holy ceremony," Kent objected.

Brandon cleared his throat and dabbed his clammy face with his handkerchief. "It's regarding my accusations surrounding the death of my daughter for which I, er, have come to extend my apologies."

"I understand," the chief said. "And your apology is gratefully accepted."

"In fact," Brandon continued, "there are fields that might be salvaged for planting if you know anyone wishing to work it like in the old days."

Muni shot a surprised glance at Wëli.

"I just might know someone. That's very, very kind." Wëli's face returned to its natural color. "What would you think of our holding bi-annual powwows there, on the northeast corner of the land, where we once lived in our wigwams?"

"I wouldn't allow it," Brandon started, causing Wëli's face to redden again, "unless you permitted me to help in any way possible."

The relieved listeners smiled, as the chief replied, "We would be honored to have you attend as well, so that we might teach you more about our ways. But don't worry. We no longer practice the once sacred custom that offended you years ago. We understand we must consider the sensibilities of those we live among."

"And in that way, you, too, are kind and generous, Mr. Nisha."

Samantha sighed with relief as Donna came bustling in from the kitchen offering pie and ice cream.

Before the group from Gellermann Manor left with Jes in the limousine, Wëli said to Tuki, "You've got our approval. Go ahead and tell him."

During the limousine ride back to Lebanon County, Pennsylvania, Samantha was surprised when Tuki put his arm around her in front of the others.

"Grandfather," Tuki started.

"Yes, dear boy?"

"There's something I need to tell you."

Brandon smiled and shook his head. "No need, Charles. I'm not blind."

Tuki frowned. "What do you mean?"

"I recognize love when I see it." Brandon laughed. "You have my blessing."

Samantha's face blazed as she tried to hide behind the collar of her coat.

"Actually," Tuki said, smiling, but not blushing, "that's not what I meant. I have something else to tell you."

Brandon's face became serious. "So sorry, Charles. I hope I didn't embarrass you or Samantha."

"Let's not make it worse, shall we?" Tuki said.

Samantha shrank further into her coat.

"Of course. What is it you want to say?"

"There's something I need to show you, actually."

"And what might that be?"

"Something ancient that has been a part of my family for centuries."

"Is that so?" He looked at Claire who nodded.

"Yes," Claire said. "It's something that dates back to as early as 700 A.D., if not earlier."

"Seven hundred A.D. did you say? Dear Lord, what is it?" He sat forward in his seat with wide eyes.

Tuki removed his arm from around Samantha and leaned forward as well. "An ancient catacomb filled with the history of my people."

"Good gracious, where?"

"On the other side of the creek from the manor, on the northeastern part of the property."

"Good gracious, on my land?"

"Yes, Grandfather. On *our* land."

"Of course, dear boy. *Our* land."

"Would you like to see it?"

"Do you really have to ask? Yes, I want to see it." He slapped both hands across his thighs. "What man in his right mind wouldn't? Can we go right away?"

"We can go tonight, if you're up to it."

"Then let's go!"

As Brandon, Claire, Samantha, and Tuki made their way down the stepping-stones of the grassy hill at the back of Gellermann Manor, each with flashlights and jackets (and Tuki with a lantern), Brandon, a bit winded from the exercise, asked, "I say, must we run a race? Might we slow down just a bit?"

"Sorry," Tuki said.

"Here, take my arm," Claire offered.

The cool wind hurled fallen leaves across their shoes as they neared the creek.

"Tell me something, my boy. Why is it," he stopped to catch his breath, and the others stopped, too, "why is it the other archaeologists don't know about this place?"

"I made a promise to my father to protect it."

"From what?"

"From being defiled and exploited by the government. Samantha promised not to tell anyone."

The group continued along the creek toward the part that narrowed and then stepped across to the other side.

"Are you okay?" Claire asked Brandon.

Panting and slowing down considerably now they were moving uphill, Brandon said, "Yes, dear girl. But why? Why would a young, ambitious archaeologist full of idealistic dreams of giving voice to the dead agree to such a thing?"

Neither Tuki nor Samantha replied. Brandon gave them each a knowing smile.

"So, I was right, back there in the limo."

"This way, Grandfather."

A few moments later, they approached the boulder, which Tuki pushed away with the thick stick from the ground. Then he helped his grandfather step down into the smaller chamber.

Tuki lit his lantern.

"Good God!"

"Wait. There's more," Tuki said.

Though it was late when the party returned to the manor from the ancient catacombs, Brandon convinced everyone to join him in the parlor before a raging fire for hot coffee and scones.

After Jes served them, Brandon said, "There's something I wish you would consider, my dear boy. I want you to think long and hard on this. What I just saw is perhaps the greatest archaeological find in North America. I don't understand why you would want to keep such a treasure a secret from the rest of the world."

Tuki's eyes narrowed.

"Just consider this. The whole problem with land ownership being confiscated by the government and what not, that was all a danger when federal grant money was behind the excavation. If a private foundation were to research and publish findings—"

"There would be people crawling all over this place."

"But it's private property. They would need to seek permission, in writing, and be granted an interview. Only the most learned scholars would be permitted."

"Like the Shroud of Turin!" Samantha said. "What a great idea!"

"What?" Claire asked. "The cloth Jesus wore when he was buried? What does that have to do with this?"

"It's heavily guarded," Samantha explained. "Every decade or so, they invite scientists and historians to apply for a private viewing."

"I made a promise to my father to preserve and protect—"

"Dear Charles, that's precisely what I'm proposing! Just think about this. I'm proposing to invest a considerable amount of money to establish a private foundation—something that will continue long after you and I are gone—dedicated to preserving the catacombs while educating the rest of the world of their ancient history. Just think on this. It's important. I would hate to rob modern man of this opportunity, wouldn't you? And who better to sit at the head of the archaeological end of things than our good natured and intelligent Samantha?"

Samantha's heart pounded in her chest. The tears welled in her eyes as she held her breath, waiting for Tuki's response. This could be the key to their dreams.

Tuki's face went through several transformations before he finally comprehended what his grandfather had suggested.

He turned to his sister. "What do you think?"

"I love it," she said. "But we'll have to take it to the council."

C H A P T E R   T W E N T Y - S I X

The Tribal Council

That night, Samantha lay folded in Tuki's arms wondering if he was thinking the same thoughts as she.

All those things she hadn't allowed herself to consider with him—marriage, a family, and a happily-ever-after—now seemed possible. She rubbed his chest and nestled closer to him.

This time, when they had made love, there was something different about it. She had thought to herself, this could be my soul mate. She had allowed herself to really look into his eyes, thinking, but not saying, Yes, I love you. I truly, deeply love you.

After breakfast, Brandon had Jes prepare the library and its conference table for the meeting. Samantha watched as Jes drew the long olive curtains and dusted the table and chairs. She pretended to be looking over Brandon's collection of books, which lined two of the four walls, while she waited for the council members. Jes had polished the silver globe, and dusted a world map and set of bookends before the council members began to arrive, one by one, filtering into the room, led by Tuki and Claire.

Samantha smiled and waved at each of them as they entered, hoping to influence the decision they had no idea at the moment they would be required to make. First came Muni, the old farmer, oldest of the Earth, wearing deerskin pants and robe and a beaded bandolier bag like a sash across his chest. Only his boots looked like they were bought in a store.

Next came Kent, the old storyteller with the missing tooth, in jeans and a leather jacket, accompanied by an old, heavy woman in a long and wide deerskin robe. Samantha remembered she was the oldest of the Fish.

Claire introduced each council member to Brandon, assuming Samantha remembered everyone. Samantha stood before the bookshelves and waved and nodded her greeting to each. The Fish's name, it turned out, was Patty.

Chief Wëli entered next, and after shaking Brandon's hand, gave Samantha a big embrace. "Good to see you, Wulik Etchilhillat!"

"Thank you, Chief Wëli. It's good to see you, too."

When the last of them arrived—Harley Dan, the biker tennis instructor, and two others whose names Samantha didn't get—Tuki asked Samantha and Brandon to leave the room.

Brandon led her to the kitchen and offered her a chair at the little table, which surprised her. She had expected they would wait in the study or the parlor, or perhaps the media room upstairs. But the kitchen? Jes was bustling around the sink, cleaning and putting away breakfast dishes, and making trays of snacks for the council members.

But it wasn't long before Samantha understood why Brandon had led her to the kitchen, for over the speaker, she could hear every word spoken in the library!

Brandon explained. "This way, we don't have to wait for a report."

"But is this ethical?" she asked. "Does Tuki know?"

"Claire does. She saw me turn it on. She didn't object, so it must be okay."

"Are you sure she knew what you were doing?"

"Positive. I could tell by her expression."

The council had gotten past the preliminary hellos and thank-you-for-comings, so Samantha and Brandon stopped talking to listen.

Tuki said, "I called you all here today to listen to a proposal my grandfather has made that will benefit our tribe tremendously." He then went on to explain Brandon's idea of forming a private foundation.

"I knew it was a mistake to let Gellermann know about the catacombs," Kent, the old storyteller, objected. "I warned you all something like this would happen."

"We'll lose all control!" Muni, the wiry old farmer, bellowed. "We can't just sit back and let this guy take over. Sure, he'll say it's in our best interest. Sound familiar?"

"I agree," Patty said. "Look to the past. Every time a rich white man offered Native Americans a deal, it weren't no good. How can we trust a man whose wife murdered two of our own in cold blood?"

Brandon's face turned red, and he whispered, "Perhaps listening in wasn't a good idea after all."

Nonetheless, the two listened on.

"Men can't be held accountable for what their wives do." Samantha thought this might be the voice of Harley Dan, the single, middle-aged biker. Tuki had told her Harley Dan gave tennis lessons at a country club to married women, giving them a lot of personal attention.

Wëli spoke up. "We can trust Brandon Gellermann. He's offered his lands to us again for farming. He wants to put the past behind us. Besides, the archaeologist is one of us, a descendent of Chief Wëli Kishku, for whom I was named."

It was Samantha's turn to go red in the face.

"Wait, Uncle."

"What?"

"I found out after the powwow the archaeologist was adopted. Her father is a descendent of Kishku, but his blood does not run in her veins."

Several members of the council spoke out "What?"

"This is an outrage!"

"Can this be true?"

"What did you say, Tuki?" Wëli asked carefully. "Please, nephew, say it again."

"Samantha Beck is not of Lenape blood."

"Mother Kukna, this is a catastrophe!" Kent wailed. "She tainted the Rite of Misink! The spirits will have their revenge, to be sure!"

Samantha glanced at Brandon, who patted her hand and shook his head.

Muni added, "If we approve this foundation idea, and we put that imposter at its head, the spirits will certainly have their revenge against us. Last week one wall of my barn collapsed without warning and killed my best dairy cow. Now I know why! Listen to the signs! I say we have no choice but to decline Gellermann's offer."

"It was an old barn," Tuki muttered.

Samantha and Brandon both chuckled.

Claire then spoke: "Let's all sit down and talk about this some more. Everybody needs to take a deep breath and calm down."

"My grandfather wants to put the foundation in my name. He plans to relinquish all of its control to us. He's just going to give us the money, that's all."

"That's what he says, friend, but how do we know that's what he'll do?" Kent challenged. "What's in it for him?"

Brandon shook his head.

"I think things are fine the way they are," Muni added. "We have nothing to gain from this foundation."

Tuki quickly said, "Let's not vote today. I'd like the council to think on this for a week or two, and then we'll reconvene and have our vote. What say you, Chief?"

"That's a wise idea, Tukihëla. We'll meet here in two weeks. But before we go, please help us to understand how the foundation might benefit the tribe."

Tuki seemed at a loss.

"Come on, Tuki!" Samantha whispered, wishing she could barge into the meeting.

Then Harley Dan spoke up: "You gotta tell us what's in it for us. You can't argue the point of your grandfather's character. I think he's nice and all, but that just won't do it. You've got to tell us what we'll get out of it. And there's plenty, if you think about it."

"Like?" Wëli asked.

"For one, what would happen if his grandfather ever decided to sell the land? What if a developer wanted to make a goddamn mall here or somethin'? You gotta point out that this foundation would preserve the land as it is forever. As long as the foundation is in place..."

"A mall? The spirits would never let that happen," Muni said.

"They let us get banished," Harley Dan said.

"Because Attie married unwisely!" Muni shouted.

"How dare you!" Tuki shouted back.

"Wait a minute," Harley Dan interjected. "Just listen. This foundation will get our ancestors in the history books, instill pride in the younger generations, who don't give a damn anymore. Lot of 'em don't even come anymore. Make the young ones proud. Put Chief Kishku next to goddamn George Washington, know what I'm sayin'?"

"Hmm."

"That's a thought."

Samantha gave Brandon a hopeful glance.

Kent argued, "We can instill pride in the young ourselves, through our stories. We've been doing it for centuries and don't need some imposter archaeologist to do it for us."

"But the archaeologists might be able to fill in the gaps, you know?" Harley Dan continued. "Tell us what we can't figure out for ourselves about our people. It'll legitimize our tribe, man. Know what I'm sayin'? No more sneakin' around. Let us be known and let us be proud!"

Claire joined in. "The foundation will also provide money to maintain and maybe even improve the structure of the catacombs. Mother

Earth won't hold still forever. A foundation would bring in revenue and make money available to the tribe for maintenance and repairs. We could even send representatives to conferences with that money, let people know more about us, let us have a presence, too."

Harley Dan added, "Maybe put in electrical lighting down there!"

Muni snorted. "Who needs conferences and electric lights? And we already have a presence. Who cares if the rest of the world is ignorant of it?"

"There's jobs, too, right?" Harley Dan asked. "The foundation would need an accountant, a secretary, a publicist, a groundskeeper, a board of directors. Let's see, what else? Anyway, we'd hire our own, right? Provide some good jobs to members of the tribe."

"That's right," Tuki said. "Just think about this. Without the foundation, the future of our catacombs is like a roll of the dice. We've been lucky so far. With the foundation, we can preserve our history and the catacombs and guarantee prosperity for the tribe. As long as the foundation protects the catacombs, they'll be safe. Now, there's nothing protecting them."

"Blasphemy, you traitor!" Muni cried. "The spirits protect them. That's all we need!"

"I'm no traitor, Muni!"

"You ruined our sacred rite with your imposter girlfriend!" Muni shouted. "You should be forced to marry her, to make her Unikwëti, and appease the spirits, who are angry with us!"

Samantha shifted nervously in her seat.

"If I marry her, will you vote in favor of the foundation?"

Samantha's face flamed as she avoided Brandon's glance.

Muni replied, "I don't know."

"I would," said Kent. "I would trust the foundation if the archaeologist were bound to the Unikwëti by marriage."

Wëli spoke: "We have much to consider over the next two weeks. Let us think hard on this and pray to the almighty one for guidance."

The speaker system went off for a few minutes. Samantha and Brandon exchanged worried glances.

"Hello?" Tuki's voice came over after a few clicks and garbled sounds. "Jes, if you can hear me, would you bring in the refreshments?"

Jes left the kitchen with trays of food and drink. The speaker no longer carried the voices from the library into the kitchen.

"I guess all we can do now is wait," Brandon said.

Later that evening after dinner, Samantha and Tuki went for a walk in the cold night along the creek.

"Did I tell you the nightmares have stopped?" she asked.

"Yes, you did."

She searched for something else to say.

"Beck, I want to ask you something."

Oh, God.

"About what?" She shined her light on the path in front of her, careful not to look in his eyes.

"About us. About our future."

Damn him. Why couldn't he have asked before the council pressured him?

"Wait, Tuki. Listen. I know what you're going to say."

"Then why are you stopping me?" He turned to face her, standing still on the path.

"You want to increase the chances of the council approving the foundation."

"What?"

"Your grandfather and I overheard the council meeting. We should have mentioned it at supper."

"So? It's not like I didn't already want this for us."

She wrapped her arms around his waist and pressed her cheek against his coat. "I've figured something out today."

"Tell me." He stroked her hair.

"I love you more than the catacombs. I love you more than my career." She looked up at him.

He kissed her. She closed her eyes and relished the warmth and gentleness of his mouth against hers, his sweet breath, his strong hands caressing her face, her neck.

"Then say you'll marry me."

It was thrilling—hearing him say those words, but she needed to know she was first in his heart, before the catacombs, before his promise to his father, before anything else.

He hadn't said he loved her.

A gust of wind chilled her. She took his hand and walked toward the manor. "Let's go inside."

"But you haven't answered my question."

"Let's go inside."

"There you two are," Brandon said as they entered the backdoor to the kitchen. "I wondered where you had gone off to. I'm going to bed, but I wanted to make sure you knew, Samantha, that Jes will be ready after breakfast to take you to the airport. That is what you wanted, isn't it?"

"Yes. Thanks. I appreciate it." She avoided Tuki's surprised look.

"See you at breakfast then." He started up the backstairs.

"Good night," Samantha and Tuki said.

As they walked through the foyer, Tuki asked, "I didn't realize you were leaving in the morning. I knew you couldn't stay indefinitely, but I hoped it would be later. We have a lot to talk about. Can't you stay another day?"

"Let's sit down."

"Let's go upstairs, to your room."

"I'd rather go in here." She led him to the parlor and flipped on the light. "I like that picture of your mother."

"She looks like a bride."

Samantha cleared her throat. "Come sit with me." She sat on one of the couches and patted the cushion beside her.

"Do you want something to drink?" he asked.

"Do you?"

"I'm okay."

"Me, too." She took his hand.

"Well? Why haven't you answered my question? Don't you want to marry me?"

"Yes. I do want to marry you."

His eyes lit up and he gave her a huge grin. "That's great!" He leaned in for a kiss, but she pulled away.

"Listen."

"What's wrong?"

"I need time to think. I want to wait for the council's decision."

He covered his face with his hand and sighed. "So you lied."

"What?"

"I don't mean more to you than the catacombs. If I did, it wouldn't matter what the council decides."

She shook her head. "You've got it all wrong. That's not it at all."

"Then tell me why you want to wait."

She couldn't admit she didn't trust his motives. What if he were only marrying her to appease the tribal council members?

She looked up at the painting of Rebecca in her white dress in a field of daffodils.

Tell me what to do.

"Well?" Tuki demanded.

"This is happening way too fast. We just met four months ago. Let's take it slow, okay?" She patted his thigh.

He narrowed his eyes but nodded. "Okay. We'll take it slow."

Tuki didn't ask to stay the night, and she didn't invite him. He gave her an awkward, gentle kiss at her bedroom door.

She arrived late to breakfast, issuing her apologies as she took her seat.

"You don't look well," Brandon said. "Are you coming down with something?"

Samantha pressed her warm coffee mug against each red, swollen eye.

"A cold, I think. Maybe allergies. My eyes won't stop running." Tears threatened to fall down her cheeks, so she quickly dabbed them with her napkin.

Tuki cleared his throat. "Sorry to hear that. Hope you feel better."

"Thanks." She didn't look at him.

"Perhaps you shouldn't travel, if you're congested," Brandon said. "The altitude could make it worse. You're welcome to stay as long as you'd like."

Samantha smiled as her eyes flooded over with tears. Quickly, she dabbed her cheeks. "Thanks. I wish I could. But I need to get home. Thanks anyway."

Tuki tossed his napkin on his plate. "I've gotta run. I told my supervisor I'd come in to work today."

The blood left Samantha's face as she straightened in her seat and looked up at Tuki. She hated that he would be leaving her like this.

"Have a good day," she said because she could think of nothing else. What she wanted to say was much too complicated.

"You too. I'll let you know what the council decides." Without a kiss, a handshake, or touch of any kind, he walked out of the dining room.

She watched him disappear from her sight, and then she dropped her face in her hands and wept.

CHAPTER TWENTY-SEVEN

A Special Guest

Two weeks after Samantha left Gellermann Manor, her mother burst into her bedroom where she had been reviewing the galleys for one of her articles entitled "The Lost Tribe of Delaware."

"Someone's here to see you," her mother said. "A very special visitor."

"Just a minute, Mama." She pulled the earphones of her iPod away from her ears and jumped from her bed. "Give me a minute, will you?"

Samantha rushed to her bathroom and brushed her hair and teeth and applied more deodorant and perfume. She stepped out of her sweats and threw on a pair of jeans lying over a chair. She started to leave the bathroom and stopped.

Okay, maybe some powder. She quickly patted her face and started to leave the room but stopped.

Okay, blush, too. And lipstick.

She looked herself over in the mirror.

Had he really come for her?

Giddy with excitement, she left the room and headed for the living area where her mother stood waiting.

As Samantha turned the corner, her mouth dropped when she saw, not Tuki, but Josephina Schmidt sitting on her mother's divan.

"Hello." Josie stood.

"Oh, Hello."

"What do you think of this one?" Samantha asked Josie two weeks before Christmas as they stood in front of The Magpie, Winter, painted by Claude Monet in 1869, on loan at the McNay Museum in San Antonio from Musée d'Orsay in Paris.

"I love the appearance of the snow on all the branches. And see here, these shadows, and look at the sky. It's impressionistic, but it looks so real, like I could be standing before such a scene in real life. You know what I mean?"

Samantha nodded. "Oh, yeah. What draws me to it is this lone bird sitting there on that rickety gate in the midst of all the winter beauty."

"What do you think of this Picasso?" Josie moved down the gallery to a separate display.

"I have mixed feelings about Picasso. There are a few paintings of his I like, but there are many that I, maybe 'detest' is too strong."

"Actually, I know what you mean."

Samantha smiled. "It's almost uncanny, how similar we are."

Josie put an arm around her shoulders. "It's called DNA, my dear."

They walked further down the museum to the last room, full of modern art.

"Too stark," Samantha said.

"That's just the word I would have used."

The two women laughed as they exited the museum and stepped onto a balcony overlooking the grounds, where three different photographers took shots of bridal clients posed among the natural beauty outside.

"That bride looks nervous," Josie commented.

Samantha made no reply.

"Something's bothering you. Am I trying too hard? Do you need more space?"

Samantha shook her head. "No. It's nothing like that. I've enjoyed getting to know you." She leaned against the rail beside a white Grecostyle column and stared out at the lily pond and the weeping willow overhanging it.

"Just let me know if you need more space. I don't get down this way often, so when I'm here, I want to see you as much as possible." She leaned her elbow on the rail and looked out at the view.

"I feel the same way. Really."

"Is there anything you want to talk about?"

"I don't know. There's this guy. I haven't heard from him in two months."

"I knew it. You're in love." Josie gave her a smile.

"It's so complicated."

"Tell me about it."

A week before Christmas, Samantha lay in her bed one evening after dinner listening to music on her iPod when her mother burst in and said, "You have a very special visitor."

Samantha sat up with a smile. "That silly woman. She was just here."

She spat her bubblegum into her wastebasket, unruffled her sweatshirt, and walked, barefoot, without makeup, hair half in and half out of its ponytail, into Tuki.

"Oh my God! Tuki!" She looked at him to be sure he was real. "I don't believe this! You're really here!"

He gave her a hug, wearing a big grin. "God, it's good to see you."

"I've missed you." She eyed her mother standing across the living room. "You remember my mother, Dorothy?"

He nodded. "Yes, we've said our hellos. Your parents were expecting me."

"What? Mama! Why didn't you tell me? Look at me!"

"He told me not to tell you. I tried to get you to take a shower before dinner, remember? What else could I do?"

"You look adorable." Tuki hugged her again.

She looked at him, beaming and thinking she could die right then and have lived a good life.

"Well, aren't you going to ask him to sit down?" Dorothy asked.

"Of course. I'm just in shock. Please, come and sit down. Are you hungry? Thirsty?"

Tuki shook his head. "I'm fine." He sat on the divan and Samantha sat beside him. "You're probably wondering why I haven't called."

"Yes, actually. I've been wondering that for weeks."

"Excuse me," Dorothy said. "I'll just leave you two to talk."

"Thanks, Mama."

Dorothy left the living room.

"Well, I've been arguing with the council all this time about establishing the foundation. The first time we reconvened, after you left, it was voted out, but it was close enough, that I got them to agree to another vote. I went out gathering information all over the country about other foundations and what they've accomplished for historical properties and landmarks. I put this huge case together, which I presented to the council last week."

"And?" Samantha held her breath.

"They turned me down. There's nothing I can say to convince the tribe."

She looked down at her hands and bit her lip. "Thanks for coming all this way to tell me."

He took a deep breath. "That's not what I came to say."

She looked up at him.

"I came to say I love you and I want you to be my wife."

She sat there, stunned. Even as he got down on one knee and brought a tiny box out of his jacket, she sat there, dumb.

"Beck? Will you marry me?"

Samantha smiled. "Will the tribal council change its decision if I marry you?"

"No," he said. "It's never going to happen. I tried everything."

"But you know I'm never going to give up on making the catacombs public. I"ll keep writing to the tribe. You're okay with that?"

"I want you to be my wife because I love you more than anything," he said with a steady voice. "What do you say?"

She got down on one knee beside him and said, "I say yes."

He took her in his arms and held her, she with her arms around his neck, he holding her at the waist, her face nestled at his neck.

He pulled back and opened the box, exposing a beautiful two-karat oval diamond. He took it from the box and slid it onto her ring finger.

"I'm so relieved you said yes."

"You mean you thought I might turn you down?"

"Because of the council's decision. I was afraid everything hinged on the foundation."

"But I told you I love you more than all that." She gave him another hug.

"Then why didn't you say yes two months ago?"

It was her turn to take a deep breath. "Don't be hurt, okay? But, well, I needed to know that you wanted to marry me because you loved me and not because it was good for the tribe or because of the promise you made to your father." She took his face in her hands. "Please don't be angry. I, I…"

"I understand." He smiled.

"Really?"

"Yes. In fact, I've done the same thing to you, a kind of test," he said with a mischievous smile.

"What?"

"I lied to you just now."

"What are you talking about? You don't want to get married?" She sat back on the divan.

"No. I mean Yes. I want to get married. I lied about the council's decision."

"What?" She stood up. "Do you mean?"

He nodded. "The tribe approved the foundation. We've just formed it. Wëli's the president of the board. I'm vice president."

She flapped her hands as her mouth dropped open. "Are you serious? Oh my God!" She gave a little bounce as tears welled in her eyes. "This is so, so, awesome!"

"We want you to be the head of the archaeology division. You'll do it, won't you?"

She jumped up. "Oh my God!"

"I'll take that as a yes."

He stood up and took her in his arms. Then she lifted her head and pressed her lips against his, savoring the moment she hoped would last forever.

Four months later, on a Saturday in April, Samantha stood in a field of daffodils in a white, sleeveless wedding gown, holding a shovel in one hand.

"Come on, Dad! It's time!"

Luther came from the back porch of Gellermann Manor, lifting the trousers of his tuxedo to avoid the patches of dirt on the hill leading to the creek below.

"You're going to get dirty. You may as well face it!" She laughed.

She put her free arm in his, and together they walked through the eastern wood toward the grounds of the Unikwëti, her full white gown dragging against sticks and rocks and dirt.

They could hear the drums and wooden flutes singing from down below as they reached the edge of the clearing, where the women waited. Her grandmother, the oldest among them, came forward and placed a deerskin cape trimmed with quillwork around Samantha's shoulders. Gale gave her a kiss on the cheek, followed by kisses from Dorothy, Josie, and Claire, as two tribeswomen dressed in traditional deerskin robes placed a wreath of flowers on Samantha's head. The other women carried candles, including the bridesmaids, two friends of Samantha's from Trinity.

"Congratulations," Claire whispered.

"Thank you."

Gale held on to Luther as they, followed by Dorothy, Josie, and Claire and the two bridesmaids, led Samantha down the dark passage to the catacombs. The men's voices below could now be heard chanting to the flutes and drums: "Heya, heya. Unikwëti hach ki? Heya, heya. Unikwëti hach ki?"

When they reached the balcony of rock overlooking the main chamber of the catacombs, Samantha nearly lost her breath at the beautiful sight below.

"Oh my God!" she cried.

A center fire was surrounded by four water drums, upon which four young men beat a slow cadence. A huge circle of people stood around the fire, tribesmen and friends and family of the Beck's, including Dorothy's best friend, Maggie. Many of them held up lit candles toward the bride. Some of the tribesmen played turtle shell rattles and wooden flutes. Tuki stood next to Brandon at the far end of the cave in the center of the ring wearing deerskin trimmed with the same quillwork as that on Samantha's cape.

Luther handed Samantha's shovel to Claire and then he and Gale led Samantha down the path to the floor of the cavern. The music increased in volume as she neared the ring of tribesman, Wëli and Donna and their children among them, surrounding the fire. Gale led Samantha to the center in a dance.

Two shakes down, two shakes up, twirl around, clap. Two shakes down, two shakes up, twirl around, clap.

As Samantha maneuvered around the fire, the rest of the tribe danced in their places in the human ring and chanted: "Heya, heya. Unikwëti hach ki? Heya, heya. Unikwëti hach ki?"

Epilogue

Samantha sat in her second-floor study in the east wing of Geller-mann Manor opening the last of the packets sent by scientists and journalists from all over the world hoping to be selected for the next public tour of the ancient catacombs of the Unikwëti of Lenni-Lenape. Before she could finish reviewing its contents, the telephone rang.

"Hello?"

"Mija! I've got the lab results in on the latest samples we took from the catacombs!"

"Wonderful, Professor! And how old does the lab think they are?"

"Get this. Are you sitting down? This has been corroborated by three separate labs. Hold on Mark, I've got Samantha on the line. Are you sitting down, mija?"

"Yes! I'm dying here!"

"You know last year's samples took us back to 300 B.C., right?"

"Professor, will you just spit it out?"

"All three labs date all ten fossilized bone specimens and the artifact collection to 4000 B.C."

"What? Did you say 4000 B.C.?"

"That's what I said!"

Samantha couldn't speak.

"Hello? Are you still there?"

Mark must have taken the phone from the professor.

"Sam? This means the whole theory about the Lenape crossing over the Bering Straight and coming from Africa or the Orient is completely undermined. This might mean that North America was populated much earlier than any of us originally believed!"

"I can't believe it! I can't believe it!"

"Mommy? What can't you believe?" Four-year-old Becky asked from the hallway.

"Listen, Mark. I'll call you guys back later. I can't wait to tell the others. And don't forget to send me a report of all these findings in writing when you have the chance, so I can present them to the board."

"Sure thing, Captain!"

"And Mark?"

"Yes?"

"Congratulations again on your new baby boy. Please give Millie my warmest wishes."

"Thanks, Cap. Will do!"

Samantha hung up the phone, trembling a bit and feeling light-headed. A picture of Rebecca Nisha fell over on her desk, so she set it right again, as always.

"Mommy, Jes says dinner's almost ready, and you're not even dressed."

"Come here, Pumpkin, and give your Mommy a kiss." She took the girl into her lap and exchanged a quick peck on the lips. "Is Daddy home?"

"Here I am. I'm on my way to the shower."

"Don't I even get a hello?"

"Daddy! Daddy, we want a hello!"

Tuki rushed into the room, swept his Nisha girls into a big embrace, and said, "Hi sweethearts! Sorry I'm late." Then to Samantha, "We were working on a really good bill we hope to have ready for the next congressional meeting."

"That's okay. I've still got to dress myself."

"Hmm, care to—"

"Shhhh!" Then she gave him a flirty look. "I've got big news."

"Oh? What is it?"

"Follow me." She took her husband and daughter's hands and led them to the balcony overlooking the foyer.

"Granddad, can you hear me? Granddad?"

Brandon limped from the parlor into the foyer with Baby Charlie in his hands. "What is it, dear girl?"

"Jes, can you hear me?"

"Jes, old man! Samantha has something she wants to tell us!" Brandon called through the foyer.

Jes came hobbling in from the kitchen. He looked up. "Madam?"

"What's going on, Beck? Tell us already," Tuki complained.

"Four thousand B.C.! The specimens from the catacombs date back to four thousand B.C.!"

"Did you hear that, Jes? Four thousand B.C.! By golly, break out the oldest wine in the cellar! This calls for a celebration! I'll call Claire right away and ask her to join us! We've got enough food, don't we Jes?"

"Yes, sir. We've got plenty."

"Charlie? You want Auntie Claire to come for dinner?"

The baby cooed in his great-grandfather's arms as his parents and sister laughed overhead.

"Wëli will be flabbergasted!" Samantha said as she and Tuki went to dress for dinner.

"If he ever had any fears over forming this foundation, you can bet they will be laid to rest tonight when he learns what we've been able to tell him about our people."

"Our people?" Samantha glanced back at him.

"Of course, Wulik Etchilhillat. Yours and mine." He smiled, putting an arm around her shoulders.

A soft, plump arm wrapped itself around his leg.

"And mine, too, Daddy?"

"Yes, Wisawtayas. Yours, too."

THE END

Thank you for reading my story. If you enjoyed it, please consider leaving a review. Reviews help other readers to find my books, which helps me.

Please enjoy this excerpt from another dark thriller romance, *The Purgatorium.*

Chapter One: The Island

A morning fog was just beginning to thin in the sticky, ocean breeze. Whether it was the sharp smell of dead fish or lingering anxiety from the plane ride, Daphne could not eat when Cam offered to buy her a snack at a stand in the harbor. He bought himself a baked pretzel, and then the two of them followed Dr. Hortense Gray up the ramp and onto the catamaran, pulling their bags behind them.

They maneuvered through a crowd of school-age children in matching yellow t-shirts. Of the twenty or so other passengers, most were men in their thirties and forties. She and Cam were the only teenagers aboard.

Daphne stood at the railing overlooking the water with Cam on one side of her and the doctor on the other. The wind whipped her brown hair around her face despite her efforts to tuck it behind her ears. She missed this beauty. She'd forgotten how breathtaking it was. Her parents used to take her and her brother and sister to the beach all the time. There was nothing like gazing at the ocean where it met the sky on the horizon.

But the beauty could not stop her from trembling, could not stop the dread gripping her chest. Cam had said a wildlife refuge and a resort with pristine beaches. He hadn't said a thing about therapeutic exercises. She'd had to hear it from this strange doctor who had met them at the airport in Ventura. Was the doctor like a life coach? Would Daphne have to climb a rock wall or plunge down a zipline? She should have known her parents wouldn't let her go with Cam to a getaway resort just for fun. She should have been more suspicious. Tears pricked her eyes. She felt betrayed. Betrayed by her parents and her best friend.

As the catamaran reached the open sea, a pod of dolphins leapt ahead of them, as if guiding them to their destination.

"Look!" Cam pointed at the group of four leaping in turns from the water beside the boat.

Daphne's cheeks stretched into a smile in spite of everything. The dolphins were amazing.

"Just wait," Cam said, his blond hair flattening against his head with the wind. "We might see a humpback whale. Keep your fingers crossed."

She stood close to Cam's tall, wiry frame as though the two years they had rarely spoken had never existed. She hadn't even so much as texted him a happy birthday wish last month when he had turned eighteen. For the millionth time, she wished she could go back to that night she had failed to get out of bed.

An hour passed with no humpback sightings, but soon a great mound of rock could be seen—bald, solid, smooth like the skin of a whale, and round like a bowling ball. Daphne couldn't imagine how such a rocky place could hold any kind of paradise. Then a long, narrow pier became visible, and beside it, a rocky beach. The boat docked at the end of the pier, and all but Daphne, Cam, the doctor, and the captain climbed out.

Where were the pristine beaches?

The captain then turned the boat north and skirted around to another part of the island, where there were more rocky crags with waves crashing into and away from them, tossing the boat side to side, until they came into a large harbor full of other boats.

To Daphne's right were hundreds of pelicans roosting on a rocky beach of shale. Some slept standing up, others cleaned their feathers, and still others walked around inspecting the shoreline and the shallow waters surrounding it.

Kara would have liked this, she thought.

"They're looking for sardines in the kelp beds," Cam said.

Daphne used her hand as a visor. "Look at them all."

An even longer pier than the first shot out into the harbor, and they were now moving to it.

"Prisoners Harbor," Cam said.

This side of the island was certainly more beautiful than the eastern point at Scorpion Anchorage, but Daphne still saw no evidence of pristine beaches. A wildlife refuge this island may be, but where was the resort?

Once they docked, Daphne and Cam followed Dr. Gray up five rungs on a ladder to the pier, and then they dragged their luggage across the narrow row of boards toward several flights of steps. Descending from the steps ahead of them were two people, an African-American boy and girl in their teens. The girl was bald as the rock at Scorpion Anchorage, as though she had undergone chemotherapy.

"Look at me!" the girl growled at Dr. Gray, and Daphne thought perhaps they were related, having the same round dark eyes and high cheek bones.

"Come along, Daphne," Dr. Gray said, ignoring the girl.

The girl grabbed Daphne's wrist and started to say something, but Cam moved between them.

"We don't want any trouble," he said.

"Are you okay?" Daphne asked the girl, trying to see around Cam, but the bald teen turned away, scuttled down the pier, and quickly boarded the boat.

"What's her deal?" Daphne asked Cam.

"Don't know," he said, leading her onward.

"That was odd."

"Yeah. It was. Come on."

The squawking of the pelicans could be heard from the several flights of wooden steps, but they were less visible until Daphne reached the summit near a dirt road, where a jeep and its driver waited. The driver was an older man, maybe in his forties, with tanned skin and a straw cowboy hat. He nodded at them as they approached.

"Hello, Roger," Dr. Gray said.

"Nice to have you back, Hortense," the driver said with a southern drawl. "The island ain't the same without you."

From this point, Daphne looked out over the ocean and, although the view was spectacular, she frowned. This wasn't what she had expected.

It wasn't like she hadn't asked a lot of questions. Cam had gone the summer before, and then, this summer, one rare evening while she'd sat in her tree in the backyard, the thick oak leaves forming a shield around her, he had told her about it.

She hadn't seen him in the treehouse on the other side of the six-foot wooden fence that separated their two yards. When he called out to her, she'd been crying again, and although she had wanted to scramble down the trunk and run inside and hide, he'd asked her a question that had made her pause.

"If you could spend your final days anywhere in the whole wide world, where would it be?"

"Are you drunk?" she had asked.

"No. Just curious. " Then he had added, "I miss you, Daph."

"I'd spend my last days on a beach somewhere beautiful," she had said.

"I know just the place." He had jumped from his treehouse, had bolted over the fence, and had landed at the base of her tree faster than she had been able to wipe her eyes.

"I'm sorry you didn't get to see a humpback," Cam said beside her now. "Maybe on the way back."

They drove by picnic tables, trees, a kayak rental, and an outhouse as the driver took them along a canyon ridge toward the center of the island. A few minutes later they came up on two other buildings with solar panels turned toward the sun, a long wooden deck, and two greenhouses. To their right was a deeper valley with a stream running down the middle and pine trees.

"Look there!" Hortense Gray pointed above the valley. "A bald eagle. See it?"

"Oh, yeah," Daphne said.

"Isn't it fantastic?" Cam handed her a pair of binoculars from his bag. "Use these."

She took them and looked closely at the majestic bird as it soared through the sky above the valley.

"See if you can spot any foxes," Cam said, full of enthusiasm.

Daphne scoured the landscape for wildlife. Gulls flew to and from the sea up high above where the eagle soared. The valley looked like a manicured fairway on a top-notch golf course with a stream running down the middle of it and branching off into smaller ones. Along the sides of the "fairway" were pines and shrubs and grassy knolls. The spring ran heavily from the highland but narrowed in places where it gently rushed over rocks.

A figure stepped into her view through the binoculars, but it was no fox. She watched it, focused the lenses. It was a person. A hiker? A girl with long black hair trailing behind her ran along the stream, turning back to look, as though she were being followed.

Just then a man grabbed the girl by the hair and dragged her back up the hill and into a copse of trees.

Daphne's stomach dropped. "Oh my God!"

"What?" Dr. Gray asked.

Daphne's tongue twisted in her mouth as she stammered, "A man….and a girl! He's hurting her!"

The doctor took the binoculars and pointed them toward the valley. "Where? I don't see anything?"

"I swear they're out there," Daphne said, her stomach forming a knot. "I saw them. We have to do something!" She gave Cam a pleading look, and said again, "We have to do something." Why wasn't he more alarmed? "We have to go down there and help her. What are we waiting for?"

"Roger, take us down into the valley, please," Dr. Gray said.

The driver sped downhill. The road ended about twenty yards from the spring. Roger stopped the jeep, and all four climbed out.

Daphne pointed to the ground, insistently. "They were here, I swear I saw them. He was pulling her by the hair."

When the adults looked back at her blankly, she took off running through the nearby trees, her heart beating wildly. Why wasn't anyone taking her seriously? Panic had overtaken her, and she couldn't think. She couldn't think. "Hello?" She saw and heard no one.

The others also called out and began to search the trees.

After several minutes, they all met up again.

Dr. Gray said, "Oh, this is no good."

"What should we do?" Cam asked, out of breath.

The doctor put a hand on Daphne's shoulder. "Please don't be offended by what I'm about to say."

Daphne couldn't believe the patronizing look on the taller woman's face. "I didn't imagine it," she said, panting.

"It's been a long, tiring trip, and islands are famous for their mirages, especially this one," Dr. Gray said.

"Not mirages," Roger said. "Ghosts."

"Please, Roger. Don't start." Dr. Gray shook her head.

"What ghosts?" Daphne asked. Even though she didn't believe in ghosts, goosebumps popped up along her arms.

"Let's go on to the resort," Dr. Gray said. "I'll phone the naval guards when we get there and tell them what you saw."

"What ghosts?" Daphne asked again in the jeep in the backseat beside Cam. She twisted back with her eyes held up to the binoculars, scanning the stream and nearby woods for signs of the girl and her attacker as the jeep climbed toward the canyon ridge.

"We aren't going to talk about nonsense," the doctor said.

"She has a right to know about the island's legends," Roger objected.

"Is this the one about Misink?" Cam asked. "The guy who threw the men in the ocean and took the women on his rainbow bridge?"

Hortense Gray turned from the front passenger seat. "The Chumash believed the first people grew from seeds planted on this island by the

Earth Goddess, Hutash. When the island became overpopulated with people, she sent down Misink, the guardian of nature, to set things right. They say each year Misink threw six young men into the ocean where they turned into dolphins. That's why the Chumash consider the dolphins to be their brothers.

"Misink also took six unmarried women and had them for himself. They say he took them into the sky by way of his rainbow bridge, and they were never seen alive again."

"What does this have to do with ghosts?" Daphne put down the binoculars, the deep valley now out of view.

Roger said, "People say Misink comes for women about your age to take with him to the skies, and sometimes they come back and wander this here island."

"Interesting legend, but you don't expect me to believe that was Misink out there in the valley, do you?" Daphne smelled a set-up. "Is this some kind of joke?" She expected one of them to say, *Bwahahahaha*, any minute now.

Roger coughed and cleared his voice.

Cam whispered, "Apparently Roger is a believer."

"Like you can talk," she whispered back. Cam had made plenty of claims throughout their childhood of having seen his grandmother in his attic. Her brother, Joey, a year older than Cam, still believed Cam's grandmother spoke to him.

Roger said, "I dare you to spend one night at the old Christy Ranch, and then you can laugh at me all you like."

"What's old Christy Ranch?" Daphne asked.

"It's on the western end of the island," Roger said. "That there ranch house is haunted by the wife of a slave trader."

"Have you seen her ghost?" Cam asked.

"No, but I've heard the screaming."

"What screaming?" Daphne asked.

"Out on Haunted Bridge," Roger replied. "I've heard the screaming with my own ears. My pal and I searched all over in the morning and found no trace of anyone and no explanation for the screams. People say the wife of the slave trader was horrified when she learned what her husband done, and, once when he was headed back for more slaves, she sunk his ship with him and his crew aboard. They say she went crazy until she died. They say she's responsible for a lot of the ships that wreck in that there part of the sea."

As they made their descent into the canyon, no one said more about the incident Daphne may or may not have seen. Daphne was tired and had eaten little. Maybe she *had* imagined the figures in the valley.

Joey, her brother, saw people who weren't there all the time. Daphne worried one day she would begin to see them, too.

No. She knew what she had seen. They'd been real, flesh and blood, living people. But something gave her the feeling that Dr. Gray and Roger were messing with her.

EVA POHLER

Eva Pohler is a *USA Today* bestselling author of over thirty novels in multiple genres, including mysteries, thrillers, and young adult paranormal romance based on Greek mythology. Her books have been described as "addictive" and "sure to thrill"—*Kirkus Reviews*.

To learn more about Eva and her books, and to sign up to hear about new releases, and sales, please visit her website at www.evapohler.com.

www.ingramcontent.com/pod-product-compliance
Lightning Source LLC
Chambersburg PA
CBHW072029220726
48293CB00016B/600